THE
FOXFIRES
TRILOGY

About the Author

E. C. Hibbs is an award-winning author and artist, often found lost in the woods or in her own imagination. She adores nature, fantasy, and anything to do with winter. She also hosts a YouTube channel, discussing writing tips and the real-world origins of fairy tales. She lives with her family in Cheshire, England.

Learn more and join the Batty Brigade at

www.echibbs.weebly.com

Also by E. C. Hibbs

THE FOXFIRES TRILOGY
The Winter Spirits
The Mist Children
The Night River

THE TRAGIC SILENCE SERIES
Sepia and Silver
The Libelle Papers
Tragic Silence
Darkest Dreams

Blindsighted Wanderer
The Sailorman's Daughters
Night Journeys: Anthology
The Hollow Hills Tarot Deck

Blood and Scales (anthology co-author)
Dare to Shine (anthology co-author)
Fae Thee Well (anthology co-author)

AS CHARLOTTE E. BURGESS
*Into the Woods and Far Away: A Collection of Faery
Meditations*
Gentle Steps: Meditations for Anxiety and Depression

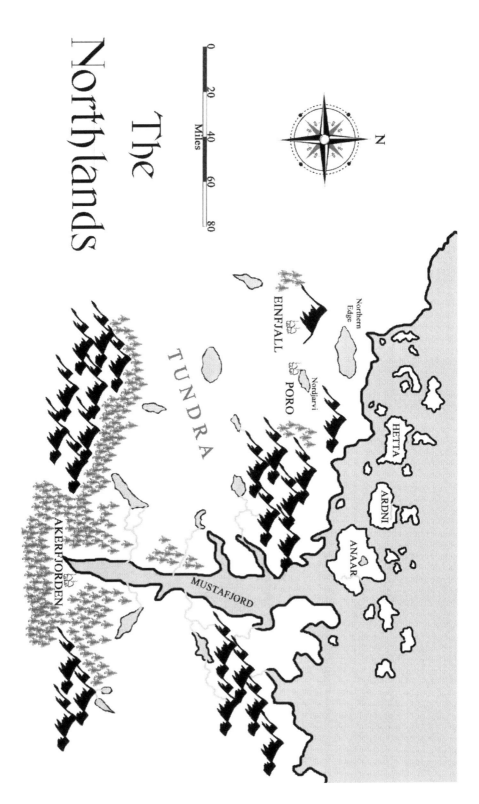

The Northlands

The Night River

The Foxfires Trilogy
Book Three

E. C. Hibbs

This is a work of fiction. Names, characters, businesses, places, events, locales, and incidents are either the products of the author's imagination or used in a fictitious manner. Any resemblance to actual persons, living or dead, or actual events is purely coincidental.

For Maiken,

A wonderful person with a wonderful smile.

Thank you for your encouragement and friendship.

Prologue

The stars twinkled and the Moon Spirit was bright, but despite the glow they cast over the snowy tundra, Mihka felt like he had never known a night so dark. Somehow it seemed even blacker than at the height of winter. The air was sharp around him; not from cold, but something else which ran deeper, through the very veins of the Northlands. It left him breathless, as though he'd climbed to a mountain summit where the oxygen thinned and he had to struggle to fill his lungs. He was no mage, but even he could sense the Worlds moving away from each other, like currents pulling water in different directions. Overhead, the sky was torn clean in two and the edges of the abyss waved like a spiderweb in the breeze.

The sight was terrifying, but he forced himself to concentrate. He had only fled Anaar the night before, but already the island was a dark blue speck in the distance behind him. He'd crossed the channel in a boat, then emptied it of his belongings and strapped them all into a small sled made from lightweight birch planks. Attaching it to his belt and slipping his shoes into a pair of skis, he had set off in the direction of Akerfjorden's winter camp. The only things which he hadn't tied to the sled were his bow and arrows. Those were slung across his shoulders, in case he came across a hare or ptarmigan.

He had decided to take the long way. Keeping to ground level meant he could stop at the Poro winter camp, rest and perhaps trade for some food if he failed to catch anything. Going through the mountain passes was a definite short cut, but with spring approaching, he didn't want to risk it. Spring was the most changeable and dangerous season of all. If he became trapped up there, alone, nobody would ever find him.

It wasn't even late in the evening, but the nights were still coming early. The hours of daylight wouldn't catch up for several more weeks. It was time to stop and pitch camp.

There was a forest in front of him, branches heaped with snow, their ends feathered by the glistening of ice crystals. Boulders peppered the ground here and there – he supposed they had broken off the nearby mountains in some long-ago avalanche and crashed down into the trees. Perfect. They would block a little of the wind.

Mihka stepped out of the skis and untied the eight long poles lashed to the top of the sled. He arranged two in front of the largest boulder, balancing them against each other in the air, then added the others until he had a skeletal cone structure. Finally, he opened a length of reindeer-skin tarp and wrapped it around the whole thing to create a tent. It was smaller than a typical one, but it would do. He only needed room for his sleeping sack.

Usually he would have carried the poles in a sleigh, to make things easier. But for a sleigh, he needed a reindeer, and they were all still on Anaar. He wouldn't have been able to leave so quietly if he'd had to urge one of the animals across the channel.

Mihka thanked the Spirits and chopped a few branches off a nearby birch tree; then he ducked inside the shelter and woke a fire. It took a while; the wood was damp with snow, so he peeled the papery bark off for kindling and split the logs into smaller pieces with a knife. That gave the flames more purchase. Satisfied, he huddled close to warm his hands and tucked into some salted salmon cakes from his pack. They weren't much, but would keep him going until he reached Poro.

Unease bit at him. He'd never been out on his own before. Now, miles from his people, he realised how truly alone he was. It was an isolation he had brought on himself, but that didn't make it any easier.

The space opposite him was empty: just the shadows of flames flickering on a blank tarp wall. His father Sisu should be sitting there, as he always had.

But his father was dead. Gone forever. Mihka wasn't even sure if he would see him again in the other Worlds.

As he worked through the cakes, chewing them slowly to make them last longer, he held a hand to his chest. It was still hurting from the illness which had ravaged him. The plague had vanished from his lungs practically overnight, but at the back of his mouth, he remembered the taste of blood; heard the rattle of his own breath in his ears. All his ribs felt as though they had cracked like rotten twigs. And his head had been filled with images of a little boy with white eyes and scars down his cheeks…

The same little boy Tuomas had appeared with on the beach.

Mihka's anger swelled with the force of a spring tide. Having stopped walking, there was nothing to distract him from it. He kicked at the fire with a snarl and sent sparks shooting into the air. Tears prickled his eyes, but he hurriedly wiped them away. No matter that nobody would see them fall. He couldn't bear to cry. That would make it too real, too soon.

He touched his hair; pulled a few of the strands straight so he could see their whiteness in his peripheral vision. How could so much have happened in such a short space of time?

First, he'd been struck by the Spirit of the Lights and trapped in the World Above; then he'd come back and caught the soul plague; and now he was orphaned. All in a single winter.

And then there was Tuomas.

That brought a new wave of fury as his face floated in Mihka's mind. He had loved that face once: his best friend, with whom he'd grown up and laughed. Now there was only hatred. All they had shared, which drew them together, was severed like the rip in the sky above. It hadn't been a clean cut; it had been rising for a while, ever since Tuomas began to change. Now he wasn't even human anymore and the final straw had come not a day ago, when Mihka had overheard everything.

He thought of the red fox ears, the tail, the way Tuomas spoke of Spirits. *He* was the reason Mihka's father was dead, as well as all the others who had fallen sick. He might not have murdered them with his own hands, but he had still killed them.

And despite everything, Mihka couldn't stop thinking of how the entire nightmare had started. Tuomas had gone into the Northlands by himself, risked his own life in the Long Dark, just to save Mihka's soul. It had all been for him.

Mihka's hands curled into fists so tight, his knuckles went white. Would it be worth asking the Poro caretakers if he could stay in their village? There was nothing left for him in Akerfjorden now. He could separate his reindeer and integrate them with the Poro herd. Then he wouldn't have to see Tuomas again; wouldn't have to think about him, or anything, ever again.

He kicked the logs, harder this time. They spilled out of the pit he had made for them and sizzled as they hit the snow. Smoke instantly began to fill the tent.

"No!" Mihka gasped. He quickly snatched one of his ski poles and manoeuvred them all back into the centre. Then he flung the flap aside and stepped out to tie it open. Now he'd near to air the place before he could bed down for the night. Idiot.

He closed his eyes. That was what Tuomas used to call him, in an affectionate way. Deep down, he supposed there was some truth in it. He was an idiot, but he didn't know any other way to be. Playing around, cracking jokes and pranks… But there was no place for that now.

Above, close to the cleft in the sky, the Moon Spirit let out a pulse of silvery light.

A long, low groan suddenly floated through the boughs.

Mihka looked up in confusion. He was the only person around here for miles – Poro was still several days' walk away.

He pulled his bow off his shoulder and nocked an arrow.

"Hello?" he called. "Is someone here?"

His fingers curled around the sinew bowstring, ready to draw. Was it a wolf? He'd never heard one make a noise like that, but their howls could be twisted by wind and distance into something eerie.

He thought quickly. He hadn't seen any tracks. Maybe he was hearing things.

The groan came again. It was closer this time, but he couldn't figure out the direction. And while it definitely wasn't a wolf, something about it didn't sound human, either.

Mihka swallowed nervously. The sound swept through him as though he wasn't there; the branches seemed to present more of an obstacle than his body did. His bones chilled, and beneath his coat, the hairs on his arms stood on end.

His initial wariness gave way to fear. Not wasting a moment, he ducked behind the nearest tree.

He had barely pressed his back against it when a great bang came from the other side. Mihka's heart pounded. Moving carefully, he peered around the trunk.

He bit his lip to stop himself from screaming.

The boulder he'd propped his tent against was moving. It uncurled like a huge snail; the rock splintered and rose into the bulk of a giant creature.

As it stirred, it seemed to soften into something lifelike. Its skin turned a horrid green-grey colour, more stone than flesh. It stood fifteen feet tall, long-limbed and stocky, its torso covered by moss and fronds of ice. It snatched at a tree for balance and sent snow cascading from the crown in soft whumps. With its other hand, it reached to its hip and withdrew a vicious flint blade as long as Mihka's arm.

Terror rooted him to the spot. It was a troll.

He had heard of these things before, in the old fireside stories, but had never really taken them seriously. They hadn't been seen for generations. It was thought they had all died long ago.

The troll turned around and poked at the shelter with its knife. Then it snatched the tarp and tore the whole thing off the skeleton of poles. It grabbed the sleeping sack and shook it hard. When nothing fell out, it dropped it.

With a low grunt, it slowly turned around, black eyes shining in the exposed firelight. Mihka ducked back behind the tree before it could spot him. His hands shook on his bow. Arrows would be useless against that creature. It would be like trying to shoot a mountain.

He heard the troll sniffing like a hungry beast. Then it came closer.

Mihka held his breath and closed his eyes.

Chapter One

High above the summer islands, the night sky rippled and swayed. The tear between the Worlds gaped open, sent a shower of light down from its edges. It might have been beautiful if not for the horror of the sight. It was wrong, awfully wrong. People glanced at it and turned away just as quickly.

"Is it the end?" a woman asked Enska as they sat beside the fire pit.

Enska shook his head. "Nothing is ever the end."

But he heard his own words ring hollow. Nature had a way of always keeping the balance. This, however, was exactly what happened when the balance was thrown.

He swept a hand over the symbols on the drum. It was made from reindeer hide and painted with red alder bark. His gaze lingered on the leftmost image, of his son and daughter, the Great Bear Spirit hovering above the girl.

He glanced at Lilja, standing against the wall of a nearby turf hut. Her hair was loose, and she glowered from behind it with an unreadable expression. Though the fire shone orange in her eyes, they were heavy and distant. She didn't even stir when people looked at her.

Footsteps crunched on the snow.

Enska turned towards the trees. They stretched all around in an endless swathe of stark black lines, but he could just make out the silhouette of an approaching figure. He recognised who it was at once: the gait was easy enough, but on the head were the unmistakable points of fox ears.

Tuomas stepped out of the shadows. Then he moved aside, and everyone around the fire leapt up in alarm.

Behind him was another: a girl, with the same large ears and bushy tail as him. But she was pure white, clothed in stardust rather than furs, and her eyes shone the colours of the aurora.

Enska and Lilja lowered their heads, but the others shied away, muttering fearfully.

"Please don't be frightened," said Tuomas.

Lilja took a step forward. She shot Tuomas an icy glare before moving onto Lumi.

"With all due respect, White Fox One, why are you here? Like this?"

She gestured at Lumi's body. Lumi didn't blink, but her tail swept back and forth, and a miniature stream of green Lights rose where it touched the ground.

"I have returned to assist in correcting the state of affairs," she replied.

Her voice, though not as cold as Tuomas had known, still sent an involuntary shiver down his spine. Like everything about her, it was too ethereal to be human, both as soft as a snowflake and powerful as an avalanche. It was the voice of a being so much larger than the simple physical form she took; the sound of a thousand years given breath and air.

Lilja swallowed. Tuomas tried to gauge her reaction, but it was impossible; not a single muscle twitched to betray what she was thinking.

"May I please have an audience with the two of you?" she asked.

Enska got to his feet. "Me, too. If you would be so kind, White Fox One."

He muttered reassurance to those around the fire pit, then the four of them retreated into the trees, out of sight. It didn't take long for Tuomas's eyes to adjust; the light streaming from the tear in the sky reflected off the snow and turned the entire forest blue.

"Well?" Lilja asked as soon as they stopped. "Is this your doing, boy?"

"No," Tuomas insisted.

"You didn't summon her again?"

"No!"

"He did nothing of the sort," Lumi cut in. "I cannot say I am here in ideal circumstances, but my brother did not summon me. He did, however, cause me to act in a way I would rather not have done."

Enska frowned. "What do you mean?"

Lumi lowered her eyes for a moment, then turned them skywards, towards the rip.

"That is my doing," she said. "When I realised what he was attempting to do, with the draugars, I leapt across all three Worlds to save him. This is the result. And now the Great Bear Spirit has charged me to right the balance as much as him."

Tuomas shuffled his feet. Enska's mouth fell open, but he quickly closed it again.

"I wanted to inform you all that I am here," Lumi continued. "I also want the people to know they are in no danger from me. There are more important matters to deal with now than my own pride."

"*You* tore the Worlds?" Lilja repeated incredulously.

Lumi gave a terse nod. "I did."

Lilja shared a glance with Enska, then growled and ran a hand through her hair.

"And I thought all this couldn't get any better," she muttered.

"We're going to set it right," Tuomas insisted. "Lilja, please... I *know* I was stupid. I knew it from the moment I woke up. Mihka's run off because of me – I found him on the beach, tried to stop him, and he told me he never wants to see me again. I don't need to be constantly reminded of my own mistakes. I said I'd fix it, and I will."

Silence fell. The gash yawned overhead; Tuomas deliberately kept his attention on Lilja and Enska to avoid looking at it. He could sense the pressure of every single Spirit staring at him, taste the sharper edge of *taika* in the air as it spilled between the Worlds. Everything felt as thin and fragile as a crust of frost – the slightest pressure and it would break apart into splinters.

Lumi wrapped her fingers around his. It was gentle, but freezing.

"I will keep my distance, for everybody's peace of mind," she said. "And my own."

Enska nodded. "Will you be safe, White Fox One? The last time you walked among us, it was the Long Dark; you had nothing to fear from the daylight."

"I will manage," replied Lumi.

Without another word, she let go of Tuomas. Her body twisted and morphed like water, white fur sprouted from her skin, her face lengthened into a snout. Within a few heartbeats, she had transformed from girl into fox, and headed off into the trees with a faint aurora trailing in her wake. Tuomas couldn't help marvelling as she left. Even on four legs, she walked with the same inhuman grace, and not a single paw sank into the snow.

When he turned back to Lilja, her expression made his stomach clench. She hadn't taken her eyes off him, and it was like looking at stone chiselled into the shape of his friend's face. Then she turned on her heel and strode away.

Tuomas went to follow, but Enska took hold of his elbow.

"No. Let her go."

Tuomas sighed. "I just want her to know I'm sorry."

"She does know," Enska said. "But she also needs time. Things aren't exactly easy for her right now."

"I thought she'd be happy," said Tuomas. "I mean… she's got her son back."

Enska shook his head. "Don't be naïve. Aki is the least of it."

"Well… what can I do to make her feel better?"

"You can't. Just give her space. She'll appreciate that more than if you bombard her with apologies."

"But…"

Tuomas didn't bother trying to finish. Enska was right. And he was Lilja's father; he was one of the few people who she had ever opened herself to. He would know what he was talking about.

Enska pressed his fingers into his eyes with a weary groan.

"Come on. Let's go back, try to get some sleep."

"What about Mihka?" Tuomas asked. "He didn't tell me where he was going. But he had enough stuff for a long hike."

"I'd imagine he's heading for the Poro winter camp," mused Enska. "It's the closest place. If he's careful then he should reach it soon."

Tuomas wasn't sure how he felt about that. Logically, it made sense, and it was a relief to think that Mihka wouldn't be going somewhere which required walking through the dangerous mountains alone. But it still didn't lessen the guilt which gnawed at his belly. Mihka had left because of *him*. Because he had acted impulsively and let everyone else pay the price.

His body was still covered with tender bruises and bite marks from when the draugars had almost devoured him. In a way, Tuomas wouldn't have cared if they never healed. Such surface wounds were the least he deserved in the wake of what he had done.

It was difficult to believe that less than a week had passed since that encounter. The sideways glances and uneasy silences thrown at him since his return had made it seem more like an eternity. Sometimes he wondered if the winter would ever end. Since the moment it began, on that first night of the Long Dark, everything had changed. And while he had new friends in Lilja, Elin and Lumi, life hadn't also been without its share of horror.

Mihka's father and Tuomas's own brother were only two of those lost forever. All because of him.

He and Enska followed Lilja's footprints back to the huts. The crowd was still gathered around the fire pit, and Enska quickly began reassuring them about Lumi being on the island. Tuomas didn't stop, and carried on until he reached the shelter where Elin and her parents Alda and Sigurd were staying.

He knocked softly.

"Who is it?" Alda asked.

"Me," he replied.

There was a shuffling inside.

"I don't want to see him," Tuomas heard Elin whispering.

"Are you sure? He saved your life."

"I don't want to talk about it, Mother. Just please tell him to go away."

Tuomas stepped back as Alda opened the door a crack. Her face was tight and drawn – her attention lingered on his ears before it dropped to his eyes. He squirmed, wishing he could just pull the stupid things off his head.

"Are you alright?" Alda asked quietly.

Tuomas nodded. "I just… I was wondering if I could speak with Elin."

Alda gave him an apologetic smile. "She's asleep."

He bit his lip. He had a mind to argue, to insist on going in and making Elin listen to him, but the pain in her voice cut him to the quick. He had risked everything to save her, and all it had done was cause more hurt.

"Alright," he murmured. "Well… when she's ready, please tell her I'd like to have a word with her. I don't want to fall out with her, Alda."

Alda sighed. For a moment, Tuomas thought she might swing the door wide – a part of him hoped she would. However, she just nodded once, then bid him goodnight and pushed it shut again.

Tuomas didn't move. He rubbed his face with one hand, felt his ears drooping dejectedly. Not for the first time, he wished he could wake up in his sleeping sack in Akerfjorden, to the smell of Paavo's reindeer stew, and realise it had all just been a bad dream.

With a heavy heart, he left the shelter behind and headed towards his own.

Then he realised that he hadn't heard Sigurd in the hut, either.

Suspicion crept over him like cold water. He changed direction, sneaked close to where Lilja was staying. Smoke was rising from the hole in the top. However, Lilja wasn't one to make excessive noise, but he couldn't make out anything inside, not even the sound of her whittling or cooking.

Then he did hear her, along with another voice, in the trees behind the village. He pressed himself against the wall of the hut and let his ears swivel to pick up the sound better.

"I told you," Lilja was snarling, "it was none of your concern!"

"Of course it was my concern! You had a child! And I can only assume he's *my* child!"

"What does it matter, Sigurd? What could you have done? Don't you think *I* made the difficult decision by running off and living the way I have done, all for your sake?"

"You should have told me!"

"Why? What would have been the point? You're only arguing for the sake of it, because you know I'm right!"

Sigurd growled. "Lilja, for all the Spirits' sakes, was the truth too much to ask for?"

"What good was the truth when it would have destroyed everything?" she replied. "This isn't just about you and me. It's about your wife and daughter. The family you already had when we… Look, it doesn't matter. You know now, and we'll both have to live with it, not just me. But I want you to know that as soon as Aki is ready to travel, we are leaving. It's the best thing for all of us. And I won't hear anything else on the matter."

Silence fell, then Tuomas heard footsteps. He crouched down, held his breath as Lilja drew close and slipped through the door at the other side of the hut. She didn't see him.

He sank onto his haunches, reached inside his tunic, and pulled out the small bone fox head. It didn't feel like only a couple of months since he had carved it. An eternity seemed to have passed between that moment and now.

He glanced at his red tail, lying in the snow beside him, then lowered his face into his hands and wept.

Chapter Two

Tuomas gazed over the western sea as evening swept in. The Sun Spirit dipped low and bathed Anaar in gold, turning the clouds a fierce red. It was as though the entire sky was on fire. Her glow only intensified when she drew close to the rip – it passed through the Worlds and left a hole into which everything threatened to tumble. *Taika* poured from its edges like a ghostly waterfall.

When he was younger, he might have found it beautiful. But now unease gnawed at his heart. His mother was showing she was angry with him. All the Spirits were. He could feel them glaring from every tree, landform and breaking wave down on the shore. Even the wind held a cold edge to it, despite blowing from the warmer south. And within, like a terrible overture, he sensed the Great Bear Spirit turning its eyes on him.

He had defied it: the strongest entity in any of the Worlds. It had given him a task, and he'd ignored it. Could anyone else have ever done something so stupid?

A twig snapping made him turn around. A reindeer appeared out of the trees. It glanced idly at him before starting to scrape away the snow with its hoof. Before long, it uncovered a patch of grazing.

Tuomas watched it pull the lichen from the rocks. He could tell from the unique series of notches cut into its ear that it belonged to Paavo. *Had* belonged to Paavo. As his brother's only relative, all his reindeer would be Tuomas's now.

With a heavy sigh, he turned his back on the sea, laid a hand on the reindeer's neck as he passed it. The animals were already beginning to fatten up after the long migration to the coast. Now, they wouldn't be returning to Akerfjorden for a while. They needed to stay on Anaar while the females gave birth. Then, once summer was passed, and the island exhausted of its lichen and moss, the calves could be corralled and earmarked. Whoever owned the mother would also own the baby. Tuomas had already spotted some of his own reindeer foraging with their new young; he had done well this season.

But he didn't care. He would have given up every single one of them if he could turn back time.

As he walked through the forest, he noticed numerous pairs of antlers scattered across the ground. A couple of the females were starting to drop them early. He grasped the nearest one and turned it over in his hands, checking it for weathering and any marks where small animals might have gnawed at it. There were none. It hadn't long been shed.

Perfect. He could leave it at the shrine.

It didn't take him long to reach it. The rock in the middle of the frozen pond looked black in the fading light. The Moon Spirit was beginning to rise behind it. Her cold glow mixed with the warmth of her sister, and for a few moments, there was a strange blend of day and night.

Tuomas deliberately didn't look at her. He could almost feel her at his back, trying to wrap him in her silvery embrace, so she might whisper tempting words in his ear…

He shook his head, knelt at the water's edge, and pulled some kindling from a pouch. He struck flint until it caught, fed the flame with twigs. Then he laid the antlers down, cut off some of his hair and closed his eyes. It didn't feel like the best offering to the Great Bear, but he doubted anything would be worthy of the penance he owed.

He untied his drum from his belt and went to warm it, but paused and shuffled closer to the fire. He reached out a hand.

The flickering orange tongues wrapped themselves around his fingers. He didn't wince. There wasn't even a semblance of pain; only a delicious warmth which called to him deeper than just flesh in the shape of a human. He felt his *taika* swelling, his souls swirling around each other within his heart. The flame was him and of him. It always had been.

He focused on it. The fire spread, and when he withdrew his hand, it stayed there, nestled in his palm. He held it before his face in awe.

"What are you doing, boy?"

Tuomas looked up. Henrik was hobbling towards him, clutching a lit torch. Tuomas made a fist and the flames extinguished. His skin tingled, but remained unburned.

"Trying to make things right," he replied.

"It's a little late for that, don't you think?"

"Henrik, please. I get it. I made a huge mistake, and I'm sorry. How many times do I need to say that?"

The old mage eyed him. He shifted the torch to his other hand, then his gaze drifted to the antler at the edge of the pond.

"You made an offering?"

"To the Great Bear Spirit," said Tuomas. He didn't bother trying to hide the anxiety on his face. "How did you know I was here?"

"I had a hunch," Henrik said. "It seems there are few places on the island right now where you feel comfortable. But I'm quite surprised that your… that the Spirit of the Lights hasn't joined you."

Tuomas glanced at the sky. All the colour of dusk had vanished now to leave only a soft twilight.

"She wouldn't have been able to come out any earlier than this."

"Where is she concealing herself?"

"She mentioned something about an old fox burrow," said Tuomas, then he ran a hand across the skin of his drum. "Henrik, can I please talk to you?"

"What about?"

Tuomas faltered. At that moment, he would have gladly talked about anything. This was the first time Henrik had openly approached him since the mages' meeting, before Mihka had run off.

Henrik noticed his turmoil. He shuffled to a nearby log, brushed the snow off it, and sat down with a groan. He stuck the torch into the ground beside the fire. The orange glow hung between the two of them and encased them in a flickering circle. Beyond it, every shadow seemed darker: a blackness which might have stretched away beyond the boundaries of the Worlds.

"Well, go on," Henrik said. "Talk."

Tuomas closed his fingers around the antler hammer of his drum.

"I'm scared."

"We all are. I'd consider you a fool if you weren't. Well, more of a fool."

Tuomas looked at him. "Please."

Henrik sighed and laid a hand on his shoulder. Tuomas tried to take comfort from it, even from the stench of shockingly strong tea which followed him everywhere, but nothing worked. It felt as though he were a hundred miles from his own body, and yet trapped within it at the same time.

He gloomily remembered what it had been like to be in the World Above, uncontained, formless, completely free. What he wouldn't have given to have just stayed up there with Lumi, and never looked back.

But his heart slowed at the thought. If he'd done that, he never would have seen Paavo again, or Mihka, or Elin…

"I'm sorry for the way I spoke to you," said Henrik, cutting across his thoughts. "I know all the mages were quick to assume you were the one who tore the sky. But Enska told me that the White Fox One did it."

Tuomas nodded, glanced again at his tail. The red fur seemed to shine in the firelight, as though it were made of sparks rather than hair. He brushed it to make sure it was still real. It and the ears had only appeared a few days ago, and he couldn't quite believe they were attached to him; that he could move them as freely as any other limb.

"I need to reach the Great Bear Spirit," he said dejectedly.

"It will come to you," said Henrik. "You can't force a Spirit like that to just appear. I'm sure there's a reason why it's letting you sit in silence right now."

"So I can feel guilty."

"So you can reflect. That's something all mages must do, not just you, Son of the Sun."

"Please don't call me that."

"Why not? It's the truth."

"It's also truth that I'm still Tuomas. To be a mage is to live divided; people respect and fear you in equal measure. Well, amplify that. Imagine what it's like for me. Then imagine it's all happening when you've barely come of age. Can you blame me, Henrik?"

His voice broke. He drew his knees to his chest and lowered his head.

"I just… I don't know how much more I can take! I wish none of this had ever happened! Why did it have to be now? Why did it have to be *me?*"

Henrik didn't lift his hand, only rubbed it back and forth across Tuomas's shoulders.

"There, there, boy," he said gently. "It will all be alright. You know that, don't you?"

"No. I don't," sniffed Tuomas. Blurred by his tears, he watched the *taika* fall from the edges of the cleft.

"The Great Bear will have a plan," Henrik assured. "I trust in that. And I trust in you."

Tuomas's heart jumped. "You do?"

"Absolutely," replied Henrik. "You're lucky you got a second chance, and I hope you won't waste it. You're still the only mage who can go into trance, remember. We're all counting on you."

"I know," Tuomas said. "And I won't waste it."

He turned his attention to the shrine. Beside it was a mound of stones concealing Paavo's shallow grave.

More tears welled in his eyes. Henrik squeezed his shoulder tighter.

"I might not be a Spirit in human form, but I understand your pain," he said. "I had no siblings, but I remember how hard it is to lose family. Never forget how much he loved you, Tuomas. He would have done anything for you."

Tuomas tried to swallow, but it felt as though a cord had been wrapped around his throat.

"I want him back," he whimpered. "I need him here with me, Henrik. And I trapped him with those monsters!"

He trembled where he sat. Even the fire seemed cold now. A part of him hoped that Henrik might reach out and hold him, hug him like a child and let him feel some warmth. But the old mage stayed where he was, a stoic expression on his face. So instead, Tuomas clutched his drum, reading all the symbols painted across the skin.

He remembered the day Henrik had pushed it into his hands, when he had set out from Akerfjorden at the beginning of the Long Dark.

"This was your drum," he said. "Why did you give it to me, and not ever let me make my own?"

"Because if you made your own, the *taika* might have overwhelmed you," said Henrik. "It would have been like lighting tinder from both ends. Taking mine, with my age and experience inside it, you had a chance."

He gave a long sigh which rattled his lungs. "I tried my best to shield you, boy. I knew what soul – what Spirit – you carried inside you. And I had a feeling that you would discover it when you undertook your mage test. I just didn't expect you to pull the White Fox One out of the sky."

Despite everything, Tuomas managed a small smile. Nobody had expected that. He and Lumi, least of all.

A gust of wind blew across the island. The fires flickered wildly and sent sparks shooting towards the Moon Spirit. Then a long, low groan rattled Tuomas's bones.

He winced, glanced at Henrik.

"Did you hear that?"

Before Henrik could reply, another sound drifted from the village.

Screams.

Chapter Three

Tuomas picked up his drum and hammer, snatched the torch and helped Henrik to his feet. He cursed himself for not having his bow and arrows with him. There was scarcely a need to carry weapons on Anaar, save for knives. And whatever had made that noise was large – too large for the blades at his belt.

He and Henrik hurried through the trees as quickly and quietly as they could. Several reindeer bolted past them towards the higher ground. More sounds joined the screams: awful grunts, the crashing of falling trees. And a horrible crunch. He didn't want to think about what might have caused that.

The huts came into view. Alarm struck Tuomas so hard, he fell over.

Three giants were stomping between the shelters. They were over twice the height of the tallest man, icy coats glinting in the low light. One had seized a reindeer calf and was stuffing it into a sack. The animal bleated in terror, legs kicking vainly at the thick material. Tuomas could tell from the weight of the bag that there were more inside, and a terrible red stain on the snow confirmed what the crunch had been.

Amazingly, it seemed most of the people were safe. Many had started to fight back. Tuomas noticed Maiken; then Sigurd and Elin, all wielding bows, but their arrows did hardly any damage and bounced off the creatures like pins. The giants weren't even fazed. A few knives were stuck in their legs, but from the angle of them, it was clear the blades had been thrown. Nobody was going to risk getting to too close.

"What are those things?" Tuomas cried. But deep down, he knew.

Henrik shuddered. "Trolls."

The giant with the reindeer suddenly paused and sniffed the air. Then it turned its head and looked straight at Henrik. It let out a growl, ripped a sapling from the soil and hurled it at them.

Tuomas jumped on top of Henrik and pushed him over. The tree scarcely missed his head. He grabbed the drum and hit it hard. A shockwave flew out, so powerful, the troll was blown off its feet.

"Get under cover!" Tuomas snapped at Henrik.

He didn't waste time and bolted into the fray, beating the drum as he ran. The two other trolls immediately spun to face him. Their black eyes grew wide, grey mouths twisting into horrible smiles.

Tuomas shuddered. It was like looking at a boulder which had somehow come to life. Where had they even appeared from? All the trolls had been petrified by the Sun Spirit long ago…

He gathered his *taika,* let himself feel the warmth of summer on his back, the taste of lingonberries upon his tongue… then brought the hammer down with a cry. The resulting blast slammed into the nearest troll and knocked it backwards. But it wasn't enough. The creature was upright again in moments.

Elin ran in front of Tuomas and shot an arrow. It rebounded off the troll without making a dent in its skin. She snarled and went to nock another one, but Sigurd took hold her bowstring so she couldn't draw.

"It's no good!" he cried.

"Everyone, take cover!" Maiken yelled. "Now! Go, hurry!"

Nobody argued. They all started fleeing into the forest. Only Elin and a couple of others occasionally twisted to shoot more arrows.

Tuomas went to follow, but then noticed Henrik wasn't among the crowd.

The trolls lumbered in his direction. He hit the drum again to keep them at bay, then looked around frantically.

"Henrik!"

The old mage appeared out of the trees where Tuomas had left him. He was running, but each step shook with his age, and one of the creatures was encroaching on him. It raised a blade of cold black flint.

Tuomas sent a shockwave at it and threw it onto its side. He sprinted towards Henrik and pulled his arm across his shoulders.

"Are you mad?" Henrik hissed. "Get out of here!"

"I'm not leaving you!"

"Stupid boy!"

"You can be angry at me later!"

"You're more important than me!"

Tuomas ignored him and bundled him back into the forest. He could hear the troll close behind, coming after them, but the taller pines and spruces were harder to shove aside than the saplings by the shore.

More reindeer ran past, eyes rolling, bellowing in fear. Tuomas didn't dare stop, just pulled Henrik along. Panic blinded him. He couldn't even figure out which direction he was heading in anymore. The Moonlight reflected off the snow, but it was barely enough to see by.

The trees thinned. Tuomas made for the opening, and his heart sank.

They were at the cliffs, on the west side of the island – a stone's throw from where he had watched the Sun Spirit go down. Over the rocky lip was a sheer thirty-foot drop into the crashing sea.

There was no way out. They would have to fight.

He turned around and held his drum ready. Henrik did the same.

The troll appeared. It peeled back its lips to expose terrible grey teeth: rocks protruding from green mossy gums.

Together, Tuomas and Henrik struck the skins. A shockwave raged forward and hit the monster squarely in the face. It tumbled over with an angry grunt. The sound made Tuomas shudder – it was like two stones grinding together.

He glanced at Henrik. He'd never been more thankful that it was only the trance abilities which the other mages had lost.

Suddenly, another of the trolls tore through the trees and grabbed Henrik by the legs. His drum went flying. The creature held him upside-down, leering at him. Then it snatched his arms in its other hand and wrenched.

Henrik didn't even have time to cry out before blood rained onto the snow.

Horror paralysed Tuomas. The scene narrowed to tunnel vision. His head spun, vision blackened, and then he felt himself falling backwards. The ground disappeared from under his feet.

Air tore past his face. He hit the water and disappeared under the surface.

The waves drained through the shingle in a thousand tiny whispers. Tuomas lay motionless as they lapped around him.

He stirred, slowly at first. Then the memory of the trolls and Henrik exploded back into his mind.

He awoke in an instant, looked around, but there was no sign of the creatures. That did little to calm him. The pebbles were reddened with blood, as was his sodden coat. There was a gash on his cheek, and somehow, he had managed to keep hold of his drum. The front of it was splattered with gore. He couldn't tell if it was his own or Henrik's.

Henrik...

He'd shot enough prey and slaughtered enough old reindeer in his life, but never had he seen anything like that. Everywhere he turned his eyes, it replayed over and over again, made his entire body shake. So much blood, the crunch of bones...

He exclaimed in horror, clapped a hand over his mouth. What if he alerted the trolls?

He ached from landing in the sea, but ignored the pain and staggered to his feet. He couldn't see the monsters anywhere; couldn't hear them, either. In fact, the whole island was silent.

A terrible thought came to him. Was everybody dead?

He rounded the cliffs, clambered off the beach, through the forest. Every step brought a new terrible sight worse than what came before it.

Half the trees were flattened; either snapped in two or torn completely free of the ground. Naked roots stuck up in the air like giant spider legs. The snow was churned, blackened with earth – here and there, red stains splattered across it. A couple of reindeer were strewn among the destruction, their bodies broken.

Tuomas struggled not to vomit. The reindeer were so much more than just animals. They were everything to the people. And to see them killed like this, without respect, left to rot...

He swallowed. At least, so far, he'd come across no human corpses. If everyone had managed to escape with their lives, it would be nothing short of a miracle.

Eventually, he reached the village.

The entire place was razed to the ground. Not a single hut remained standing. Among broken doors and scattered firewood, he could make out a few possessions: cups, sleeping sacks, leather pouches and clothes. Everything was muddied and trampled – the clear tracks of massive footprints were embedded through the whole settlement.

Tuomas sank to his knees in despair. Where was everybody? Where were the rest of the reindeer? They couldn't all be gone...

He didn't even have the strength to call out, too afraid that no-one would answer him.

He suddenly noticed a flash of green in the trees ahead. It flickered and rose around the trunks like fire.

He gasped with relief as Lumi ran into view. She drew to a halt in front of him and grabbed his hands.

"Where were you?" she asked.

Tuomas shook his head, tried to force his mouth to work, but he only managed a horrified cry.

Lumi hauled him upright.

"Come with me," she said. "We have no time."

He stumbled after her through the wreckage. Even now, she managed to walk on top of the snow; her bare feet didn't disturb a single flake. It was as though she weighed nothing, her skin as thin as the sheerest ice.

Then, amazingly, he heard a voice.

"Tuomas! Are you here?"

It was a woman. She was close.

He spotted two figures in the distance, scarcely visible against the black sea. He almost fell over again, but Lumi kept tight hold of his hand and pulled him forward.

"I have him!" she called.

The smaller figure ran over, shouldering a bow as it came. Tuomas realised with a jolt that it was Elin.

"You're hurt," she said, noticing the blood on his cheek. Her eyes were huge, voice flat with shock.

"It's nothing," Tuomas breathed. "Are you alright?"

"Fine," Elin said. "Thank you so much, Lumi."

Lumi didn't reply, just led the two of them towards the second figure. When they broke free of the trees, Tuomas recognised it as Niina: the apprentice mage from Einfjall village. Her face was bruised and dirty, and she was shaking, but otherwise seemed unharmed. Lumi was the only one without a hair out of place.

"Are the others safe?" Tuomas asked. "Where are the trolls?"

Elin glanced at him. "That's what they were? Trolls?"

"Henrik said so."

"Where is Henrik?"

Tuomas's breath caught in his throat. Elin and Niina immediately understood and lowered their heads. Lumi's eyes transformed red with anger.

After a moment, Niina spoke.

"We can't look for him, it's too dangerous."

"Is anyone else hurt? Are the trolls still here?"

"Not that we can see, but the elders said not to take any chances. And most people are alive, but a lot of reindeer were taken. We rounded up those which were left and drove them to Ardni. We've all gone there. Elin and I came back to look for you."

Tuomas nodded woodenly. "Thanks."

He knew he should say more, but it was impossible. He was too dazed, his mouth too dry, and his muscles smarted with pain. And beyond that, he read the meaning beneath Niina's words. It was too dangerous to take chances… except for him. Because he was the Spirit in human form. Once again, that was all that mattered.

In subdued silence, Niina and Elin led the way to the beach. A lone boat lay on the shingle. Lumi shrank to her fox form, to save space, and leapt inside. Tuomas followed her, then Niina and Elin pushed it into the water. As soon as it was afloat, the two of them grabbed oars and paddled off.

Tuomas threw a glance at Elin. This was the first time he had properly seen her since the day the two of them had woken on the shore. She was still thin and a little pale from the soul plague, but had recovered her strength incredibly quickly. Her oar sliced through the water with no effort – though part of him wondered if she was just making it look easy to prove a point.

Had their argument worn off? It was difficult to tell. She had clearly been glad to see him alive, but now she kept her attention straight ahead. He decided against trying to strike up a conversation. This was no time to talk.

It was only a few miles to Ardni, but in the aftermath of the attack, it felt like they were moving towards the ends of the earth. Tuomas tried to focus on the slapping of oars on the water. The waves sparkled as *taika* rained from the gash in the sky.

Slowly, Ardni drew closer: a black silhouette against the stars. It was the neighbouring island, and the ancestral summer grounds of Poro. Lilja and Enska's village would traditionally come here during the migration, rather than to Anaar, but as the largest in the archipelago, Akerfjorden's island had been chosen to house everyone, in light of the troubled winter.

Tuomas trembled. The whole point of merging the villages was because Anaar was meant to be safe.

"I don't understand," he whispered, afraid of speaking too loudly. "Where did they come from?"

"I don't know," muttered Niina. "They just… appeared out of the earth. What about those boulders in the mountain pass? They're supposed to be trolls. The Sun Spirit touched them and they turned to stone."

"But that was ages ago," he said. "How did they break free? We always left offerings, asked the Spirits to keep them contained…"

Lumi growled. Tuomas looked at her.

"Do you know something?" he asked.

She turned her eyes on him. They danced between green and blue: the colours of the Lights on a clear winter's night. But at their edges, he could still see a trace of crimson. However, she didn't reply. She was unable to in her fox form; he remembered that from when she had first taken it at the end of the Long Dark.

Nobody spoke again as they drew close to Ardni. Kittiwakes screamed from their nests on the high cliff faces. Puffins darted around in flashes of black and white. The trolls might not have come here, but their presence had sent waves through the night. All the animals, plants, and rocks were on alert. Tuomas could feel it like a pressure on his chest.

Everything was shaken, struggling to keep purchase on the unsteady, torn Worlds.

Niina and Elin drove the boat onto the shore, beside all the others from Anaar. Lumi changed back into her human form. Then Niina led the way inland, following a line of trampled snow. Tuomas could tell from the mess of footprints that all the survivors had come this way.

"Do you know something?" he asked Lumi again.

"The Spirits heard the people's pleas about those creatures," she replied grimly. "I cannot say why they have been reanimated. But I have my suspicions as to who has done it."

With that, she turned her eyes skyward, to the Moon Spirit.

Tuomas touched his drum, trying to take some comfort from it. But he recoiled when he realised the surface was still damp with blood.

"Why her?" he whispered.

Lumi shook her head. "My mother is a dark entity. Trolls cannot survive in the daylight. It appears to make sense to me. I just hope I am doing her an injustice."

Tuomas shivered. Like all Spirits, the Silver One was not inherently good or evil, but she was dangerous, and he had quickly learned she had her own agenda. Twice, she had tried to convince him to renounce his soul to her and accept her as his mother. At his lowest point, she had even encouraged him to give up his life.

Her words shot through his memory like the cracking of ice.

If I cannot have you, Red Fox One, then no Spirit will.

His mind raced. What good would unleashing the trolls do in making him surrender? Hadn't he made it clear that he wanted nothing to do with her?

Like Lumi, he hoped he was wrong.

Soon, the four of them reached the village. A fire was burning in the central pit, and people were busy airing out the huts and cooking food. Tuomas wrinkled his nose at the smell of it. Seaweed. Escaping like they had, there wasn't much choice for anything else.

But he ignored it and let out a sigh of relief. Niina had been right. Most of the herders were all here, looking dazed and a little bloodied, but alive.

He quickly took stock of the faces. They all paused when they saw him, muttered in apprehension. He pulled his tail and ears as far back as he could, to hide them, but soon gave up. It wouldn't be of any benefit when Lumi was standing right next to him.

"How many did the trolls take?" he asked.

"Amazingly, nobody," said Niina. "They just went off with reindeer. We guessed it's probably for food."

"How many?"

"We haven't had a chance to count yet, but I think everyone's lost at least two animals."

Tuomas grimaced, then frowned as he continued to check who was around the fire.

"Then where's Aslak? And Stellan?"

"With the herd," replied Elin. "Alright... now we're back, I need to go and help my parents."

She hurried off into the throng. Tuomas watched her go, went to call after her, but stopped himself.

"Are Enska and Aino up there, too?" he asked instead. "Or are they healing people?"

Niina's face turned even paler.

"Come with me," she said tightly.

She led them away from the fire pit. Tuomas clutched his drum nervously, by the back beam, so he couldn't touch the blood. He would have to wash it soon, before the skin could stain…

It wasn't long before they came across some men, slamming axes into the trunk of a tree. Another had already been felled nearby, and a woman was chopping it down to firewood. They all nodded their heads as Niina and Tuomas walked by. Even amid the horror, it was important to still show respect to mages. But Tuomas noticed a spark of fear come into their eyes when they saw him and Lumi. It was as though they were looking at something inhuman.

His stomach clenched. He did his best to ignore it and instead fixed his attention on a spot between Niina's shoulder blades. She paused every now and then to check on people as she passed. Tuomas could tell several of them, like him, had been in the water: they had changed into dry clothes, but their hair stuck in all directions after being towelled on strips of fabric. Others were visibly injured, with broken fingers bound to twigs, cuts covered by poultices. The mages hadn't wasted any time seeing to the wounds.

Then they rounded the last line of huts, and Tuomas's heart leapt into his mouth.

A makeshift litter had been erected, surrounded by a protective circle – he recognised its *taika* as being Niina's. Two bodies lay atop the wooden platform. Lilja was standing outside the barrier close to the nearest figure, tears streaming down her cheeks.

It was Enska. And beside him: Aino, Niina's mentor.

Together with Henrik, the chief mages of all three villages were dead.

Chapter Four

Lilja approached. Her face was almost as pale as Lumi's. A glaze had come over her eyes, as though she had retreated deep inside herself, and left only what was needed to function. Her sleeves of white reindeer fur – the mark of a mage – were spotted with blood.

"Thank you for bringing him back," she said to Niina, so quietly, Tuomas strained to hear her. "Where were you? You're soaking."

"I fell off the cliff," Tuomas said. "I was with Henrik. The trolls… they…"

He couldn't bring himself to say it. Just remembering the sight of his old teacher being pulled apart made his stomach flip.

Lilja shuffled uncomfortably. "Did they take him away?"

"I didn't see."

"Did they kill him there and then?"

"Yes. Why?"

"Then they won't have taken him. They don't bother with things which are already dead. At least, that's what the old stories say. They didn't try to take Aino and my father, either. They just killed them. Put those huge knives through their stomachs."

She broke off with a shudder.

At Tuomas's side, Lumi bristled. She swept her tail so hard, a miniature aurora drifted around her. There was no green in it; the Lights were the colour of blood. Several people drew away at the sight; even Tuomas struggled to stay still as her power pressed against his skin.

A man stood up. Tuomas recognised him: Frode. He had lost his son and daughter to the draugars.

"What's going on?" he asked tearfully. "Son of the Sun… please! Do you know what sent them?"

"Tuomas. And no, I don't."

"Did you summon them?"

"No!" Tuomas cried. "I would never do that!"

"You summoned *her!*" another man cried, pointing at Lumi. "What have you done? Are they here for you?"

"They took the reindeer! Killed the mages!"

"What do they want you for?"

"Silence!" Lumi shouted.

At once, everyone became quiet. Lumi moved in front of Tuomas and glared at everyone who dared meet her eyes. The Lights intensified until the air glowed bright red.

Niina threw her a nervous glance, then spoke.

"I… We don't know. But please just bear with us. Speak with the elders while we… well, sort this out."

She tried to sound strong, but her voice wavered like leaves tossed about in the wind. She was afraid; only a couple of years older than Tuomas – and unlike him and Lilja, the only mage who was still an apprentice.

Slowly, everyone shuffled away from the litter and returned to their work. Lumi lowered her tail and the Lights faded, but Tuomas could tell she was still angry. He was just glad she hadn't decided to strike anybody.

He turned to Enska and Aino. They had been covered by reindeer skins to hide their injuries, but nothing could disguise the amount of blood. They didn't even look like the people he'd known: their faces were drawn, jaws slack, eyes open and already beginning to cloud over.

Lilja brushed his hair aside to see the gash on his cheek.

"That needs cleaning," she said. "Come with me."

"I'm fine," Tuomas protested.

"Shut up," Lilja snapped. "I'm not in the mood for false modesty. Come on."

Without another word, she snatched his wrist and pulled him away. He only had time to throw a brief glance at Lumi before she bounded into the forest.

Lilja dragged him to the outskirts of the village. Tuomas wasn't surprised to find that she had settled so far from everyone else. The shelter was small, set against a snow-covered hillock, and looked as though it hadn't been touched for years, even among those who would have come to Ardni every winter.

Lilja pushed the door open, then shoved him through. The hut stank of mildew and smoke. A fire burned in the centre, contained by flat hearth stones, and the floor underfoot was laid with overlapping birch twigs. Reindeer skins and sleeping sacks had been strewn at the back, and on one of them sat a small boy, knees clutched to his chest.

He stared with wide eyes. In the flickering firelight, Tuomas could see lines of vicious burn scars down his face.

Aki. Tuomas recognised him straightaway. But before he could say or do anything, Lilja elbowed past him and hurried to her son's side. She pulled him against her chest, caressed his hair. It was the same sandy blonde as her own.

"Mama, have they come after us?" he asked in a tiny voice. Tuomas's heart wrenched at the sound of it.

"No, no," Lilja replied softly. "We're safe, baby. I'm here now. Try to get some sleep, alright? You still need to rest."

Aki looked at her. "Please don't go away again. Will you stay here now? Please?"

"For a little while. Unless someone calls me."

"Will they?"

"I don't know. I've seen to most of the people who were hurt," said Lilja. "But don't worry. You're safe."

Aki pressed his face close to her to whisper. "Why is he here?"

Tuomas shuffled. This was the first time he had seen Aki awake. And while he was truly a five-year-old child, Tuomas couldn't shake the memory of what he had inadvertently been responsible for. When he looked at him, he could still see his eyes as sightless white globes, his flesh puckered, water pouring from his mouth…

He put his hands behind his back to hide the nervous fists they had curled into.

He's just a boy, he reminded himself. *Nothing more, just a little boy…*

"You remember Tuomas, don't you?" Lilja said. "He's our friend. And he's got a nasty cut which I need to fix."

"Why does he have big ears and a tail?"

"Because he's special."

She planted a kiss on Aki's forehead, then eased him into one of the sleeping sacks, tucking it high around his chin. As he settled against the soft fur, his eyes became heavy, and he let out a yawn.

"Go to sleep now, baby," Lilja said. "I love you."

"I love you too, Mama," Aki muttered.

Lilja stroked his hair, sang a gentle wordless chant until his breathing became slow and steady. Then she rummaged in a sack and flung a bundle of clothes at Tuomas.

"Get out of those wet things before you freeze," she said, turning her back to give him some privacy.

"I'm not cold," Tuomas insisted as he untied his shoes.

"Of course you're not, Son of the Sun," Lilja snapped sarcastically. "But change anyway."

Tuomas didn't reply and focused on tugging his tunic and trousers off. Once he was free of them, he wiped himself down and wriggled into the new clothes. They were a little large, but fit well enough. It was lucky that there were even dry garments to go around.

His temperature was the same as before, but now he was more comfortable. He hadn't genuinely felt cold since halfway through the migration, not even when he had gotten wet or been outside for an extended period. He couldn't remember the last time he'd worn mittens or a hat.

It was all because he had accepted who he was. That, combined with the mass of *taika* inside him, meant the elements had practically no effect now. As the Spirit of the Flames, he couldn't be too hot, and even the icy winter didn't bother him much anymore. He remembered the night when Lilja had taught him how to walk through fire. Just like when he'd held the flames at the shrine, he had felt no pain; his skin hadn't even reddened.

He cleared his throat to tell her he was dressed. She looked him up and down, then nodded.

"Sit," she ordered.

Tuomas settled on the hide. He noticed a small bucket of melted snow nearby and washed his drumskin as carefully as he could. As he worked, Lilja produced a small box and rummaged through it for her herbs. She dropped a handful into a pot over the flames, waited for the smell to fill the hut, then dipped a cloth into the mixture and began wiping the blood off his cheek.

"Any broken bones?" she asked.

"No," he replied, careful to keep his voice low in case he woke Aki. "I think it's just bruising."

"You're lucky. If you fell off the cliff, it's a wonder you're not in pieces."

Her choice of words made him flinch.

"How many reindeer did you lose?" he asked instead, needing to get Henrik out of his head.

"I don't know yet," she said. "But nobody came through this unscathed, even if they don't have any injuries themselves. I think about a third of the entire herd is lost."

Tuomas closed his eyes so he wouldn't cry.

"Not all the reindeer were taken, though. I saw some on Anaar."

"Well, it doesn't really matter. They're still dead." Lilja dipped the cloth back into the pot and wiped it across his cheek again. "Listen, I saw the way you were looking at Aki. And I know what you were thinking. Stop it."

"I wasn't thinking anything," Tuomas said quickly.

Lilja glared at him. The fire only lit half of her face, yet her eyes glowed like embers.

"Everybody has been alienating him," she said. "I don't need you doing the same, especially after you saw him like none of the others did. He's just a child. You know that."

Tuomas's shoulders slumped. "I'm sorry. You're right. They're doing the same thing to me."

Lilja scowled for a moment longer before resuming her work. She gripped his chin so he couldn't move.

"You're doing it, as well," Tuomas said.

"Well, forgive me if I'm still angry with you," she snapped.

"Why?" he asked. "I don't know how many more times I can apologise to everyone. Didn't Lumi tell you there are more important things right now?"

He winced as the cloth drew close to the gash. He was sure Lilja didn't need to press so hard.

"If it will put your mind at ease, then I accept," she muttered. "I'm not stupid, I know these trolls aren't your doing. So, let's draw a line under this now, shall we?"

"Gladly."

She let go of him. Tuomas moved his eyes towards Aki while she wrung out the cloth. His eyes were still closed, and around the burns, his cheeks bore a healthy glow. He looked a little chubbier than the last time he'd seen him. Lilja and Enska mustn't have wasted any time giving him his first proper meals in years.

Tuomas recalled the argument he'd overheard between her and Sigurd. He had a mind to ask her if she still intended to leave, but bit it back before the words could form. There would be a better time and place to talk about that.

He groaned under his breath. He still needed to speak with Elin, too. Why did so many of those he was close to suddenly feel so far away?

Lilja pulled out some more herbs and ground them into a poultice. Their spicy scent flew up Tuomas's nose and he fought not to sneeze. He noticed her hands were shaking.

"I'm so sorry," he said softly. "About your father."

Lilja pressed her lips together. Her eyes glistened with tears, but she blinked them away.

"If there's anything I can do," he offered, "you know I'm here, right?"

"Thank you. I suppose I'm completely like you now. Neither of us have any parents anymore."

Tuomas gave her the best smile he could, then the two of them sat in silence as she smeared the poultice on his cheek. It stung at first, but numbed his skin until all he could feel was warmth. Lilja wiped the excess off her hands and sat back against the earthen wall.

"I take it you haven't found a hut yet," she said. "You can stay here if you want."

"Thanks," Tuomas smiled. "You're sure?"

"I wouldn't offer if I didn't mean it."

"I haven't got my sleeping sack, though."

"Don't worry. Some spares were brought over from Anaar when we all left. You can get one."

She twisted around, grabbed the sack which the clothes had been in, and pulled it into her lap.

"I brought this with me," she said. "I was making Aki some new clothes on Anaar – ones which would actually fit him. I finished quicker than I thought. So I... made this for you."

She drew out a coat. It was decorated about the neck and hems with beautiful bone beads. They didn't just show the designs of Akerfjorden, but also of Poro and Einfjall. Tuomas realised she must have taken note of the different ways the three villages expressed themselves, and integrated them all.

But that wasn't what stunned him. It was pure white reindeer fur: the material reserved for mages. That was one of the most sacred animals, second only to a bear. But none of the other mages had an entire garment of this size made from it.

"It's beautiful," Tuomas gasped.

Lilja shrugged nonchalantly, but her eyes shone.

"I thought it was about time you had something worthy of who you are. Tradition, and all that stuff."

Tuomas glanced at her. "Who I am?"

She sighed. "Face it, boy. You need to own it now."

Tuomas gripped the coat tightly. The Great Mage had worn something just like this.

He managed a mirthless smile, then pulled it on. It billowed around him like a thick cloud. As soon as it touched his skin, he sensed its power – not just being from a white reindeer, but also from the symbolism he now wore. It pressed upon him as though he had clothed himself in stones, not fur.

He went to move towards Lilja, but she held up a hand.

"Don't you dare hug me."

Tuomas smirked. "Fine. Can I thank you?"

She cocked an eyebrow in response. That was enough.

A soft knock sounded on the door. Lilja jumped to her feet and eased it open.

"What is it?"

"Sorry to disturb you," said a voice – Niina. "The elders have asked you, me, and Tuomas to come and see them."

Lilja hesitated, glancing over her shoulder at Aki. A torn expression fleeted across her face.

Tuomas could tell she wanted nothing more than to curl up with her son and be left alone. He knew exactly how she felt: after Paavo had died, he'd barely been able to function. And even though Lilja had spent so many years away from her people, Enska was one of the few she had ever forged a bond with. To be without him, mere months after finding the strength to return to Poro…

He tapped her leg to get her attention.

"It probably won't be for long," he assured. "Aki won't wake up. Don't worry."

He took a log from the pile by the door and added it to the fire. He placed it carefully, so the embers wouldn't break under the weight.

Lilja sighed, then gave a single nod and stepped past Niina. Tuomas followed, closed the door behind him. As the three of them walked away, he scanned the trees for sign of Lumi, but there wasn't a trace, not even a tiny wave of Lights.

Chapter Five

Niina led the way to a large hut close to the central fire pit. Several people were still huddled around the flames and threw the mages anxious glances as they passed. Tuomas offered the best polite smile he could, but he knew it hadn't reached his eyes. Everyone was still too stunned, too overwhelmed, to do anything except breathe and cry.

Stepping inside the shelter, they were met by the elders of all three villages. Tuomas instantly recognised Maiken from Akerfjorden, and her cousin Anssi; as well as Birkir, from when he had stayed in Einfjall. All of them wore clothes decorated with fine bone and antler beads to show their rank, and the patterns seemed to dance in the shifting light cast by the fire.

A wave of sadness washed through Tuomas when he saw them. Sisu should be in the hut, right next to Anssi and Maiken. But he was dead, too. Lost. Another soul trapped beyond life, with the monsters from between the Worlds.

The elders stiffened when they saw Tuomas's coat. He squirmed and flattened his ears in discomfort.

"Son of the Sun," said Anssi awkwardly. "It's good to see you."

"Tuomas. And you, too," he replied.

"We were worried we'd lost you, as well. The mages…"

"With respect," Lilja said tersely, "what would you like to speak to us about?"

Everyone shuffled. Maiken gestured to the other side of the hearth, and Tuomas, Niina and Lilja sat on the reindeer skins

– Lilja closest to the door. She twisted her fingers and slouched, trying to make herself look as inconspicuous as possible.

"Alright, to the matter at hand," said Anssi. "We're sorry to call you like this, but… well, you're the only mages left now. The only three who survived."

A lump formed in Tuomas's throat like a stone.

"So you want us to lead the funerals?" Niina asked.

"Well, yes, that too. But you're also the only ones with *taika*. We need you to put a protective barrier around the entire settlement, in case those things come back."

"Trolls," Tuomas muttered. "They're trolls."

All the elders gasped in horror.

"I thought the trolls were gone!" protested Birkir.

"Let's be honest," Lilja said with a hint of scorn. "Nothing should be surprising us by this point."

Maiken shrugged dryly in agreement.

"Do you think they're the ones from the mountains?" Niina suggested, turning to Tuomas. "Maybe they weren't happy that you were able to split the avalanche they sent. I didn't see it, but I heard about it."

Tuomas grimaced. Everybody had heard about that.

"If that was the case, they would only have come after me," he said. "It makes no sense why they… well, you know."

"Maybe it's because the other mages are weakened," volunteered Birkir. "Aino mentioned she couldn't enter trances for the whole of the migration."

"None of us could," Lilja said, with a pointed look at Tuomas.

He sighed. "That was my fault. After I came back from the World Above, I made a hole in the boundary between there and the World Between. Not the rip which is up there now, but it was enough to cut off all the other mages' *taika* except mine."

"But what could that have to do with the trolls?"

"I don't know. I think Lumi has an idea."

At mention of her, everyone except Lilja recoiled.

"She's really not going to hurt anyone?" Maiken asked uneasily.

"No," Tuomas insisted. "Just stay out of her way and do what she says. It's me she's here for. I'll speak to her after we're done."

"Very well," said Anssi. "But now… we need to talk to you about something else, all three of you. The trolls only killed the mages. We don't think they left you alive except out of pure luck. They might come back, either for you or for the reindeer. And if they don't realise yet that we're trapped on these islands, they will soon enough."

"We're sitting ducks," said Niina.

"Yes."

"So what do you suggest?"

Maiken laced her fingers together under her chin.

"We need to leave. If we go together, and head south, we can all look after each other."

"That's a good idea," Niina agreed. "Trolls can't survive if the Sun Spirit touches them. That's in all the old stories. It's why they turned to stone."

"Exactly," mused one of the Poro elders. "And the Sun Spirit is growing in strength every day now. So if we go south, we'll be in a place where she'll shine for longer. The nights will be shorter, and there's less chance of the trolls being able to attack."

"We should all move as one," said Maiken. "Einfjall and Poro can come with us and shelter at Akerfjorden. It's the furthest south; it will be the safest place. Then, maybe when day and night are equal, you can return to your own villages. Once the summer takes hold, we will have the Long Day; the Sun Spirit will never set for two months. That will certainly kill any trolls."

"You want to go through the mountains again?"

"No. Spring is on the way; it will be too unstable up there. What if we just walk on the sea ice and then down the Mustafjord? That's a direct route to Akerfjorden."

"Terrible idea," Lilja said.

The elders looked at her to explain, but Tuomas realised her point immediately and stepped in.

"The sea ice will already be melting," he said. "The mouth of the Mustafjord will be open water by now."

"Well, I personally don't want to take the herd back through the mountains," said Anssi. "I think we should go around them. It's the long way, but it would be less dangerous for the calves, now the thaw is coming. Once we've cleared them, we can turn due east and head for the Mustafjord. It should still be frozen enough to hold us halfway down, that far from the sea."

Several heads nodded in agreement, but then another of the elders spoke up.

"But the reindeer!" she protested. "We've barely finished the migration! The females have only just recovered from giving birth, and the calves are still young! How are they supposed to survive a journey like this?"

"And what about the lichen? It won't have had a chance to grow back yet in the south. Even if the herd does get to Akerfjorden, they'll starve."

Tuomas frowned. It was a good point. They couldn't leave the reindeer here either, not with the trolls stealing them. Without them, the people would have nothing. They depended on them for their livelihood, for their very survival. It was why the villages always accompanied them on the migration, twice a year, to ensure the animals would be safe. Even though this wasn't the time to naturally move them, going south without them was out of the question.

"Then we'll collect every bit of lichen and moss we can from across the islands," Maiken suggested.

"She's right," said Anssi. "We can't risk the herd by leaving them here. We'll have to take our chances."

The elders muttered amongst themselves, but it wasn't long before they all nodded in agreement.

"These are exceptional circumstances," Birkir said eventually. "We have no choice."

"You three lay down a circle, and prepare for funerals in the morning," Maiken said. "Then we'll bury the dead. Tonight, when we leave this shelter, spread the word that we set off in two days. That's the quickest we can get everything done. In the meantime, everybody will take turns on watch duty, and keep the reindeer as close to the village as possible. The less time we can spend rounding them all up, the sooner we can start moving."

Anssi leaned forward. His eyes were heavy.

"And there's one last thing," he said solemnly. "We might be elders, but mages are equal to us in leading our people and keeping them safe. You're all that's left now. One for each village."

Niina gasped nervously.

"We need to step up? Be resident mages?"

"Yes."

"But…"

"There can be no buts," said Maiken. "You three are the only ones with *taika*, with the knowledge of how to use it."

Niina let out a tiny whimper. Tuomas squeezed her hand in comfort, but he didn't feel much better. Only now did the true gravity of the deaths strike him. He fancied himself back in the mountains, with the avalanche barrelling towards him, and was powerless to stop it sweeping him away. Henrik had been a frustrating curmudgeon, but knowing his guidance was gone, the void between the Worlds seemed closer than ever. It was as though the very air itself was pulling apart.

His insides felt hollow. No elder mages, no Sisu, no Paavo... and even though Mihka and Elin were still alive, they might as well be a thousand miles away.

At that moment, he realised how truly frightened he was. Since winter began, it had been one bad thing after another. He thought he'd had terrible luck when Kari tried to kill him, but the worst hurt of all came after. Like he'd thought when he offered himself to the draugars, his own death was the easy, painless option. Living on while his loved ones were in danger... that was much harder.

He looked at Lilja out of the corner of his eye. She was gripping the hem of her tunic so tightly, her knuckles had turned white. She had been planning to leave, to get away from people forever. How could she do that now?

She glanced at Birkir. "Are we finished here?"

Her abruptness caught him off guard, but he nodded. In an instant, Lilja was on her feet and disappeared out the door.

Tuomas sighed, then stood and extended a hand to help Niina.

"Thank you," he muttered. "Goodnight."

The two of them stepped into the open. As soon as they were away from the crackle of the fire, Tuomas heard an anguished cry, deep in the woods.

Niina blinked in alarm. "Is that Lilja?"

Tuomas nodded. The sound cut through him like a blade. He had a mind to go looking for her, but Enska's advice rang in his ears. She wouldn't appreciate being comforted; it would likely make her angrier. And he had only just managed to repair their friendship – approaching her now could break it straight back down.

"Come on," he said. "Let's do the circle."

"But what about Lilja?"

"She'll be alright. Leave her be."

Niina swallowed, but nodded, and allowed him to lead her towards the fire pit. They both held their drums close to the flames until the skin was tight, then began to walk in opposite directions around the edge of the village, beating as they went.

Tuomas raised his voice in a chant, let his *taika* consume him until it twisted his souls around each other. He didn't form words, just allowed the power to take form in his breath, undulating up and down. He heard his own pain in the sound, trembled at the desolation which poured from his lips.

The wind whistled in the treetops and matched the rhythm. The Spirits were listening to him, answering back. But he wasn't sure if it was in comfort or accusation.

A crowd of people emerged to watch him and Niina. Everyone was bleary-eyed, yet wide awake, all too aware of the danger to risk sleeping. Tuomas did his best to ignore them and kept his attention on his work.

With every step, the barrier grew, strengthened; he felt his power entwining with Niina's. As they worked, they laid down intent: only humans could enter. That way, Lilja would be able to get back in.

When he was done, he lowered the hammer with trembling fingers, and stepped outside the circle. It would hold until dawn, when everywhere would be safer.

He went to turn to the litter, to start preparing the bodies for the funerals, but then he noticed movement in his periphery. He knew it was Lumi before he even turned around. She was standing in the shadow of a large spruce, just out of sight of the village.

She didn't need to speak. Tuomas followed her into the trees.

Chapter Six

Lumi glowed in the darkness. Her entire body shimmered like a thousand snowflakes; even at a regular walk, she seemed to dance. Green sparks flew from her tail as it moved.

Soon, they reached the Ardni shrine: the stump of a massive ash tree carved into many strange shapes by decades of wind and weather. The sky was open around it; the other plants knew the sacredness of the site and refused to grow too close. This was a place where the Worlds touched, powerful in how different it was to everything around it. Tuomas had never visited this place before, but he sensed its magic, as clearly as though it were the warmth of a fire after a cold night in the tundra.

The rip waved overhead; the night seemed to have no end. For a moment, he felt as though he was in the middle of the Long Dark again: that time in deepest winter when the Sun Spirit didn't rise above the horizon.

"I wish it was still midwinter," he said. "Everything was simpler then."

"Indeed. You only had me to concern yourself with," replied Lumi. "And a demon, of course."

Tuomas winced as he thought of Kari. He held a hand to his chest, remembering the cold flint blade as it sliced towards his heart. Then he noticed all the healing wounds on the rest of his flesh: his hands, wrists… beneath his clothes, even more of them covered his body. Draugar teeth. He had known nothing sharper.

Thus far, all his enemies had managed to draw blood. What would it feel like when one of the trolls ran that huge sword through his belly?

"Are you afraid?" he asked.

Lumi turned her eyes on him. They were a soft twilight blue; it chilled him just to look into them for too long.

"Yes."

Tuomas wasn't sure if that brought any comfort. She was a Spirit: one of the most revered of all. She intimidated everyone who saw her. He had never known her to be scared – and never thought a time would come when she'd admit to it.

A bead of water ran from her hairline. She quickly wiped it away and shifted her focus to her mother's silver face. A harshness descended upon her expression like ice.

"Come," she said. "I do not wish to remain ignorant to these matters a moment longer."

"Me, neither," said Tuomas.

He spun a protective circle around the shrine, then they sat beside it. Several offerings had already been laid there; he supposed people had already visited upon arriving on the island. He saw beads, blades, small carvings of bone and antler, strands of hair tied onto the exposed roots.

Tuomas went to cut some of his own, but decided it wasn't good enough – he'd already left some hair earlier that night, and the Great Bear hadn't come. Instead, he drew his smallest knife and dragged it across the end of his finger. Lumi watched wordlessly as he let the blood drip onto the snow.

He went to untie his drum, but she shook her head.

"There is no need," she said quietly, and instead held took his hand.

At once, he felt her power reaching for him, plucking at his souls. It was freezing cold, but didn't repel him; he allowed his own to rise with the sharp taste of lingonberry and delicious warmth of the Sun Spirit at midsummer.

He spun in darkness. Weight left him as he entered a trance, and his body slumped back against the ash tree. He was no longer contained, but was a Spirit, shining brighter than anything else.

Then he sensed an enormous presence, as though the energy of all three Worlds were swirling around him and Lumi. But it wasn't the oppressive, dangerous kind which he knew was caused by the cleft. It was something beyond that, almost beyond comprehension. Neither dead nor alive, male nor female, completely uncontained.

The stars swirled into the face of the Great Bear.

Tuomas shrank back in reverence. Lumi did the same.

Thank you for coming to us, he said, in the silent formless language of Spirits.

It is time for you to hear what must be heard, replied the Bear. *Firstly, White Fox One, I wish to settle you. The souls in the World Above are safe. They wander and search for you, but they are aware of why you are not dancing with them. They wait for your return.*

Lumi pulsed bright green at the words, but her relief vanished as quickly as it came. Tuomas realised why. There was a gravity to the Bear's tone, firmer than he had ever perceived before. It felt as though he were underwater: pressure on all sides, twisting his gut and pulling at his mind. He was going to hear some uncomfortable truths tonight, he knew it.

I have seen the trolls ravaging the people, the Bear continued darkly. *I watched the destruction of Anaar, of reindeer and mages.*

They are not powerful enough to have reanimated by themselves, said Lumi, with the edge of snarl. *Who sent them? Am I correct in my assumptions?*

The Great Bear turned its nose towards the Moon Spirit, but Tuomas could tell she was too far away to hear. This was a conversation which didn't involve her.

You are, it said. *But why she has awakened them, I cannot say.*

Tuomas felt Lumi's grip tighten, and for a moment, he worried she might crush him. A furious red aurora blazed around them both, wove itself with the ethereal shape of the Bear and the falling stardust around the rip.

Is it to do with me? Tuomas asked anxiously. *She wants me back.*

I know. But I cannot say.

Lumi growled. *Then what must be done?*

What has already been decided, replied the Bear. *The people are not fools and are reacting in a sensible manner. Go south. Take shelter in the Sun Spirit's light. Rely on the mages to protect all which can be protected.*

Can't you stop the trolls? Tuomas asked. *Please! You can do anything!*

You know, Red Fox One, that my power is in righting imbalances, nothing more. And before I may act upon anything, nature and those within it must take the first step. Which brings us to the two of you. I set you a charge, Son of the Sun, which you ignored.

I know. And I'm so sorry, said Tuomas. *Can you forgive me?*

Forgiveness is immaterial. Your decision was dangerous, one which I was barely able to correct, and now there remains only that which must be done. Do you realise why

I told you to merely draw the draugars out, and not attempt to bargain for the souls they had taken?

No. Why?

Because with them contained, I would have been able to save the boy, Aki. And Aki is a human who has died and returned to life in the same body. He could have then crossed into the Deathlands and freed the souls. Balance would have been restored.

Tuomas's blood turned to ice. The Great Bear had had a plan all along? He should have known… this being was all that had been and all that would be. It saw everything, knew everything, from the surge of the greatest avalanches to a tiny moth crawling out of a chrysalis. Of course it had anticipated a way to set things right. And then he had tried to play the hero, second-guessed it, and brought only more problems.

But… that wouldn't have saved Elin, would it? he asked. *If I hadn't done what I did… she would have died.*

Yes, she would, said the Bear. *And I will not force you to consider whether that was the wisest decision. You berate yourself well enough for that. And the actions your sister took to save you stand in testament to it.*

Tuomas flinched. The words held no form, yet they struck him heavier than if an entire mountain had been thrown onto his shoulders.

Lumi hadn't let go of him. He tried to take comfort from her, and, sensing it, she swept a stream of Lights around him.

All is not lost, Red Fox One, said the Bear, gentler now. *Now, will you do what I ask you?*

It's not a request, and I take it gladly, replied Tuomas at once. *Tell me.*

You and your sister are the only ones able to open the gateway into the World Below now. Take Lilja's son there, to the border of the Deathlands. Cross the Night River with him and enter the domain of the Horse-Riding One. Let him do what I bid, and separate the trapped souls of the mist children from their captors. And then all will be free.

Tuomas's heart grew heavier than a stone as he thought of Aki. He was just a child – five years old, finally returned to his mother after so long as a puppet and prisoner. And now he would have to be taken from her, walk into the place where no living person had ever stood? Even Tuomas himself was terrified of that shifting black water. When he'd seen it, every fibre of his being had screamed at him to not take a single step closer.

Why do you fear the Deathlands? asked the Bear. *Even before you remembered the White Fox One was your sister, you viewed her with the same respect and fear as you do the Horse-Riding One. Neither of these Spirits are evil.*

Tuomas twisted around himself anxiously. *I know the World Above. I know her Lights. I knew them long before I went up there this winter. I don't know what lies across the Night River.*

And you shall soon learn it, was the reply.

But why does it need to be Aki? Tuomas asked. *That's not fair on him. Why can't it just be me, so he can have some peace with his mother? I've died and come back to life, too. I caused all this misery; it should be me.*

But you have not, luckily, been in the grip of the draugars, the Bear said. *Aki will be able to separate them and the souls in a way even you cannot. But I charge you, for the time being, not to inform Lilja.*

What? Why? He's her son, she deserves to know.

Yes, she probably does. But if you tell her now, she will refuse to leave him. And there are other matters she must attend to, from which she cannot be distracted. Do you understand?

Tuomas squirmed. No, he didn't understand. But he needed to trust. That was one thing he had been forced to learn.

Alright, he said. *I'll figure out a way to take Aki to the Northern Edge.*

The people depart in two days, Lumi cut in. *We will follow around the flank of the mountains, then separate from them.*

Very well, said the Great Bear. *And there is another reason why I do not wish for you to separate the souls from the draugars, Son of the Sun. When you return to the World Between, I have another task for you. It is the very reason why I allowed you to be reborn once again as the human called Tuomas.*

It drew close, surrounded him with starlight. Far away, in his body, Tuomas felt his heart pounding.

When you first walked among the people, as the Great Mage, you opened the gateway to the World Below, unleashed the draugars, and they killed you. Now, I charge you to finish what you could not, all those generations ago, Tuomas Sun-Soul. Close the gateway. Seal off the Northern Edge of the World forever. And then, White Fox One, you shall do the same with the tear in the sky. If you both do this, balance will be restored.

Tuomas trembled. *So... nobody else will be able to go to the World Below again?*

No. This is the way it should always have remained.

And then everything will be safe again? Forever?

Forever is a concept for myself alone, the Bear replied. *There will always be dangers and fluctuations. It is a part of the riddle of existence. But it will all occur as it should, with every end heralding a new beginning. And the two of you must make this so. If you do not, oblivion will sweep through the Worlds, turn them inside out and devour them until nothing is left. Do you accept this charge?*

Tuomas glanced at Lumi. She swirled closer to him; he felt her protectiveness sweep through him like a cold wind.

I accept, she said.

As do I, added Tuomas. *But please, help us with the trolls. We won't be able to do anything if they kill me.*

It is beyond my control, the Great Bear reiterated. *It is the work of the Silver One. I can sense that they do not have their sights on you alone, but all you may do is endure, Red Fox One. Learn your lessons. There will be a solution yet – in the palm of your hand.*

It enveloped them in a wave of starlight and darkness. Tuomas and Lumi cartwheeled around each other, caught in the current.

The Worlds hang together by a thread, because of you. I charge you, once again, to repair them.

Sensing that the conversation was at an end, Tuomas bowed his head. Then he drew himself away, felt himself becoming heavier as he settled into his physical body. Cool snow appeared under his knees; his weight pressed through it to the grass beneath.

He opened his eyes.

He was back at the shrine. His breath misted in the air; there were no clouds to hold in the heat and a new layer of frost had begun to form over the trees.

He glanced at Lumi. She let go of his hand and jumped on top of the ash tree.

"I am glad the souls are safe," she said in a small voice. "I cannot describe how difficult it is to be parted from them, down here, like this."

Tuomas nodded grimly. He recalled how tenderly she'd held them when the Spirit of Passage brought them to her Lights; the way she swept them up and danced with them through the night, so they could look upon the World Between and see their descendants. It was what she was: compassion behind a frozen exterior. The only Spirit who had learned what it was to love, even as it threatened to destroy her.

"Have you ever met the Horse-Riding One?" he asked.

"No. His domain and mine are of different Worlds."

"I'm scared," Tuomas said. "He's the Spirit of Death."

"There are worse things to be afraid of than him," replied Lumi, and she looked at the Moon Spirit again. Her eyes flashed angrily. "I wished I was not correct. But now I know I am, we must ensure the trolls do not reach you."

"Can you not speak to her?"

"No. I attempted to reach out just now, but she refused to reply. Once again, it seems she wants nothing to do with me."

Tuomas's head rang with confusion. "This doesn't feel right. The Silver One reanimates trolls and sends them after me and the other mages, when she knows how important it is that I finish my task? Why? It makes no sense."

Lumi scowled and a hint of red appeared in her eyes. "I am sure she will make her intentions known soon enough. And fear not, I will not let her anywhere near you."

Tuomas managed a small smile. "It's nice to know I've got you on my side, at least."

"You always did," said Lumi, and for the first time that evening, her voice became a little warmer. "Remember, brother, I told you I would save you a thousand times."

He sighed. "Thank you."

Lumi regarded him for a long moment, then walked across the top of the shrine. Tuomas didn't worry about her slipping. He doubted such a thing was even possible.

Instead, he turned his attention to his fingers, regarded the stumpy ends where frostbite had taken its toll. He would have let the cold ravage his entire arm if it might bring Paavo back. His brother had only been twenty-five when the soul plague had choked the life out of him. Now he was trapped with the draugars, too.

Tuomas closed his eyes. At least when he and Aki returned from across the Night River, Paavo might know freedom, even if it were in death.

"What do you think the Great Bear Spirit meant?" he asked. "About a solution in the palm of my hand?"

"Your powers," Lumi replied at once. "I know you can hold fire. And the trolls will petrify if exposed to Sunlight."

"What are you saying? I'm... well, the Spirit of the Flames," said Tuomas bitterly. "What do flames have to do with that?"

"You are also the Son of the Sun," said Lumi. "The Sun Spirit herself is the brightest fire of all. You must continue practising to hone your power, Tuomas. It will grow. And your people will likely need it, in the middle of the night, when the trolls will attack."

Tuomas's stomach tied itself in knots. He turned his hands over, ran his thumb over one of the teeth marks. It was normal human flesh: warm, firm; he felt bones and tendons when he pressed. And yet, beneath it, there was so much more. More than anyone else could know.

Lumi stepped down so she was at his eye level.

"How am I supposed to do that?" he whispered. "Are you saying that I'll be able to channel Sunlight as well?"

"There is no reason why not. The Great Mage could do it."

"I'm not the Great Mage."

"Yes, you are."

"But I've never been able to handle my power, not fully."

"Because you had not accepted it before," Lumi said. She touched one of his ears, flicked her own at the same time. "Now, you must, Son of the Sun. It is not an insult and does not diminish your identity. It is so important."

She placed a finger under his chin and lifted his head.

"Sometimes, Tuomas, the best way forward is through endurance, not sacrifice. And we are Spirits. We have endured forever. We can do so again."

Tuomas frowned. There was still a glow to her expression, but he could see something raging within it: a darkness at the edges, like the promise of night behind a dancing aurora.

"What is it?" he asked.

She shook her head. "Nothing. Come, now. You must take shelter within the village until the Sun rises."

Without another word, she turned and walked away. The protective barrier dissipated as she passed through it. Tuomas hurried after her, watched a faint stream of Lights drift from her tail towards the Moon.

He shuddered. What could she want?

Chapter Seven

Lumi saw Tuomas to the edge of the settlement, then transformed into a fox and vanished into the trees. He didn't worry about her – she was more than capable of looking after herself. But, just as much as the trolls, she would have to take shelter during the hours of daylight. She was a Spirit which could exist only in darkness; the touch of the Sun in the World Between had almost spelled her end on several occasions.

Tuomas raised his hand to the men on watch, then beat his drum and stepped through the barrier. His own *taika* tugged at him for a moment before it let him pass. Then the circle sealed itself behind him, as though it hadn't ruptured at all.

Most people had retired to bed, in an attempt to get some sleep, but others still huddled around the central fire pit. They eyed him as he passed. He tried to smile, but knew it wasn't very convincing. All he wanted to do was run off, hide somewhere, and weep at the burden crushing his shoulders.

He looked at his palms again, remembered the feeling of holding the fire. Could he truly do as Lumi had suggested, and conjure Sunlight as well? Unleash it at will, like she did with her aurora?

He thought of his sister, throwing the Lights from her hands, sweeping them with her tail. She had defended him with them, attacked Kari and his demon and the draugars. She had even struck Mihka with them and stripped all the colour out of his hair. A flame just as strong as his, but of cold rather than warmth.

Could he have the same power inside him? The ability to control so much?

He scoffed at himself. Control almost seemed like a joke. Gossip about splitting the avalanche had spread quickly, but a part of him worried that had just been luck. He could barely control his own anger and rash decisions, let alone his power.

He pushed it to the back of his mind. He would ponder it later. For now, there was work to be done. Dreadful, necessary work.

He reached the litter holding Enska and Aino's bodies. Lilja and Niina were already there. He could tell from their faces that both had been crying.

"Where did you go?" Niina asked quietly.

"To the shrine," replied Tuomas.

Lilja regarded him, but didn't say anything.

Niina gazed at Aino through the circle. In the low light cast by torches at each end of the platform, she looked younger than her seventeen years; more like a child who had lost her mother. Tuomas wondered how close she and Aino had been – he hadn't seen her earlier that winter, when he and Lilja stayed in Einfjall. But from her expression, it was clear the two of them had shared a true bond.

None of them spoke another word. They walked among the birch trees and peeled the bark off in large curling strips. When enough had been gathered, they set to work.

First, after waking a small fire, they drummed and chanted, calling forth the Spirits to protect and guide. They burned herbs until the air swam with heady scents. Then they made a red alder bark paste and daubed it on the bodies' chests, to mark the place where the souls would have resided in life. They sewed the birch pieces together with bone needles and sinew thread, until they had two thin shrouds, in which they wrapped Aino and Enska.

Once the open edges were stitched shut, they painted powerful symbols onto the surface with the rest of the paste: reindeer, shelters, fish, trees – everything the dead would need. Then they drew the Sun, the Moon, and the Great Bear Spirit, as well as a figure on horseback and a trail of dancing swirls. Those were for the Spirit of Death and the Spirit of the Lights: both bearers of passing souls.

They worked through the night, and by the time they were finally finished, the eastern sky held the faintest glow of dawn. The Sun Spirit would be up soon. Tuomas had never been so relieved to see his mother's light.

With a shaking hand, he picked up some ash from the central fire pit, mixed it with melted snow, and swept it across his face in a series of circular symbols. Niina and Lilja did the same, then Lilja retrieved a headdress from her hut. It was the one Enska had worn at major ceremonies: two magnificent reindeer antlers.

Tuomas was glad she had managed to salvage it. Henrik and Aino's headdresses were nowhere to be found. He assumed they were still on Anaar, strewn amongst the wreckage.

He felt sick. Henrik was still there, too. Like at Paavo's funeral, when others had also died, the Akerfjorden mage would be laid to rest without a body. Even if the people did manage to find Henrik when they returned to gather lichen, there likely wouldn't be enough to bury.

The herders followed the three mages towards the shrine. The corpses were carried on the shoulders of men from Poro and Einfjall. Tuomas, Lilja and Niina chanted as they walked, each holding a flaming torch.

Tuomas let his voice mingle with the others; it was a dissonant sound at first, but then their *taika* braided together and it grew into an outpouring of grief. It echoed the howling wind through the mountains, the hiss of rain cascading from an autumnal sky, the empty hole which had been left in everyone's hearts. There was no need for lyrics. To give it words would only diminish its power.

When they came to the ash tree, they spun a circle with their drums, cut a lock of hair and scattered it. The villagers stepped forward and deposited offerings of food and antler. Tuomas kept his eyes firmly ahead so he couldn't watch. It was too much… he had only done this for Paavo a few weeks ago…

How many more would have to die before this terrible winter was over?

Lilja struggled to keep her composure. Her breaths came shallow and hard; the muscles in her jaw tensed as she gritted her teeth. Tuomas realised she wasn't looking at the shrouded corpses, either. Her attention was fixed on Aki, hiding behind a tree at the back of the procession. Nobody had gone near him, but Sigurd kept throwing him anxious glances, as though worried the little boy might run over and bite him.

A girl walked past. As she did, she lifted a clod of soil and threw it at Aki's face.

Tears welled in Tuomas's eyes. He was just a child…

He shook his head. He had to concentrate. This was a sacred rite: the final honour for their fallen mentors. And the sooner it was done, the sooner everyone could prepare for what would come after.

He laid a comforting hand on Lilja's shoulder, then did the same to Niina on his other side. Both of them tensed, but didn't pull away.

"Alright," Niina muttered eventually.

Her voice was the cue they all needed. They raised their drums and began to beat. Tuomas's souls stirred inside him as the *taika* rose like a tide. It was overwhelmingly powerful; he planted his feet on the ground, but even that was scarcely enough to contain it.

He thought of Henrik: the one mage who wasn't here. This was *his* drum he was beating: the only thing left of the crabby old man who always brewed his tea too strong.

Tuomas felt so sorry for ever thinking him boring. All he had done was try to prepare him and protect him.

It was true that life in the Northlands was fraught with danger. It took strength and care to survive in such an unforgiving place, and safety was never a guarantee. But that was supposed to be because of wolves or bears, or the sheer risk of the elements. Not creatures out of fireside tales.

Yet, as Tuomas watched Enska and Aino being lowered into their graves, what did it really matter how death came? There were certainly good and bad ways to be taken, like old age compared to falling into a ravine. But could anything really be considered natural or unnatural? When the last breath was let out, the souls all took the same journey. The body was returned to nature no matter what happened.

Perhaps, in its own strange way, that was the best comfort to take. The dead would give life, and life would return when the soul was ready. Nothing really ended, because nothing really began either. And so it would be for everything, forever.

The rest of the day was spent preparing for the departure. Salvaged belongings were packed and loaded into the boats. Men crossed to the mainland, gathered the sleighs from where they had been left near Anaar, and hauled them along the coast to be closer to Ardni. People walked into the forest to locate the reindeer and drive them towards a corral near the village. Others scoured the trees, ripping down clumps of stringy grey lichen and stuffing it into sacks. More rowed through the archipelago, heading back to Anaar and to Einfjall's island of Hetta, to collect whatever was there. The animals would need as much food as possible.

Tuomas set aside his new coat and helped Aslak butcher a line of dead reindeer. Some had drowned during the frantic escape from Anaar, and it was unacceptable to see them go to waste.

As he opened a cow's belly to expose its guts, Tuomas threw a glance at the earmark. He recognised the pattern of notches instantly. This was one of Sisu's. Technically, it would be Mihka's now.

"Aslak?" he said.

"What?"

"Do you think Mihka's alright?"

Aslak hesitated. "I hope so."

"If he made it far enough away…" Tuomas mused. "How far do you think he could have gotten in three days? If the trolls came for us – the mages – he might not have run into them. He could have reached Poro."

"I'm sure we'll find out soon enough," replied Aslak. "I imagine we'll be gathering the winter caretakers from Poro and Einfjall along our way. If he's not with either of them, and he's not at Akerfjorden when we get there, then we'll have our answer."

Tuomas's heart grew heavy. He wasn't sure what it would be like between him and Mihka if they met again, but he hated the idea of his old friend coming across those monsters. Just because he wasn't a mage didn't mean they might not kill him. In the old stories, if there was no other food around, trolls wouldn't think twice about taking people.

He turned his attention back to the reindeer. He stripped the bones, packed everything which was edible into sacks and covered them with generous helpings of salt. The fresh meat would serve the people well during the first week. The cold temperatures would keep it from spoiling, and only when they ran out would they need use the dried food.

Once he was done with the butchering, he walked towards the beach to wash himself. A stream was closer, but he wanted to try speaking to Elin, and he knew she was on watch duty.

He rounded a tree near where she had been, then stopped himself. She was gone. Stellan was standing in her place, an arrow already nocked on his bow. Hearing Tuomas, he tensed and went to draw.

Tuomas held up his hands.

"Easy!" he cried. "It's just me."

Stellan lowered the bow. "I could have shot you! You're too light on your feet. What are you doing down here?"

Tuomas brandished his hands again in answer. They were slick with blood.

"Oh. Right," Stellan said, a little flustered. "Are you alright? You look awful."

"I fell off a cliff," replied Tuomas pointedly.

He knelt by the water's edge and started to scrub the gore off his skin. He could feel Stellan's eyes on him, knew he was looking at the red tail as it lay in the snow.

"Can you... well, really move that?" asked Stellan. "And the ears? Are they a part of you, I mean?"

"Yes," said Tuomas in a sour tone. "Courtesy of the Great Bear Spirit."

Once again, he wished he could tear them off his body. It was one thing to carry the responsibility, but to have it marked on the flesh made him want to curl in on himself and never stand up again.

Stellan must have realised his discomfort, because he cleared his throat and flicked his bowstring with one finger.

"You should try to get some sleep when you're done. I know you, Lilja and Niina were working all night. Let some others take it from here."

He was right. Tomorrow was going to be another hard day, and migrations were difficult and tiring at the best of times. This one, so close to the last, with everyone scared, would be even worse.

"I will," said Tuomas. "Thank you for going on watch. It's appreciated."

"Not as appreciated as you," replied Stellan.

Tuomas gritted his teeth as he washed the last of the blood off his fingernails. When he was done, he threw Stellan a friendly smile, and made his way towards Lilja's hut. When he stepped through the door, he found her already asleep, one arm curled around Aki.

Then he realised that she had fetched him one of the spare sleeping sacks and spread it out next to the fire.

With a small sigh of gratitude, he wriggled into it, and had barely laid his head down before slumber engulfed him like warm water.

Chapter Eight

When Tuomas opened his eyes, he saw stars through the smoke hole. The rip waved from left to right, like the thinnest fabric floating in water. He turned away from it and glanced at Lilja.

Aki was mumbling softly in his sleep; she heard it and pulled him closer. Tuomas had never seen her so protective, so contented… and yet so worried. It was as though he was looking at a mother wolf with her cub.

She shivered – the fire had receded to grey embers. Tuomas grabbed a log from the woodpile, peeled the bark off to awaken the flames again, then added the whole thing. After a few moments, it caught, and heat swam back into the shelter.

He laid his head on his arm and watched the orange tongues dance and twist around themselves. Then he held a hand over them. The fire ticked his skin, wrapped about the frostbitten stumps of his fingers. He played with it, wafting it this way and that, blowing on it to make it brighter. It didn't hurt at all. It called to him: a secret song which only he knew.

Restlessness bit at his heart. There was no point trying to get back to sleep now. The very air around him felt too heavy to even breathe.

He crawled out of his sleeping sack, emerged into the forest. It was still dark, but he could tell from the positions of the stars that dawn wasn't far away. It had been a cold night and spikes of frost had formed around the smoke holes. Nearby, he caught the musty scent of reindeer in the corral. The sounds of them floated on the wind: antlers knocking together, tendons clicking in their knees, bells jingling around their necks. But he knew, just from listening, how few were left compared to a few days ago. The combined herd of all three villages should have been almost twice as large as this.

Then he spotted Lumi, just outside the barrier which he, Lilja and Niina had laid down the evening before. He walked over to her, stood inches away, separated by a sheer wall of rippling *taika*.

"Any sign of the trolls?" he asked.

She shook her head. Her hair glittered with the movement.

Tuomas twitched his tail anxiously. "That doesn't make me feel any better. What are they waiting for?"

"I wish I could tell you," Lumi said. "Today is the day you will move south?"

"Yes."

"I will go to the beach to wait for you, take my fox form and conceal myself under a tarp in the furthest boat. Instruct the people to not draw it back completely. Then, when we reach the other side of the channel, you shelter me in a sleigh. Nobody is to disturb me whilst the Sun Spirit shines."

"Don't worry, I'll make sure of that."

Lumi gave him a tiny smile, then ran around the edge of the circle towards the other end of the village. A stream of green Lights drifted into the sky as she disappeared.

Tuomas didn't have to wait long before everyone woke up. The elders emerged first, followed by those who had been on watch duty during the night, and went from shelter to shelter. The entire island exploded with urgency.

Tuomas pulled on his white coat, found the boat Lumi had indicated, loaded it with reindeer skins and rowed across the channel. He threw an anxious glance at the lapping waves, and for a moment, fancied he heard the slithering sound of draugars, but he forced that idea away. They were all gone. Now there were new monsters to outrun.

When he reached the other side, he piled the skins into his own sleigh, used one to cover Lumi and carried her to safety. Only when he was sure she was concealed did he return to the island.

By the time all the items had been transported, the Sun Spirit had broken the horizon and transformed the water to liquid gold. The elders summoned everyone around the central fire pit and counted to make sure none were missing. The flames had burned low, but nobody bothered to add any more logs. There was no point now they were leaving.

Tuomas stood at the front, next to Anssi, and looked across the sea of heads. He spotted Elin with her parents, and for a fleeting moment, she met his eyes.

He wished he could somehow communicate with her in the language of Spirits – just think what he wanted to say and let her understand it. But she turned away and busied herself by checking the tightness of her bowstring.

"We're all here!" Birkir called from the back of the throng.

Maiken nodded, then raised her voice. "Alright, we'll release the reindeer in a moment. When we get to the mainland, stay close and move fast. We need to cover as much ground as possible before nightfall. When it gets dark, we'll pitch camp, take turns on watch, as we've done here. And, if the Spirits are kind, we'll reach Akerfjorden in good time."

A murmur passed among the herders. Tuomas's ears swivelled at the sound. He couldn't make out individual comments, but the nerves were palpable in the air and hung like a heavy mist.

A sudden thought came to him. He was standing here, in white reindeer fur, the ears and tail of the Red Fox One on his body, about to lead the people into the south for safety.

Lumi was right. He was more than just Tuomas now, more than just the apprentice who had set out at the beginning of winter to save his friend. He was the Son of the Sun, the Great Mage of old fireside tales.

Above, the cleft seemed wider than ever: a gaping maw which threatened to swallow him whole. Just looking at it for too long made his souls tremble. It tugged at his *taika*; his head swam and his belly tightened, until he had to gasp for breath. It was so awfully wrong…

His hand strayed to his belt and touched the knives hanging there. He had made those blades with Paavo, when he was a child. Back before all this had begun, when his only cares were helping around Akerfjorden and dreaming of the day he might be a mage.

Lilja's words rang through his memory.

"You live constantly in two. Not just with the physical and the unseen, but because everyone will come to rely on you and fear you equally."

Holding Paavo in his mind, he cleared his throat.

"We can do this," he said, as confidently as he could. "It might not have happened in our lifetimes, but we've done it before. We're strong enough, all of us."

A cool silence descended when he finished: an empty space where words should have been. Men, women and children glanced between each other and whispered.

Tuomas's heart hammered at the sight. So many of these faces were ones he'd known since childhood. He couldn't remember the last time they had looked at him as anything other than a Spirit.

Anssi gave him a smile and squeezed his shoulder.

"Thank you for telling them that," he whispered. "They'll believe it, coming from you."

"They're scared of me," Tuomas replied sadly.

"That doesn't mean they don't respect you."

"I'm still me. Please respect that, too."

He stepped down and walked towards the corral. The elders followed, then opened the gate and let the reindeer out. The herders stood in long lines, holding lengths of tarp to create walls on either side. It formed a clear path for the animals. They thundered to the beach, but hesitated. There was no instinct driving them to cross this time, and the air filled with the bleating of uncertain calves.

The villagers sprang forward, closed the tarps behind the herd and urged them on. Eventually, the reindeer at the front took the plunge, and the rest followed until the channel was filled with furry heads and white water. The boats rowed close, making sure they kept going.

At the halfway point, the calves began to struggle. One tried to turn back towards the island, but Maiken leaned over and snatched it around the neck. She forced it around; the calf took the hint and carried on swimming.

After several long minutes, the last of the reindeer clambered onto the far shore. They trembled from the effort. Some had grown too exhausted and drowned, but most had made it across safely. Those which had died were lashed to the backs of the sleighs to be butchered later. The calves were given time to find their mothers again and suckle, then the tame animals were lassoed, so the others would naturally follow.

Tuomas drew close to his sleigh.

"Lumi, are you alright?" he whispered.

A faint bark answered him, and he patted the skins before pulling a pair of skis out. He slipped his shoes into them and pushed off, towards the front of the herd.

As he moved, he searched for Lilja and Aki. Across the heaving caravan of bodies, he spotted them. Everyone gave them a wide berth, until they were left walking alone in a circle of snow. Aki clung onto his mother's arm for comfort, and Lilja's face was as dark as a thundercloud, eyes blazing with tears.

Tuomas was reminded of how she had admitted becoming a wanderer in order to protect her son. Aki had never known anything of community. And now it was thrust upon them both, the community didn't want them.

And, in only a few days, Tuomas would have to separate them and take Aki to the most terrifying place in any of the Worlds. How was he even supposed to get the boy away from Lilja? The Great Bear had said not to tell her yet, but she would never forgive him…

He shuddered. He couldn't think about that now. Spring might be coming, but the hours of daylight were still brief, and there was a long way to go.

He drew parallel to Niina. Her red hair shone like a trail of fire down her back.

"How are you?" he asked quietly.

"Fine," she mumbled, not looking at him.

"I'm sorry about Aino. I know I haven't really had much of a chance to speak to you, but it looked like you were close."

"Yes. She was my aunt."

Tuomas blinked. "Really?"

"I did see you, when you came to Einfjall in the Long Dark, but you were always asleep. Aino told me you had frostbite and hypothermia."

Tuomas winced at the memory. That had been after Kari had kidnapped him, tied him down on top of the mountain and tried to carve out his heart. He raised a hand to his chest, touched the spot over his breastbone where the blade had pierced.

"How did that work?" Niina asked. "The frostbite, I mean... I haven't seen you wear a hat or mittens for ages. Aren't you cold?"

"No. I don't really feel it anymore."

"Then how come you were so sick?"

Tuomas wasn't sure how to answer. Because, back then, he hadn't accepted who he was yet? Because he had still been bound more by human flesh than the Spirit inside him?

No... he was still human as much as he was Spirit...

"It's complicated," he said eventually.

Niina regarded him. Her eyes flitted over his face, so wide that he could see all around her irises. Her hands trembled on her ski poles.

"I don't think I can do this," she said in a tiny voice. "I mean... Lilja's so powerful. You're the Son of the Sun. And I'm nothing. I haven't even passed my test yet. I'm not fit to be a mage for the whole of Einfjall."

"Of course you are," replied Tuomas. "This might be your test right now. By the time we reach Akerfjorden, I think you might be a full mage."

"*If* we get to Akerfjorden," Niina said. "If those things don't kill us first."

"We can't think like that. We just need to keep going. And don't forget, everyone will be staying together for a while. You won't be alone."

"Aren't you afraid?"

"Afraid?" Tuomas repeated. "I'm terrified. I wish I could explain how much."

Niina shook her head. "But how? I mean... you're the Great Mage. How can you feel fear? I mean... feel it the same as us?"

"I'm still the same as you," Tuomas said curtly.

Niina sucked in a breath at the expression on his face.

"I'm sorry. I didn't mean to offend you."

"You haven't. Just treat me normally, please. I've got enough to deal with, without you all worrying about how you speak to me."

Tuomas put a hand on her shoulder.

"You'll get through this, Niina. We all will. Trust yourself as much as the Spirits."

She swallowed nervously, but her eyes softened a little.

"Thank you," she said, "Tuomas."

The sound of his own name lifted his heart; it took all his self-control to not hug her. He gave her the first genuine smile he'd managed in weeks.

"Thank *you*," he replied.

Niina nodded once, then turned her attention back to her skis.

Tuomas took the opportunity to glance behind at the herd. Across the sparkling water, Ardni looked smaller already. And ahead, the huge flank of the mountains filled his vision, piercing the sky with summits as sharp as knives. Now the Sun Spirit had risen higher, their snowy peaks turned baby pink. It almost belied how dangerous the place was: filled with loose snow and crevasses so deep, a man might fall for a mile before he reached the bottom.

In a way, Tuomas himself felt as though he were tumbling down a crevasse: one which plunged through all three Worlds. Usually the people went six months between leaving the islands and returning to them. But now, the timings were wrong. The reindeer shouldn't be brought back to the mainland until autumn set in, not when spring was only just starting to break.

And, with every passing moment, the tear in the sky bore upon him, wore at his *taika*, made his chest ache under the pressure of all he needed to do.

He felt his mother's warmth on his shoulders and closed his eyes.

Please, he thought, *help us*.

Chapter Nine

It no sooner seemed that day had arrived before it began to retreat. The sky transformed into a pastel haze; the snow turned lilac, then blue, as shadows swept across the open tundra. The temperature dropped and moisture froze in the air; everywhere Tuomas looked, he saw glittering flakes. If he squinted, he could almost fancy himself back in the World Above, surrounded by stardust, weightless, exactly how he was meant to be.

Twilight came in, and the people halted the herd so camp could be pitched. The mountains were closer now; they stood massive against the inky sky – so high that Tuomas had to crane his neck to see the summits. The ground slanted a little underfoot as it sloped towards them, and cold air rolled down in bands of invisible waves.

Lilja assembled a tent by herself with practised ease, ushered Aki inside and approached Tuomas. Niina followed close behind. The three of them untied their drums and walked the edge of the camp to lay a circle, then Tuomas did the same around the herd, so no trolls could sneak close and steal the animals again. As he worked, the rest of the people woke a fire. Soon, the odour of roasting reindeer meat filled the air. Those on watch duty were given their portions first before they hurried away to take their positions.

A stream of green and blue light rose from the snow. Tuomas glanced over, watched Lumi trotting towards him on four paws. As she came closer, she grew taller; her fur shrank back and limbs lengthened, until she was once again in the form of a girl. But, as always, her ears and tail remained.

Tuomas fetched a large sack of lichen and began throwing it around for the reindeer.

"How did you manage in the sleigh?" he asked.

"It was serviceable," Lumi replied bluntly. "It is a manner of travel which I must grow accustomed to."

"Well, hopefully it won't be for too long," he said. "Two weeks out of forever. There are worse things."

He couldn't keep the bitterness out of his voice. Lumi bristled, and for a moment he worried he'd insulted her. No matter that she was his sister – he had known her as the Spirit of the Lights for much longer, a being who could strike fear into the strongest hearts simply by appearing in the sky.

But then she softened, and instead looked at the Moon Spirit. Tuomas did the same. He could feel her watching him, like a wolf in the shadows. Even the touch of her pale light sent a shiver through him; it was a million fingers sweeping over his skin, reaching for his life-soul.

He wasn't in a trance, but he could still sense her, hear her freezing voice in his memory.

I will not be kept from you. Not now you are aware, once again, of who you truly are. And where you truly belong.

He took a deep breath. She couldn't have him. He would never let her.

He noticed one of his own reindeer nearby and held out a clump of lichen. It ate from his hand, then ambled away, knees clicking with every step.

His stomach grumbled. Lumi swept her tail and a small aurora rose where it hit the snow.

"Have you eaten today?" she asked.

"No," said Tuomas. "To be honest, food was the last thing on my mind."

"You may be a Spirit, but your body is human," she said. "You must eat. You will need your strength."

"I know. I will. I just…"

He snarled and kicked at a stone underfoot. He wanted to throw his head back and scream until he was hoarse; anything to be away from this moment and all the burdens it carried.

Lumi didn't speak. There was no need to. The blue swirl in her eyes was all the response he needed: cool, and also caring; filled with the same level of power he held inside. They might have had different mother Spirits, but they were equal in all things; opposites, yet cut from the same ethereal cloth.

A little water streamed over Lumi's skin and she swept it away. Tuomas frowned.

"You're not melting again, are you?"

"It appears to have become an occupational hazard whenever I walk in the World Between," she replied cynically. "Human emotions are so troublesome. How you have abided so specific a form for two lifetimes is beyond my comprehension."

Despite himself, Tuomas smirked. He was inclined to agree with her.

"Do not fear for my safety or comfort," continued Lumi. "I will be in no immediate danger unless the Sunlight touches me."

Tuomas sighed. "That's another thing which is my fault, isn't it? I put you in this body in the first place."

"Yes, you did," Lumi admitted, a touch of ice at the edge of her voice. "But not this time, and you know that. And I can hardly remain stoic where you are concerned. I thought that would be evident by now."

"But you won't fade?"

"No. Though I will ask you to allow me to keep my distance. The people must not know me as you do."

"Why? Don't you think it will be good for them, to see they don't have to be terrified of you?"

"They should respect me."

"Fear is different to respect," Tuomas insisted. "Please don't let pride get the better of you again."

"Get the better of me?" she repeated pointedly. "We are both guilty of that. It is what we are: to be proud, and powerful. In all my thousands of years of existence, Tuomas, I could count on these fingers you gave me, how often I have terrorised them. The same can even be said for my mother, and for all the Spirits. Nature will be nature. Stories will do what they will with *our* natures. Do you not remember, when you came to me in the World Above, how the souls held no fear of me?"

Tuomas hesitated. She was right. The way they had danced around her, revelled in her Lights as she swept the aurora through the sky... it was as though they had come home.

"Until recently, when the abilities were cut off, only mages possessed the power to commune with Spirits," Lumi said. "And out of all the mages who have ever lived, only you know the absolute truth of what we are. The people have spun their own fear and stories by themselves, and I respond in kind. Let it continue, if that is where they may draw their own power. They shall need strength, as much as you will."

Tuomas swallowed. "I'd never thought of it like that before."

"Well, you have had other matters to think on since this all began," said Lumi. "And I dare say there is a limit to what a human mind is able to take, even if it is given life by a Spirit."

He shrugged. "Fair point."

Lumi put her hands on his shoulders. It was so light, he barely felt it through the thick fur of his coat.

"Now, go and eat. I will remain out here."

Tuomas shot her a hopeful glance. "Won't you come over with me? Please?"

"No."

With that, she turned around and walked away. He thought about following her, but decided against it. He was a mage, after all, and there were trolls lurking in the darkness. He needed to stay inside a circle.

With a sigh, he eased himself free of the herd, headed towards the camp and passed through the barrier. Everyone stopped what they were doing to watch him. He had a mind to flatten his ears and try to tuck the tail under his coat, but realised there was no point. There wasn't a man, woman, or child in the entire throng now who didn't know who – *what* – he was.

He went to go to the central fire and collect some food, but paused. There was a figure standing on the outskirts, staring into the darkness. A long black braid hung down its back.

Elin, taking watch again. And she was alone.

Tuomas sucked in a deep breath. It was now or never.

He changed direction and walked towards her. She heard the snow crunching under his shoes and turned to glance at him. Her face was unreadable, but her grip tightened on her bow. An arrow was already nocked to the string, ready to draw at a moment's notice.

"Hello," he said.

"Hello," she replied. Her eyes flickered to his ears.

"How are you?"

"I'm fine."

"Where's Sigurd?"

"He's gone to help my mother. One of her calves died today, crossing the channel. It needs to be butchered."

Elin shuffled uncomfortably, then bent to snatch a handful of snow. She crushed it in her mitten and took a bite out of it, letting it melt on her tongue and swallowing the water. Tuomas did the same, and the two of them gazed into the distance. The fires' glows cast a soft circle of light, but it only extended for several feet before blackness swallowed it.

How close were the trolls? They might be just out of sight, watching, waiting for the tiniest lapse in concentration. Would they roll down out of the mountains like boulders? Spring up from the snow?

Tuomas curled his toes inside his shoes. He couldn't wait to be away from this place.

"Elin, listen… I want to talk to you. Why are you avoiding me? Are you still mad at me?"

"I haven't been avoiding you," she replied. "I've just been trying to make myself useful after being sick for so long. And anyway, if I was avoiding you, why would I have volunteered to go back to Anaar and look for you?"

"I don't know," Tuomas admitted. "But… *I* don't know what else I can do except apologise."

She didn't say anything, so he tried changing the subject.

"Have you told Sigurd about Aki?"

Elin shook her head. "No. He hasn't mentioned anything to me, either. But I think he knows. I can tell. He's acting very strange. Quiet, and keeping away from Lilja."

Tuomas stepped closer. She was struggling to hold back tears. She had never looked at him like this before he'd gone to the draugars. Before she'd learned the truth about the secrets which had been woven around her.

He could almost feel her anger and hurt like a physical pressure. It was as though she had pressed a blade to his throat.

He swallowed. She was waiting for him to speak – but he knew that no matter what he said, nothing would be easy.

"Lilja kept it a secret in order to save your family from pain," he tried to explain. "She didn't want to tear the three of you apart. She told me it was her burden to bear. That's why she wandered alone for so long: to protect you and your parents."

"But *you* knew," Elin said sharply. "And you were never going to tell me."

"It was complicated."

"It was still wrong."

"I don't really know whether it was right or wrong," Tuomas said. "But, either way, it must have been for the greater good."

Elin glared at him. "So you're defending her?"

"No, but I'm not going to entirely blame her either, because neither of us can ever know the full story," replied Tuomas.

"What's that supposed to mean? She was with my father. What else is there to know?"

"She went through a lot, Elin. She carried that knowledge for ten years, exiled herself for the sake of everyone else. And until a week ago, none of you even knew. It doesn't really matter *how* it happened, but she's lived with it every day since. It's not as simple as being right or wrong. Do you see?"

"You're saying it doesn't matter?" Elin snapped. "My parents are married. They were married before I was born. But Aki is still here."

"I didn't mean it like that," Tuomas protested. "Lilja knows she messed up. She's paid the price already. I don't think anything anyone says will be worse than what she's put herself through."

He glanced towards the tent. "And for his part, Aki's innocent in all this. It's not his fault that he's alive. Please try to understand."

"I'll tell you what I don't understand," she snapped. "That kid scares me. He should be nearly as old as us, but he came back from the dead, and he's still five. And he made us all sick – he made *me* sick. He tried to kill us."

"He didn't," Tuomas insisted. "The draugars were using him. *They* were behind the plague, not him."

Elin turned her face away. "So you're standing up for *him* now, as well as Lilja?"

"That's not what I said," Tuomas replied. He could feel his own anger rising like hot water.

"You know who else I'm not fond of at the moment?" Elin carried on. "Lumi. She did that, didn't she?"

She jabbed at the rip in the sky with her arrow.

Tuomas shook his head. "Be careful. She's out there."

Elin rolled her eyes. "You realise she never would have needed to do that, if *you* hadn't been so stupid?"

His patience snapped and he grabbed her shoulder.

"I did it to save you! I know I was stupid, but would you rather I hadn't cared about you at all? I'm already feeling guilty enough! I don't need you making it worse!"

Elin shoved him away and thrust her face forward.

"I'm glad you saved me," she hissed. "But I hate what I've come back to!"

Before he could say anything else, she stormed off.

Tuomas watched her go, his hands in fists. Anger flooded his blood; his ears turned back and lay flat against his skull. His tail swept furiously… and then he felt heat.

He spun around and gasped. Sparks were flickering in the red fur, like Lumi's Lights. But they weren't the aurora. They were bright yellow and gold. Flame.

That was the final straw. Desolation broke his backbone and turned his legs to stone. With every moment, Elin grew smaller, until she disappeared into her tent. He dropped to his knees, lowered his head, and cried.

Chapter Ten

By the time he had managed to stop weeping, the majority of people had retired to bed. Tuomas dragged himself to the central fire and sat on a reindeer skin, beside Frode and Ritva. Both of them shuffled away a little. He did his best to ignore it and instead forced a smile when Maiken handed him a slice of roasted heart.

"Are you alright?" she asked.

Tuomas nodded miserably. Nobody seemed to have seen the sparks, or heard the argument. That was the only comfort he could take.

He'd hoped speaking with Elin would mend things, as he'd done with Lilja, but now it only felt as though he had made it worse. Would she ever forgive him, or talk to him again? Or was it to be a repeat of Mihka?

As he chewed, he couldn't help but think of the beginning of the Long Dark. He and Mihka had laughed as they ambled away from Henrik's hut, sat on the banks of the Mustafjord with the rest of Akerfjorden, to bid farewell to the Sun Spirit. Back then, he had known nothing. Back then, everyone had still been alive.

Paavo swam into his mind. The heart tasted delicious, but his brother would have cooked it so much better.

Tuomas's body felt a hundred times heavier than it really was. So much loss, death, destruction... and the end wasn't even in sight. Once again, he felt the urge to flee – perhaps he could convince Lilja not to abandon her plans, beg her to take him along as well...

No. That was wishful thinking, foolish, and impossible. He was just as trapped as she was. Perhaps even more so.

Lilja appeared, Aki clutching the hem of her coat. A few people glanced at the boy as she passed. Some women made the sign of the hand to ward off evil. Lilja noticed and gave them a glare harder than stone.

She collected a slab of meat and marched back the way she had come. Tuomas hurried after her.

"Lilja, stop!"

"Why?" she snapped. "I'm sick of the way they're all looking at him. It's easier for everyone if we keep to ourselves. As usual."

"Please don't be like that. Listen to me. Lilja!"

Tuomas jumped in front of her and planted a hand on her shoulder. He opened his mouth to speak, but then caught sight of Aki, staring up with huge blue eyes, and words died on his tongue. What was he supposed to say to comfort either of them?

In the end, he just shook his head. "Can I sit with you?"

Lilja shrugged, but he saw a gleam of gratitude when she looked at him.

"Baby, go inside," she said to Aki. "I'll be there in a moment. Take this and put it on the spit, alright? Keep it warm."

Aki nodded shyly, then took the meat and walked to the tent at the furthest edge of the camp. Tuomas couldn't help but smile at the sight. He was wrapped in so many layers that he could hardly bend his knees.

"He feels the cold," Lilja said in an undertone. "Being in water for so long, and… in the space between Worlds. I'm just glad that's the only lasting impact there seems to be."

Tuomas nodded. "How are you?"

"Fine. And you?"

"As well as I can be, I suppose. I'm really sorry about Enska."

Lilja drew in a shaky breath. "Thank you, boy. And I'm sorry about Henrik. I wish we'd been able to bury him, too."

"Well... it was quick. That's the best comfort I can take from it," said Tuomas. "I saw it, Lilja. The troll ripped him apart, right in front of me."

Her face turned as white as the snow. Tuomas supposed he didn't look much better.

Aki pulled the flap of the tent closed behind him. Lilja cleared her throat, then turned her attention to Tuomas.

"Your cheek's healing well," she observed. "You were so lucky."

"I know," he muttered. "Listen, Lilja... I heard Sigurd speaking to you."

"Did you? Well, I'm sure those ears of yours can pick up anything. I was straight with him. There's not much more I can do now."

"But... Well, what *are* you going to do? You can't leave."

"I know," Lilja growled. She paced back and forth, ran a hand over her head in agitation.

Tuomas threw a glance at the tent. On the other side of the skin-tarp, he could see Aki's silhouette, sitting by the fire. With the lack of detail, he looked smaller than ever.

"Does he remember what happened to him?" he asked.

"Yes." Lilja fingered the end of one of her braids. "He says... he misses his friends."

A lump formed in her voice and she quickly swallowed it.

"All this just reminds me of how much I dislike people," she admitted. "I know they saw Aki with the draugars, but he's innocent. I've tried to explain that. And the glances, the whispers... I'm used to it happening to me. I'm an adult, I can deal with it. It's awful to see it happen to your baby. You wouldn't understand."

Tuomas offered the gentlest smile he could.

"Maybe not. But the three of us – you, me, and Aki – we're all outcasts, in our own way. I can understand that much. It will take time for people to get used to him. You said yourself, they don't just accept things overnight. I mean, how long did it take for them to get used to *you* this winter, after you went back to Poro? You were under Kari's control; you were terrifying. I knew what was going on and even I was scared of you."

Lilja was silent for a moment. She didn't even blink. But then her shoulders sagged, and she gave a conceding nod.

"I forget it does me good to talk to you," she said, running a finger over the scar on her throat. "You remind me of Kari in that respect."

Tuomas's heart skipped nervously. "I remind you of him?"

"In a good way," Lilja said quickly. "As he was before. Not how you knew him. When he was... a good man. *You* are a good man, Tuomas."

She watched Aki moving about in the tent. Her eyes darted in a hundred directions, as though she was preparing herself for something painful.

"That actually brings me to something I wanted to speak to you about. You're the only person who I can trust. I'd like you to look after him for me."

Tuomas's mouth fell open. He'd never been asked to look after any children before. He'd always been on the fringes of Akerfjorden, with no real responsibilities, until Henrik took him on as an apprentice.

"Why?" he blurted.

"I'm going to the Poro and Einfjall winter camps, to collect the caretakers," said Lilja. "I don't care that they were safe from the draugars, or will be safe from the trolls; they need to be with us. Unless someone goes, they won't have any way of knowing what's happening. And it's safer for one person to go than divert this entire caravan."

Tuomas stared at her. "But you're a mage! You'll be putting yourself in danger!"

"I'm not going on foot, boy," Lilja answered, and tapped her drum. Tuomas understood at once.

"You'll travel through the fire?"

"It's the quickest way," she said simply. "Thank the Spirits that ability hasn't been taken away from me."

Tuomas went to argue further, but then bit back his protests. The Great Bear had told him Lilja had other matters to attend to. Was this what it meant? After all, if he'd spoken with her about taking Aki to the World Below, she never would have come to this decision.

There's a plan, he reminded himself. It wasn't his place to question it.

"Alright," he said. "I'll take care of him."

"I know you will," replied Lilja, with the tiniest hint of a smile. "Thank you."

She tossed her head towards the tent and the two of them ducked inside. Aki's scurried across the furs and wrapped his arms around her waist.

"Mama, I think the food's still warm. Can we eat it now? Please? I'm hungry!"

"Of course," Lilja said. She lifted the spit out of the hearth, slid the meat off and cut it cleanly down the middle with one of her knives. "Slowly, now. Don't burn your mouth."

"I won't," said Aki. He took a bite off the end. "Hello, Tuomas."

"Hello, Aki," he replied. "Has it been a long day?"

Aki nodded. "Is it always going to be this busy?"

"Only until we get to Akerfjorden," said Lilja.

"Where's that? Will I make friends there?"

A muscle twitched in Lilja's jaw. Tuomas quickly shuffled closer.

"You've already got a friend," he said. "I'm your friend."

Aki regarded him, wiped some meat juice away on his sleeve. Then he grinned.

The sight almost made Tuomas forget all the darkness the little boy had been forced to trail in his wake. He had the same eyes as Lilja, the same hair. Without the scars, he would have been a stunning child to look at. And there was such innocence in his gaze, such trust. It melted Tuomas's heart.

Lilja threw him a grateful smile, then ate her meal in a few hurried mouthfuls and cupped Aki's face in her hands.

"Listen, baby, I have to go away for a little while," she said. "So Tuomas is going to take care of you."

Aki grasped her wrists. "Where are you going?"

"To help some other friends."

"Can't I come with you?"

"I wish you could, but it's too much. You can't walk through fire."

"Let me try! You and Uncle Kari said I would be the best mage ever!"

"No," Lilja said firmly. "I need you to stay here and be a good boy. Can you do that for me?"

Aki's lip trembled, but he sniffed back a sob and nodded. Lilja pulled him into a tight hug. Her eyes flashed with tears, but she kept her chin high so Aki wouldn't see them.

"I'll be back before you know it," she promised, kissing him all over his head. "I love you."

"I love you too, Mama," said Aki.

Lilja hesitated. For a moment, Tuomas thought she might lose her nerve and not leave. But she shook her head, and forced herself to let go of her son.

"By the way," she said as she rose to her feet, "I've got something of yours, Tuomas. It was in your old tunic."

She dug into a pouch on her belt, pulled something out and tossed it at him. He caught it with one hand, stared at it in alarm. It was the fox carving. But Lilja had bored a tiny hole through it, and threaded it onto a length of leather, long enough to be worn around his neck.

"It seemed apt," she said. "And it means you won't lose it again."

Before he could thank her, she untied her drum, held it close to the flames to warm it.

"Stay back," she said, to Aki.

Then she beat the skin, chanted loudly. Tuomas felt her *taika* slam into him like a wall of heat. He saw the tundra at the height of spring, covered in carpets of heather; the sweet waters of a lake, freshly melted... heard Aki's laughter on the wind...

She stepped into the smouldering logs in the middle of the hearth. Sparks flew up around her; fire swept over her body. And in an instant, she was gone.

Aki's eyes widened.

"Mama?" he said, crawling closer to the fire. Tuomas sprang forward and pushed him away.

"No, don't," he warned. "You'll burn yourself."

Aki blinked. He raised a hand to his cheeks pensively. The soft glow highlighted the scars in ragged pink lines.

After a moment, he sighed and rested his shoulders against one of the poles holding up the tent tarp.

"She'll be alright," Tuomas assured. "She knows what she's doing."

"I know," said Aki. "Do you know she's met the Great Bear Spirit? It brought her back to life when she was a bit older than me. And then she told me I would be a mage too, just like her. You're a mage as well, aren't you? I can tell, because you've got a drum. When will I get a drum?"

Tuomas chuckled. "When you're older."

"How much older?"

"I don't know. It's different for everyone."

"Tomorrow?"

"No."

He sat down properly, pulled at his coat so there was room behind him for his tail to lay flat. Aki peered around the hearth to see it better.

"Why do you have that?" he asked.

"Let's just say your mother isn't the only one who's met the Great Bear Spirit," Tuomas replied, as he inspected the carving. With a small shrug, he slipped it around his neck. There was nowhere else to put it.

Aki looked straight at him. "Is that because you're a Spirit, too?"

Tuomas stilled. "You've heard that?"

"Everyone talks about it. Not to me, though. But I hear them," said Aki sadly. "You didn't have a tail when you came and helped me, though. When you made *them* let me go."

He plucked at the fur on his shoes, broke off a couple of strands and rolled them between his fingers.

"That's fine," he said.

"What is?"

"You being a Spirit. It's fine."

Tuomas frowned. "You mean you aren't frightened of me?"

Aki shook his head. "No. You're not scary. They're stupid if they think you're scary."

Tuomas smiled, but Aki didn't see it; he closed his eyes and yawned. Tuomas promptly shook out a sleeping sack.

"I'm not tired," Aki protested.

"Well, you should try to sleep, anyway."

Aki crossed his arms. "Are you going to be boring?"

"Look, if your mother knows I let you stay up late, I'll never hear the end of it," Tuomas said. "And you're going to need your energy. All of us are. You've never been on a migration before; it's hard."

"I'll be fine," Aki insisted, but nevertheless allowed Tuomas to pull his shoes off and slide him into the sack. "Anyway, what is a migration? Why do the reindeer need to go all over the place?"

"Because they eat all the lichen and moss, so they have to swim to the islands for more. And once they've eaten everything at the summer grounds, they go back to the winter ones."

"And they need us to help them?"

"Not really. They were doing migrations long before people came along. But we keep them safe on the way, from wolves and things. And in return, they give us meat and furs and everything else we need to live. So reindeer and people help each other."

Tuomas threw a couple of new logs onto the fire and poked at the smouldering embers. Then he sat on his own sleeping sack and faced Aki. The little boy gazed into the flames; already his eyes were drooping.

"I'm happy Mama told you to look after me."

Tuomas was taken aback. "Why?"

"You're the only one here who I remember, except her. I know you'll keep them away."

"Keep what away? The trolls?"

Aki shook his head. Tuomas instantly realised what he meant.

"The draugars?"

"Yes."

Pity welled in Tuomas's heart. He crawled over and put a hand on Aki's head.

"They're gone," he promised. "They won't ever come back."

"How do you know?"

"Because you know the Spirit of the Lights, who dances in the sky? She's my sister. And she and the Great Bear got so angry with them, they banished them to a place where no living thing has ever stood."

Tuomas's mouth went dry. They would have to go there soon. Now Lilja was gone, he would need to take this tiny boy across the Night River…

To his relief, Aki didn't speak again. His eyes closed and he nestled deeper into the sack. Tuomas stroked his hair, the way he'd seen Lilja do, until he was sure he was asleep. Then he moved away as quietly as he could and lay on the other side of the fire.

He rested his hand close to the embers as tiredness pulled him under. But no sooner had he let go when a freezing wind brushed over him. He smelled dampness and decay, felt shadows pressing on his flesh like a shroud.

And then… silver. It was everywhere; no matter how he twisted, he couldn't escape it.

A pockmarked face appeared before him; dark hair wove through the night sky. Long fingers plucked at his *taika* until he hung like a spider in a web.

Hello, my dear, said the Moon Spirit.

Chapter Eleven

She sat in the middle of the tundra, snow all around, at one with everything. She didn't need to breathe – she had no lungs or organs beneath the pristine snowy skin – but the air, though thin and cold, was a weight against her face. Gravity pulled at her; every movement felt hampered and laboured. No matter that she had taken this form before, was no longer imprisoned in it and could shift at will. By nature, she was shapeless, indistinct, uncontained. She wanted to fill the World Above with her Lights, dance through the stars and never stop…

But such a thing was impossible, so long as the rip hung overhead. The nothingness beyond it tugged at the very fabric of existence. When a wind blew past and swept up the powdery snow, the flakes hung suspended for a while, as though unsure where to settle. The souls in all living things trembled, from the strongest man to the smallest bush. Even the mountains felt like they might break apart; every crystal which made up every boulder on their mighty faces shuddered and groaned against the strain.

Stardust and *taika* poured from the edges of the gash. Every time she caught sight of it, her eyes flickered red. She had warned her brother about the dangers of crossing between the Worlds when the boundary was so fragile. And then *she* had been the one who tore it straight open. All for him.

Always, everything, for him. It would be the way of things forever. Anger each other, protect each other, until the end of time. No matter who she needed to hurt in the process.

She suddenly sensed a pulse of energy from the World Above and whirled around. Her mother was hovering over the camp, bathing it in silver light. But the pull was strongest on the tent at the edge, further from any other. Lilja's tent.

She leapt up, let her body come apart until she was nothing but an aurora, and flashed across the sky. But the Moon Spirit pushed back, flung up a barrier to keep her away. And the World Above was closed to her; the Great Bear had warned her such a thing would happen. She couldn't face her mother on equal ground, not until the cleft was repaired...

She panicked. Tuomas was in that human state between lucidity and trance. And the Silver One had him.

Hello, my dear.

She tried to push closer. *Let him go!*

This is none of your concern, White Fox One, the Moon Spirit hissed, and threw her to the ground. She burst into the fox form as she landed, and lay in the snow, shaken.

The Moon Spirit drew closer to Tuomas, pulled him against her.

I didn't summon you, Silver One, he protested.

But I summoned you, she replied silkily. Her silent voice wove around him like ropes; the creeping chill of water as ice formed on its surface; the empty darkness of a night devoid of life.

I told you I refused your offer, said Tuomas. *I am not your son.*

You lie to yourself. Do not mind the words of my sister and daughter, saying you do not belong with me. I raised you. You are everything you are because of me.

No. I am my own. And I will not return to you.

The Moon still didn't release him. *Not even to save your silly little human friends?*

Even from where she lay on the ground, she sensed Tuomas's fear: a sharpness cutting through the air. She tried to pull herself back together, focus her energy… she had to get him away from the Silver One…

The Great Bear Spirit told you that I sent the trolls, the Moon Spirit said. *Now I will tell you why. The Worlds are coming apart around us, my sweet thing. Magic falls through the cracks, I know you sense this. The only ones who may use that magic, besides Spirits, are mages. So I whispered to the trolls, deep in their stony slumber; used my own power to awaken them. And I said: kill them. Kill the mages. Let them be ended.*

She stared up at her mother, paralysed with horror.

But why? cried Tuomas. *The people need the mages! They're the healers!*

No matter how often they heal, everything will still die. Tomorrow, in a decade… it is all the same, replied the Moon Spirit coolly. *But I know you care for them, Red Fox One, in a different way. So would you have them live, for however short it may be?*

Tuomas flinched as cold fingers clutched him, trailed over his chest.

You yourself will die, said the Silver One. *This foul little human body will fail, then lie decaying in the earth. And upon that moment, your Spirit will come home. So swear that when the time arrives, you will return to me. Be my son, as you once were. Let me enfold you and call you mine, no matter what the Golden One or White Fox One might whisper to you. Do this, and I will order the trolls to stand down before they can kill again.*

Tuomas's mind raced. She saw it as clearly as though the images had been painted in the air: Niina, Lilja, Aki... the sight of Henrik being wrenched in two...

If I did, he said carefully, *the balance would not be upset?*

It was not upset when you were mine last time.

And you would spare the mages?

Yes.

Tuomas hesitated. *What about Lumi?*

Enough of the White Fox One. She is not here, just you and me, my dear. Come, do not deny me. Be my son. Swear to me.

She picked herself up from the snow and threw herself at the barrier. She could feel her brother's terror, the indecision and responsibility crushing him like a snowflake underfoot...

The Lights burst all around her and transformed the sky red.

No! she shouted, and with an almighty amount of energy, forced her way forward.

Her mother's defence cracked like ice. She slammed into Tuomas, shoved him back down towards the shelter until she felt him awaken.

How dare you! she raged at the Silver One. *Have you not manipulated him enough?*

You are a fine one to speak of manipulation. And look at you now, allowing foolish human emotions to overwhelm you again, White Fox One, snarled the Moon Spirit. *Or would you prefer the foolish human name which you have come to cherish so much? Lumi?*

You will not call me that.

I will call you whatever I wish! You are everything I never wanted! So cold, so vicious!

Then I am truly your daughter.

Her aurora clashed with Moonlight. The gash shook as though caught in a storm. Below, people poured out of the tents to watch the spectacle. Such anger… such power… Stars shot across the night like rain.

Enough!

A huge bulk appeared between them and pushed them in opposite directions. She spun through the sky, disorientated, gathered more Lights to throw into her mother's face. But then she paused when she saw a giant fathomless eye staring her down; older than her, older than any of them…

The Great Bear Spirit regarded her with a silence so absolute, it made her squirm. There were no spoken words, nothing physical, and yet the respect it commanded was as loud as thunder, stronger than the largest mountain.

You will not battle like this, it warned. *The fabric of the Worlds is too thin. Am I clear?*

The Moon Spirit shrank back. *Perfectly.*

And so you reveal your intentions, Silver One, the Bear continued. *I do not approve. It is unfair and dangerous.*

No more dangerous than what we already face, replied the Moon. *Trolls have walked the World Between before. At least, this time, their destruction is not wanton. Six may die, at most. Six, in all the millions which have ever lived and will ever live.*

She sneered at her mother. She had always known the Silver One had little respect for life. After all, she was a Spirit of shadow, misfortune and sickness: the symbol of the Long Dark, when weather was harsh and hunts were lean. Together, the two of them were among the most dreaded entities in any realm.

Two of those six has a part to play, the Bear growled. *Aki and the Red Fox One are to go to the Deathlands. Had you not acted so rashly, you would know this. You are to call off those trolls at once. Under no circumstances are they to harm either of them.*

The Silver One's light dimmed. *I would never have them harm my son.*

He is not your son! she raged, and shot a jet of red aurora at her mother. Then she turned to the Bear. *You must stop her! She wishes to steal him!*

Calm yourself, White Fox One.

No! She cannot have him!

The Great Bear glittered: a million stars against the night. She stood her ground.

She cannot have him, she said again. *Please. Stop her.*

The Silver One is at fault, the Bear conceded. *But there is a kernel of truth in her sentiment. When the Red Fox One returns to the World Above, balance will already be restored. It does not matter to whom he pledges his loyalty afterwards.*

She spun in the air, filled with disgust. It couldn't be serious. After all she had done to keep him away from her mother? After all the hardship her brother had endured, both as Spirit and human… it could be for nothing?

Are you truly willing to allow this? she demanded. *He is the Son of the Sun! He belongs with the Golden One!*

Yes, he does, replied the Bear. *But it may be his choice.*

She could scarcely contain her rage. *You knew this, Silver One. That is why you intend to force him into a corner.*

I force him into a corner? The Moon Spirit retorted. *You have a nerve to speak to me of that. You are crueller than I, and you know it. We would never have been separated in the first place if it were not for you!*

Before she could respond, the Bear turned to her again, swirled around her.

The most important thing, White Fox One, is to remember that your brother has been reborn a second time for one purpose only: to close off the opening to the World Below. Once that is done, there is nothing to hold him to this life. What comes after does not matter. Do you understand?

She trembled, and a faint wave of green washed in all directions. She looked at the camp and noticed Tuomas standing there. But beyond his living flesh and wide eyes, he was the formless golden glow she knew best, which she saw whenever she regarded him.

He was so much more than this, always had been. To be contained in a body was terrible for her; she wasn't made for it. And neither was he.

I understand, she said, so softly, she was barely aware of it herself. *He cannot be allowed to risk dealing any more damage, once we have closed the gateways.*

That is correct, said the Bear. *When all is done, I will send the Carrying One to collect his souls and bring them home. But now, Silver One, call off those trolls. This is no way to proceed. They are not to harm him or Aki.*

I shall try, the Moon Spirit replied.

No. You will do more than try. You will do whatever you must, the Bear warned.

But you will not prevent me from seeking him? He may be my son?

This feud is between you and the Golden One. You must solve it yourselves, when all is stable. And the Red Fox One may make a choice between you, should he wish, but not now. There is too much to be done.

She turned away, unable to look at her mother for another moment. Instead, she gazed at Tuomas, with his frostbitten fingers and blonde hair and eyes as blue as a summer sky. So alive…

The aurora tinted red, then lapsed into the coldest blue she had let out for generations. It sang of anguish, dripped itself across the night, as the tears she could never shed.

And I will not tell him what must come, she decided. *It is best if he does not know, or he shall be too frightened to proceed. He is human in that respect, after all.*

Chapter Twelve

The Lights turned red, then blue, then began to descend, like meltwater running over a rock. Slowly, they took the form of a girl, and Lumi toppled forward onto her hands and knees, close to the herd. Several reindeer snorted and hurried away in alarm.

People muttered nervously, made the sign of the hand. Tuomas ignored them, snatched his drum and beat it once, so he could slip through the barrier.

"Lumi?" he called.

She didn't reply, just eased herself to her feet. But she had no sooner taken her weight when her legs wobbled and she crashed down again. Her tail brushed back and forth angrily and sent a flash of crimson into the air.

Tuomas knelt beside her.

"Are you hurt?"

"No."

"Did you see that? You woke me up?"

"Yes, I did," she said. "Ignore her."

Tuomas licked his lips nervously. They were dry from cold; he fought the urge not to chew on them.

Then he realised every inch of her skin was glistening, as though she had jumped into a lake.

"You're wet," he said. "Lumi, are you sure you're alright?"

"Quit worrying," she snapped, and grabbed him. He gasped; she hadn't held him that tightly since she had tried to stop him jumping out of the World Above. For a moment, he thought she might break all the bones in his wrist.

"Do not listen to her," Lumi said firmly. "Do not even think on what she told you. Do you understand? There is too much you need to concentrate on without letting her inside your head."

Tuomas's heart rose into his throat. "But... you heard her. She'll set the trolls on the mages if I don't –"

"No." Lumi stood up again. This time, she managed to keep her balance, but still didn't let go of him. "It has been dealt with, and she will do nothing of the sort. They will be called off. Remember what I told you: it is better to endure than to sacrifice."

Tuomas swallowed, went to speak, but Lumi looked at him so earnestly that all he could manage was a nod.

"Alright," he said. "So what am I supposed to do now?"

"Keep focused, and go back to sleep. The sooner we are clear of the mountains, the better," said Lumi.

She wiped her forehead and flicked the water away. It transformed to snowflakes in mid-air and drifted to the ground. Then she fleetingly touched his cheek, turned around, and ran into the darkness.

Tuomas watched her until her Lights disappeared, and with a sigh, made his way back through the circle.

"What was that?" Birkir called. "Were the Spirits fighting?"

"It's nothing," Tuomas assured. "Don't worry, please."

But he still threw a nervous glance at the Moon Spirit before ducking into Lilja's tent.

Dawn was hardly a faint glow on the horizon when the camp was struck. Tuomas shook Aki awake, helped him to dress, then stripped the tarp off the tent until only a skeleton of poles was left. Then he packed everything into the back of the sleigh where Lumi was hiding, flung the sleeping sacks, skins and utensils on top. In only a short while, every shelter was collapsed, and the only mark that they had been there at all were the stains of ash and reindeer waste on the snow.

Tuomas took Aki's hand. Ritva, Frode and some others watched warily as they walked past. Aki noticed and lowered his eyes.

"They're staring at me," he muttered.

"Ignore them," replied Tuomas.

"That's what Mama says to do. But it doesn't stop them."

"Well, if you let them stare, they'll get bored soon enough."

Tuomas winced as he said it. He felt there was some shred of truth in it, but he hoped it could be right for someone like Aki.

He lifted him into the sleigh, beside the skins, and covered him with a blanket.

"Listen, this is very important," he said. "My sister is under all this stuff, and the Sunlight can't touch her. Do not lift *anything*."

Aki's mouth fell open. "Your sister? The Spirit of the Lights?"

"Yes," said Tuomas. "She won't hurt you, but you need to just leave her be. She's weak today. Promise."

"Alright, I promise," Aki said nervously. Then he reached out and grasped Tuomas's coat. "What happened last night?"

"I thought you were asleep."

"I was. But the *taika* feels different today. Why?"

"It's nothing. Don't worry about it."

Aki tapped his mittens together in agitation.

"Do you think Mama's alright?" he asked.

"Of course she is," smiled Tuomas. "She'll be back soon."

Niina overheard and moved a little closer, though she kept a fair distance from Aki.

"Where did Lilja go?" she whispered. "I noticed she was missing this morning."

"She's collecting the caretakers from the winter camps," Tuomas explained.

"Good thinking. But, seriously, what did happen last night? It looked like a battle."

"I don't really know all the details, but the Moon Spirit was trying to reach me. Lumi stopped her."

Niina swallowed nervously. "Well, what did she say to you?"

"I don't really want to talk about it," said Tuomas. Everyone was uneasy enough without also having to learn the mages were essentially being held hostage for his sake.

"Alright," Niina said. "Would you like me to tell the elders? About Lilja, I mean? You look like you need some time alone."

Tuomas nodded. It was impossible to be alone on a journey like this, but the promise to walk without holding conversation was too tempting to pass. He had barely slept after witnessing the fight, and the Moon Spirit's presence was fresh in his mind. He could still feel her fingers holding him, her frosty voice whispering in his ear.

He eyed her. She had faded now: a faint blue circle against the rip, but that hardly made him feel any better. What part of his refusal had she not understood? Why was she so desperate to have him as her son again? All because he had run away from her? There must have been good reason, if it had caused him to willingly come alive as a human. And now she was prepared to destroy all other mages in order to force his hand?

He shook his head. Lumi had said not to listen, and if there was one Spirit who he knew he could trust, it was her.

Niina hurried towards the elders as the herd was roused. Then the entire caravan carried on, closer to the western flank of the mountains. Tuomas wondered what they must look like from above: a giant living cloud of animals and people, sleighs and skis. He had seen the World Between from the sky before, but never at the height of migration. At least, not in this lifetime.

As the day wore on, Tuomas tried several times to catch Elin's eye, but she deliberately kept to the other side of the herd and didn't look at him. She powered ahead on her skis, bow across her back, face set as though it had been carved out of stone. She had probably gone straight to sleep, seething and hating everything about him.

That seemed to be turning into a common emotion.

He let out a sad sigh and turned his attention back to the tundra. He leaned on one ski, then the other. Each step brought him closer to the end – he had to remember that.

They travelled hard, faster than they would normally, desperate to make up the distance. Even when the Sun Spirit dipped and the sky darkened, the elders didn't give the sign to stop. Tuomas realised why. Ahead, the first promise of the forest appeared in the distance, branches bowed under the weight of snow. Camping near there would provide more shelter than out in the open.

Now they were a little further south, patches of bare rock were starting to break through in places. Soon, the thaw would be upon them. Rocks which had rolled off the mountain slopes sat slick with ice, but Tuomas knew it would shortly melt. He closed his eyes and reached out for all the Spirits of winter, begged them to hold onto their power for a little longer. The Mustafjord had to remain frozen, otherwise the final stretch of the journey would be cut off.

Finally, the convoy drew close enough to the trees. The herd was halted and the people pitched the tents. A quick meal of sautéed reindeer was passed around, then everybody went straight to bed.

But despite his own fatigue, Tuomas couldn't sleep. He tossed and turned in his sack, growing more fitful by the second. What if the Moon Spirit hijacked his dreams again and tried to whisper poison in his mind? And they were nearly clear of the mountains now. He had perhaps one more day before he would have to take Aki and leave.

With a sigh, he pulled on his shoes and stepped outside, drum in hand. The open tundra was silent. Even though he knew watchers were about, they might as well have been a million miles away.

He sat at the central fire. It had burned down and only a few lonely tongues licked through the embers. The last log which had been added was scarcely keeping its shape; the fire had made it crack and splinter.

He took a deep breath, focused on the chill of the air as it entered his lungs. There was a dampness to it now as spring encroached on the Northlands. In a few weeks, this entire place would be carpeted with heather as far as the eye could see. And then midsummer would come, and Tuomas himself would turn sixteen.

A stone dropped in his stomach. Was he still only fifteen?

Tears prickled his eyes. He lowered his face into his hands and let them fall. There was nobody to see.

He glanced at his drum – Henrik's drum. If he tried hard enough, he fancied he could almost still smell the old mage's tea. Henrik had painted most of the symbols; the skin and alder bark paint were darkened with age. But now, he found himself drawn to the tree which spanned from top to bottom.

One of the stories about the three Worlds was that they were all held together by a giant invisible tree: its trunk in the World Between, roots in the World Below, and branches up in the World Above. It connected them and kept them all in place.

Tuomas pondered the image: of the human realm caught between the two larger Spirit realms. He had been into the three of them, and even though he'd spent more time in the starry World Above, he realised that what he had seen was nothing. Simply one branch or root; others extended around it, stretching on to infinity, in the sky and under the earth.

And like Lumi cared for souls in the World Above, so the Spirit of Death did the same in the World Below, across that grey desert and the black waters of the Night River. Lumi's Lights were a river too, each flowing and weaving through the tree.

After all, as the Worlds were connected, the living and the dead were two halves of the same family. It was the fundamental reason why there always needed to be balance. Nature itself relied on it.

Soon, he would be standing on the shores of the Deathlands. When that time came, when he looked into the heart of darkness, he needed to remember this moment.

He wiped his tears away, then flexed his fingers, focused as hard as he could. He caught the taste of lingonberry, felt warmth, sensed summer flooding through his body as his *taika* awakened. He hardly needed to try anymore. It blossomed under his touch, responded like lightning. He gritted his teeth with the effort of keeping it under control.

Sparks flared in his palm. He snatched at them, forced more out. Slowly, a flame appeared.

It was tiny, only as large as his thumb, but he refused to give up and allowed it to grow. He brought his hands together and the fire spread. It slid across his flesh, softer than a feather, licked greedily at the air.

He let out an elated laugh. Yes... *this* was what he was. Spirit of the Flames. Nothing was too hot, nor too bright. He could almost feel his life-soul in his chest, alight: a piece of the Sun Spirit, shining brighter than any star.

He pushed the fire tighter until it formed a ball, tried to transform it into Sunlight. But his hands began to shake; his power wavered and the tongues began to fade. He shook his head, pressed harder. Still nothing happened, except a sharp pain in his heart.

Then he paused. The *taika* suddenly felt different. Beyond his own heat, beyond the shuddering of all three Worlds crushing each other... there was a sense of urgency; shaky breathing; something which was once warm, now cold. Too cold...

He threw the fireball away and peered at the dark shapes of the trees.

He leapt to his feet, hurried to the nearest person on watch duty: Maiken.

She frowned. "What's the matter?"

"I've got to go into the forest," said Tuomas. "There's something out there, something alive. I need to see what it is."

Maiken blinked in alarm. "A troll?"

"No."

"Then what?"

"I don't know, but it's definitely not a troll. Not big enough."

"Well, let me come with you," said Maiken. "It's too dangerous to be going out of sight by yourself."

Tuomas wanted to argue, but he could tell from her expression that it was pointless. She picked up the torch which had been stuck into the snow beside her, and held it in the same hand as her bow. Tuomas checked to make sure he had all his knives, then beat his drum, and a small hole opened in the barrier.

It didn't take long to reach the trees. At first glance, there didn't seem to be anything wrong. But as they drew closer, Tuomas felt the air change into something heavy and thick. It made him cough and the *taika* inside him pulsed like a second heart.

"Are you alright?" Maiken whispered.

Tuomas nodded.

"Are you sure it's not a troll?"

"Positive."

All the same, he kept hold of his drum, in case he needed to send out a shockwave. He hadn't sensed any wolves, but this was a perfect place for them to hide.

Huge boulders were dotted about, brought down in ancient avalanches. He could tell they had been there for a while, because mature spruces had grown around them where they sat. They broke up the maze of icy trunks and made him squint.

Then he spotted shattered branches and the shapeless humps of fallen trees. The snow itself was churned with earth. And he saw several huge footprints, each one as long as his leg.

Maiken drew in a breath and raised her bow.

"Trolls were here," she hissed.

Tuomas's throat dried up. His tail swept nervously; the more he tried to still it, the harder it moved.

They cautiously moved deeper into the woods, edged around the boulders, and Maiken let out a cry.

Sacks and broken tent poles were scattered about the remains of a trampled sled. A pair of skis lay next to it. Tuomas snatched the torch and inspected them, and his blood turned to ice.

"These are Mihka's," he said.

Maiken's eyes grew wide. "What?"

Tuomas knelt close to the mess of tracks and peered at them, trying to read them in the low light. Could he still be around here? No, surely not. If he had any sense, he would be miles away by now. This couldn't have been his last camp.

None of the tracks were fresh; ice had formed in the depressions, and they were criss-crossed with those of wolverine paws and the sweeping spread of wings where an eagle had landed. The predators wouldn't have wasted any time in scavenging any food supplies left over.

But Tuomas managed to figure out enough. Among the mess, he located the imprints of shoes. He followed them through the trees, around another boulder several feet away.

He almost fell over in horror.

A figure was lying there, under a tattered tent tarp. The dead remains of a recent fire charred the ground. A dusting of snow covered him, but the head of white hair was unmistakable.

"Maiken!" Tuomas shouted.

He flung the tarp away and checked Mihka's pulse. Amazingly, he was alive, but only just. His skin was almost as pale as his hair, ice had formed on his eyelashes and his lips were blue. The fact that he was still breathing was a miracle.

Maiken appeared. Neither of them wasted a moment. They each grabbed one of Mihka's arms, dragged him upright and ran as fast as they could.

Chapter Thirteen

"Help!" Maiken shouted when they came within earshot of the camp. "Quickly! Help!"

At once, people poured out of the tents. The others on watch duty rushed over, bows in hand.

"Where's Niina?" Tuomas snapped. "Get her! Now!"

Sigurd bolted towards her shelter. Tuomas let go of Mihka for long enough to hit his drum, then he and Maiken bundled him inside the circle. Mihka's feet dragged uselessly along the ground.

Anssi sprang forward, all blood gone from his cheeks.

"How did you know he was out there?" he asked.

"I didn't," replied Tuomas. "I just sensed *something*. I had no idea it was him."

"How long do you think he was there?"

"A few days. I don't know how he's still alive."

"Tuomas!" Niina shouted from her tent. "Bring him here!"

She held back the flap. Tuomas and Maiken hurried over; just before he ducked inside, Tuomas spotted Elin, watching from near the fire pit. Her eyes shone with alarm.

Sigurd stepped close and blocked his line of sight.

"Is there anything I can do?"

"Not right now," Tuomas said. "Thank you. We'll call if we need help."

Sigurd nodded and hurried away to take up his watch again. Niina pulled the flap shut behind him to keep the heat in.

"I'll ask questions later," she muttered, with a glance at Tuomas. "Put him on my sleeping sack."

Maiken lowered Mihka onto the furs. Niina knelt at his side, took his pulse and held her finger under his nose. Her brows knotted with worry, then she placed her hands on his chest and started to press.

"Is he dead?" Tuomas cried.

"He will be if I don't do this," Niina replied. She pushed down hard, several times, then pinched his nostrils shut and blew into his mouth.

Mihka coughed weakly. His breath came in fast, shallow gasps.

"He has hypothermia," Niina said. "We have to warm him, but not too fast. It needs to go into his bones first. We can't let the blood run back to his heart too quickly."

Tuomas threw more logs onto the fire, shrugged out of his coat and wrapped it around Mihka. Maiken pressed her body against him to get some heat into his torso. Niina laid a nearby tunic by the hearth; when the material was warm, she rolled it up and placed it under his chin.

After several agonising moments, his breathing fell into a more normal rhythm. He started shivering. Maiken tugged off a mitten with her teeth and laid her warm hands on his cheeks.

Tuomas swallowed nervously as Niina held a cup of water to Mihka's lips. This was what he had probably looked like when he'd been rescued from Kari on the Einfjall mountain. He'd fallen unconscious and developed hypothermia too. He remembered the fever dreams; the pain as his frozen skin thawed.

A dreadful suspicion crept over him. He glanced at his stumpy fingers. then back at Mihka. His face was pale and crossed with shallow scratches, but he otherwise seemed unharmed.

That didn't convince Tuomas. He crawled to Mihka's feet.

"Niina, check for frostbite."

She didn't argue. While she eased the layers back, Tuomas untied Mihka's shoes, and his heart sank. Several of his toes were grey and swollen, and hard to the touch.

"It's bad."

Niina nodded grimly and showed Mihka's hands. All his fingers were darkened, and when she dug her thumbnail into one, no redness appeared. They had frozen solid.

"I wouldn't be surprised if he loses the whole hand," she said.

"And his toes."

"How in the name of all the Spirits did you find him?"

"I just… sensed him. I think he'd pitched camp out there – his stuff was scattered everywhere. And there were troll footprints."

"It's amazing they didn't kill him," said Maiken.

"Unless they thought he was already dead," Tuomas replied. "Lilja told me that trolls won't eat anything which isn't alive."

Niina grimaced at his words.

"I wish Lilja was here now," she muttered. "Or Aino. Or any of them. I don't know what I'm doing…"

"You're doing fine," Maiken assured. "Tuomas, do you think they're close? The trolls?"

"No, the prints looked days old."

Niina felt Mihka's forehead again.

"He's starting to wake up a little. Tuomas, warm those scarves; we'll wrap them around his feet. And get some tea brewing for him. There's herbs in the box by my belt."

Tuomas pushed the hems of Mihka's trousers past his ankles to uncover his feet more. But Mihka shouted and kicked out, catching him in the chest. He fell into the tarp, winded.

"Just a reflex," Maiken said, and put one of her legs across Mihka's to keep them still.

Mihka gnashed his teeth, face screwing up in pain. He threw his head back and screamed.

The sound chilled Tuomas. It was full of pain and panic, and unbridled anger.

It wasn't long before people from the surrounding tents came running. The flap was torn open and a crowd of concerned faces peered inside. Elin stood near the front, eyes so wide, Tuomas thought they might pop out.

"What is this?" Alda cried.

"He was in the forest; Tuomas and I found him," Maiken explained. "Everyone, just give us some air –"

"Tuomas!" Mihka hissed. His voice sounded like a knife scraping along a stone.

"Can you hear me? I'm here," Tuomas assured.

Mihka eased his eyes open. They were watery and bloodshot.

"You. It's all your fault," he whispered.

Tuomas froze. "What are you talking about?"

"You doomed them all! My father... The souls, all the others, you trapped them... Your fault..."

"Quiet, now," Niina said. "You need to rest. You've been through a lot."

Mihka shook his head. "It's all your fault..."

He shuddered, gasping for breath. Maiken rubbed his arms firmly to get some warmth into them, but her gaze turned on Tuomas in shock. All the others in the doorway stared at him too.

Tuomas shuffled uncomfortably. What could he do? Deny it? If he hadn't tried to play the hero, all the souls would be free by now...

"Ravings," Elin said, breaking the awkward silence.

Niina nodded, and felt Mihka's forehead again. "She's right. He's hot. Fever will be setting in."

Tuomas swallowed. He held a hand to his breastbone, over the scar, and watched as his old friend fell into a fitful sleep.

Once the crowd had dissipated, Tuomas snatched his coat and left the shelter. He strode to the edge of the camp, looked towards the dark smudge of the forest.

It took all his self-control not to cry again. To have both Mihka and Elin hate him was almost too much to bear.

He spotted Lumi in the distance. She was recovered from her battle now: she stood with her back straight and head high, the way he knew. Her form was difficult to make out, but a faint stream of Lights drifted behind her, and backlit her against the sky. All around, stardust showered from the hole in the World Above. It seemed denser than before; the crisp air tasted strange, almost metallic. So wrong...

He heard snow crunching behind him. He glanced over his shoulder and saw Sigurd. When their eyes met, Sigurd offered a small smile and removed his hat respectfully. His black hair shone in the torchlight.

"Can I join you?" he asked.

Tuomas motioned to the spot beside him. Sigurd approached, then turned his attention to his bow. It was made from pale ash wood, beautifully crafted, and strung with a thick reindeer tendon. Elin's was exactly the same.

"Are you alright?" Sigurd asked. "I wanted to check on you. You looked really upset."

"I'm fine," Tuomas lied.

"No, you're not. Are you thinking about Mihka? Don't mind him. He's got a fever, he's delirious. You weren't much different when we were caring for you."

"I wasn't accusing my friend of being a monster."

"Well, you did rave at Lilja," Sigurd reminded him, then pressed his lips together, as though trying to suck her name back into his mouth. "Come on. What's on your mind?"

Tuomas heaved a great sigh. Out there, somewhere, the trolls were lurking in the shadows. Just because the people hadn't spotted them for a few days didn't mean safety. And despite Lumi's reassurance, he still felt the Moon Spirit watching him with her unblinking silver eyes.

Sigurd took hold of his shoulder.

"Listen, Tuomas," he said softly. "I wanted to thank you for saving Elin from those… things. I don't know what Alda and I would have done without her. We wouldn't have been able to cope. And… I know it was a huge price for you to pay."

"Do you?" Tuomas replied, a hint of anger creeping in his voice. "Mihka was right about that little detail, you know. *All the others…* that was the price Lumi and I paid. For both your children."

Sigurd gasped. He let go of Tuomas as though scalded.

"Lilja told you?" he said.

Tuomas nodded. There was no point in faking ignorance now.

"Yes, she did. I won't ask what happened, it's none of my business. But I know Aki is your son."

"When did she tell you?"

"Just before Elin was taken."

Sigurd swallowed uncomfortably. "Have you told anyone?"

"No," Tuomas said. "Have you?"

Sigurd shook his head.

"Not even Alda and Elin?"

"They don't know. I don't think I want them to."

In an instant, the questions were answered. Sigurd hadn't spoken about Aki to Elin, and she hadn't revealed it to him, either. But Tuomas wasn't sure whether that was a good thing anymore. Why hadn't Elin said anything? She was in a perfect position to let her father know she was aware of the truth.

She was annoyed, but had she truly understood the reasons why, after all?

"Lilja kept Aki a secret, for you," Tuomas said eventually. "I think you should know that."

"She sacrificed everything just to give the three of us a normal life together?"

"There were other reasons, but that was the main one. Even if she'll never admit it to you."

"Then I owe her so much," said Sigurd. "I'd… like to think that we could still be friends. At least in some way."

"Lilja isn't really one for having friends," Tuomas said pointedly.

"I'd still like to try."

"Won't that put your family in an awkward situation though? Sigurd, she made her choice. You're going to have to make one, too. You can't share your life with Alda and Elin,

Lilja and Aki, all together. It will undo everything Lilja worked to protect."

Sigurd stared at him. "How is all that wisdom in your young head?"

"I don't know. But does it really matter?"

"No. I suppose it doesn't. Who am I to question the Son of the Sun?"

Tuomas growled in frustration and flattened his ears.

"I didn't mean it like that! Please don't start with that again! All I'm saying is that your family will never forgive you. Lilja's learned to live with her burden. You need to learn how to do the same."

"But the boy... Aki..." Sigurd's eyes flashed with tears in the low light. "He's never known his father."

The sight of him softened Tuomas's heart. He offered a small smile and laid a hand on Sigurd's arm.

"I didn't really know my parents," he said. "That's why Paavo raised me; it was just me and him. But he always missed them more than I did. He had more memories."

"What's your point?"

"All Aki's ever known is wandering with Lilja, and Kari helped her raise him. That's what makes him happy. He doesn't know what he might have missed by having anyone else."

Sigurd recoiled. "That wicked mage? Don't tell me you're defending him! He tried to kill you! Twice!"

"I know," said Tuomas carefully, "and even though he's dead, a part of me is still terrified of him. But Aki never saw that side of him. He only saw his uncle. And I accept that. If you look at it in that way, Aki hasn't had it too bad. At least, until the draugars took him. But that's dealt with now, and what's done is done."

Sigurd pressed his lips together in thought. He nodded to himself, then rubbed his face with a sigh of defeat.

"Fair enough," he said. "You're more of a man than I am, I'll give you that."

Just a few months ago, hearing something like that would have made Tuomas shine with pride. But now it carried a heavier weight. No matter that he was mature enough to be a man in the Northlands – adulthood itself had arrived so fast and so terribly. It had torn through him like an unrelenting winter wind, and he suddenly felt much older than his years.

"I'm going to sleep," he said. "I need to check on Aki as well. Thanks for coming to see if I was alright."

He went to turn back to the camp, but Sigurd took hold of his elbow and stopped him.

"Tuomas, I need to ask you a favour," he said. "Please don't tell anyone about the boy's link to me. Not a word. Promise me."

Tuomas looked at him squarely. "If I was going to tell, I would have done it by now. And it's not my place, anyway. You and Lilja need to work that out for yourselves."

"I mean it," Sigurd said, his eyes hard.

"Fine," snapped Tuomas. He twisted his arm free. "I won't speak to anyone about it who doesn't already know. Goodnight, Sigurd."

He walked away, deliberately keeping his head forward, then ducked through the flap of Lilja's tent. Aki was still sound asleep. Tuomas was stunned how the commotion hadn't woken him, but he was glad of it. The last thing the little boy needed was to hear Mihka's cutting words about the souls he'd been forced to lure away.

He loaded the fire with thick logs, to burn slowly through the night, then wriggled into his sleeping sack. This was more than enough for one day.

Chapter Fourteen

The next morning, they moved again. The reindeer snorted in protest as they were pushed forward; travelling so hard with young calves was against their natural instincts. The babies had lost weight, so when the caravan found patches of grazing uncovered by melting snow, the herders relented and let the animals rest. But not for long – the ever-present threat of the trolls meant the herd was soon urged on.

The terrible creatures must have exhausted the islands now. They would have realised the people – and the mages – had gone south. Even though there hadn't been any sightings of them since leaving the coast, nobody dared to relax.

Tuomas only had to think of the forest, of those awful footprints trodden into the earth. The destruction was like Anaar all over again. The trolls had been there. They would come back. And never mind that Lumi had said the Moon Spirit would call them off; that didn't make it any safer for the reindeer, out here, miles from anything.

His eyes strayed to a sleigh near the front of the herd. Mihka was lying inside, barely conscious, among tent poles and tarps. He was still wrapped in layers of blankets and clothes. The worst of the hypothermia had passed, but every breath came out as a moan of agony. His frozen fingers and toes were starting to thaw, and the true damage of the frostbite was setting in.

Tuomas grimaced, remembering the feeling too well. Nevertheless, he hung back. The last thing he needed right now was Mihka screaming at him.

One by one, the stars faded, to reveal a crisp blue sky tinged by pink streaks. With no clouds to hold in the heat, the temperature fell, until the very air seemed made of ice. It wasn't cold enough to freeze his hair, but clouds of breath still rose from Tuomas's mouth.

After yet another tiring day, they finally broke away from the edge of the forest. The mountain flanks would continue for another twenty miles, but the same distance now lay between Tuomas and the Northern Edge of the World. Directly to the north west was the Poro winter camp, and beyond that, the lake.

He left Aki beside the central fire to get warm. As he walked off, he noticed several children shuffle away from him. One boy threw a handful of snow at the back of his head. Aki's lip quivered, but he fixed his attention on his lap and began picking at the stitches of his mittens.

Tuomas went to go back and scold the boy, but before he could, Lumi leapt out of his sleigh in her fox form. She grew with every step, until she was a girl once again.

"We have a clear path now," she said. "Tonight, we must leave."

"Tonight?" he repeated. "Won't it be safer in the day, with the trolls out there?"

"No. They will not pursue you," said Lumi. "And it will certainly not be safer for me."

Tuomas nodded. That was a good point.

"Alright, just let me help here. I need to tell the elders."

Lumi stood back and watched as Tuomas approached Mihka. He was sobbing with pain; tears had frozen on his cheeks and left them red raw. Niina was already at his side.

"We'll move you as soon as we can," she assured. "Anssi and Maiken are just getting a tent set up for you. How are you feeling?"

Mihka only moaned. Niina unwound the bandages around his fingers and winced when she saw the state of them. His skin came away with the material, leaving a blistered and bloodied mess. Whole portions of flesh were dead. Soon, they would drop off completely.

Tuomas brushed some of Mihka's hair out of his face.

"I know it hurts," he said softly. "But you're going to be alright."

Mihka opened his eyes, straining to focus.

"Get away from me," he snapped.

"I'm only trying to help," Tuomas insisted.

Mihka wrenched his hand free, threw a punch. It slammed into Tuomas's nose and knocked him over.

Niina snatched Mihka's arms. He struggled against her, but she held him fast.

"You might have a problem with him, but I'm the only other mage here!" she snarled. "So let me help, or lose both your hands, not just your fingers! Your choice!"

Mihka glared at her, but stopped fighting – whether from her words or from exhaustion, Tuomas couldn't tell.

He staggered upright and brushed the snow off his coat. Blood ran down to his lip. He carefully felt his nose, but to his relief, it wasn't broken. He pinched it, then jumped as Lumi strode over, her eyes narrowed.

A nearby crowd shied back, bowing in reverence. She ignored them and stood right next to Mihka. The ends of her fingers glowed with red Lights.

"That is no way to proceed," she said firmly. "I advise you to contain yourself."

Niina lowered her head; Mihka did the same. Nerves flashed across his face. He knew what it was like to be on the receiving end of her anger.

"You won't... pull my soul out again, will you?" he whimpered.

Lumi didn't blink. "No. But I expect you to extend your newly-learned respect to *all* Spirits, not just me."

Mihka swallowed, looked at Tuomas. "But... he doomed my father..."

"He did not," Lumi replied, in a voice like ice. "The choice was *mine*, foolish boy. Do you wish to attack *me?* Again?"

"Lumi, don't frighten him," Tuomas whispered.

She glanced around, twitched her tail. But, to his relief, the aurora in her hands faded to green.

"My brother is kinder than me," she said to Mihka. "You have learned your lesson, but I still impart a new one. Together, we shall save your father, but in order to do that, we must remain in one piece. Do you understand me?"

Mihka nodded timidly. "Yes. I'm sorry, White Fox One."

"You are forgiven," said Lumi. Then she walked away with a final sweep of her tail, and approached Tuomas. Niina wasted no time gathering Mihka in her arms and bundling him towards the tent.

Tuomas bit his lip. Gone was the prankster who always got under people's feet; the fool who had dared to try his luck. Now, his white hair was only the surface of all which had changed since winter began.

It twisted Tuomas's belly into a knot. For some reason, that showed him, more than anything else, how life would never be the same.

Maiken, Anssi, Birkir and a couple of the Poro elders came closer. Tuomas looked at Lumi, half-expecting her to run off, but she stood still.

Birkir removed his hat.

"White Fox One," he greeted. "Is there anything we can do for you?"

"No, apart from keeping yourselves safe," said Lumi. "The two of us must leave you tonight. The Great Bear Sprit has set us a charge which we must complete."

"Leave?" Anssi repeated. "And go where?"

Tuomas felt the bleeding beginning to slow and lowered his hand from his nose.

"The Northern Edge of the World," he said. "We have to close the gateway."

The elders glanced among each other in alarm. Tuomas knew they wouldn't dare refuse, but the anxiety on their faces was difficult to stomach. These were the people responsible for all others; just the sight of the beads on their clothes was enough to command respect.

"Why didn't you mention this earlier?" asked Birkir.

"There was no point adding to all the stress," replied Tuomas. "We couldn't have separated from the group before now, anyway. So if you'll let me take my sleigh and one of my reindeer, we'll go tonight."

"How long will you be?"

"A week, at most. Don't worry, we'll be safe."

Maiken didn't look happy about it, but she nodded.

"I'll trust your judgment over my own. Do you want anyone to come with you?"

"Aki," said Tuomas.

Anssi blinked in surprise. "Aki? The draugar boy?"

"Lilja's boy," Tuomas corrected. "He has to. I don't want to say why yet, I think it's best if it stays quiet."

Birkir squirmed uncomfortably. "I dare say it's best if he does go with you. People are nervous of him. Of what he did."

"He didn't do anything," Tuomas said. "He hasn't got an evil bone in his body; he's just a little boy who was kidnapped and used. He doesn't deserve to be treated as anything less than a normal kid now. Please... while we're gone, try to make everyone understand that. *He* did not kill the children, or Sisu."

At mention of their fallen elder, Maiken and Anssi's shoulders slumped. Lumi noticed and took a step forward.

"*I* chose to save him," she said. "Knowing what we do now, it appears doing so was among the luckiest decisions I have ever made. Hear it from my lips: the boy is an innocent."

A bead of water ran down her neck, but she didn't wipe it away.

Anssi heaved a sigh. "Very well. Let us help you get ready."

Without another word, they rearranged Tuomas's sleigh, so the tent poles and tarp were at the sides. Then they loaded it with furs, his and Aki's sleeping sacks, and a supply of food and firewood. Tuomas also made sure to shoulder his bow, in case they came across any prey on the route. Finally, he approached the herd, lassoed one of his reindeer and reeled it close.

Niina emerged from the tent. She saw what was going on and ran over.

"Tuomas?" she asked anxiously.

"It's fine," he assured. "I just need to make a diversion. You stay here and we'll meet you on the Mustafjord as soon as we can."

Niina's eyes grew wide with worry. "But... you're leaving? I'm... Tuomas, I'm not a mage like you! I can't look after everyone, make an entire circle by myself!"

"Yes, you can," Tuomas said. "I know you can. And you've got the elders around you, you're not alone. Lilja will probably be back soon, too."

Niina hunched over; wove her fingers together so tightly that her knuckles cracked. She looked so small, even younger than Tuomas, and terrified.

"I promise you'll be fine," he said. "Listen, just do what you've been doing: cast a circle each night, take your time, then help anyone who needs it. I'll be as fast as I can. And don't let Mihka punch you, alright?"

At that, Niina managed a grin. "Alright."

Tuomas washed the blood off his lip with some snow, and called for Aki. The little boy immediately stood and hurried from the fire. A couple of the children threw snowballs after him, their parents making the sign of the hand.

"They're teasing me," he whimpered, then threw his arms around Tuomas's middle. Maiken blinked at the sight, clearly taken aback. Tuomas was, too. This was the first time in over a week that anyone had hugged him.

"Aki? Will you look at me?" Maiken said. "They won't tease anymore. I'll tell them to stop. And they'll listen to me."

Aki wiped his nose on his sleeve. "Thank you."

Warmth came into Maiken's face. She gave him a smile, then tentatively patted his head. Aki pressed himself against Tuomas like a timid mouse.

"What's going on?" he whispered. "Why's your sleigh hitched up?"

Tuomas thought quickly. "We're going on an adventure."

Aki's eyes settled on Lumi. "Is she coming as well?"

"Yes," said Tuomas as he lifted him into the sleigh and wrapped a blanket around him. "This is Lumi. You haven't met her properly yet, have you? She saved your life."

Aki leaned closer and peered at Lumi's ears in wonder.

"Are you Tuomas's sister?" he asked. "The Spirit of the Lights?"

"I am," replied Lumi. Her voice was the softest Tuomas had heard for days.

Aki reached out a hand. Lumi regarded it for a moment, then touched her fingers to his. He gasped at how cold she was.

"You're like snow," he said. "Isn't *lumi* the old word for snow? Uncle Kari told me that. And I thought Spirits didn't have names."

"I made an exception," said Lumi.

Without another word, she stood back and shrank down until she was a fox. Like before, every part of her was completely white, save for her eyes, which shone the crisp green of the aurora.

Tuomas realised that was the cue to move. A group of people wandered close and watched as he climbed into the sleigh beside Aki. Among them were Sigurd, Alda and Elin. Sigurd stared at Aki, and the boy hurriedly turned away, trying to hide under the blanket.

Elin's eyes were blazing. Tuomas thought she might cry, or even run towards him. He was tempted to wave her over and beg her to come along; she had been so adamant about joining him in the past. Never mind that she was the best shot with a bow and arrow; he wanted her company, wanted to see her smile again…

But she stayed still, and just twisted her white hare mittens in her hands.

Tuomas sighed. It was probably for the best that she stayed. They were going to a place where she couldn't follow, where he would never want to lead her.

Anssi fetched a flaming torch and passed it to him.

"Be safe," he said. "And go in peace."

"Stay in peace," replied Tuomas. "Don't worry. We'll be back soon."

"We can't *not* worry," said Birkir. "You're the Son of the Sun. You're leading us, for all intents and purposes."

Tuomas shook his head. "You don't need me to lead you. All of you are strong enough."

Lumi shot him a wry glance, then swept her tail so a stream of Lights billowed around her. Tuomas snapped the rope, and the reindeer trotted off into the darkness, Lumi sprinting at its side.

Chapter Fifteen

Her paws skimmed the ground, barely coming down before she lifted them again. She didn't leave so much as the slightest indent. She was like a feather, like a snowflake, like light itself. The only mass she bore was that which she willed into existence.

Boulders from the mountains dotted the tundra in places, glistening with half-melted icicles. The cold was still clinging on, but she could feel the difference as the World Between stirred with the changing seasons. The Spirit of the Winter Winds was slowing, to hand the great bellows over to her cousin for spring. The tiny Spirits inside every single blade of grass were stirring beneath the snow; those within the trees pushed baby buds to burst from the wrinkled branches.

The change was coming, as it had every year, since the Great Bear had first run through the fabric between Worlds. Soon, it would be here.

She looked at the sky, watched the cleft float across the starry labyrinth. It seemed larger now; pulled at her, like invisible fingers dragging across her skin. To make herself feel a little better, she flicked her tail. The aurora streamed upwards in a river of frozen fire.

She glanced behind at the sleigh. Aki had fallen asleep and huddled close to Tuomas, to share his body heat. Tuomas himself held the torch with one hand, the rope with the other. He encouraged the reindeer on, as fast as it could go without breaking into a full gallop. The animal sensed the urgency and complied. It was too open out here, too dark…

Tuomas sighed, lowered his eyes. She heard him sobbing.

At once, mid-step, she cast off the fox form and became a girl again, so she could speak.

"What troubles you?" she asked.

Tuomas wiped his cheeks. "I'm tired of doing this. Leaving in the middle of the night to sort something out."

He looked so weary; more than she had ever seen. The marks had faded a little now, but his flesh was still marred with lines left by draugar teeth. The way they shone on his skin, highlighted by the flame, made his face appear older than she knew it was. He almost reminded her of the previous human he had been: the Great Mage, who grew for decades before being dragged under the Mustafjord.

He pulled a salmon cake out of a pouch and half-heartedly chewed it. His eyes were starting to droop.

"Stop," she said.

Tuomas frowned. "Stop? Why?"

"You are still human. You must rest."

"I can keep going. We can't afford to camp!"

"Stop arguing," she snapped, and snatched hold of the reindeer's harness. At once, it drew to a halt and dipped its head.

Tuomas ground his teeth, but didn't protest. He woke Aki, gave him the rest of the salmon cake and some reindeer jerky. Then he grabbed the tent poles, rested three against each other for balance before applying the others, until a conical skeleton protruded from the tundra. He stood on the side of the sleigh to bind them together at the top. She helped him place the tarp, stood back as he tied it with cord made from braided tendons.

When everything was secure, Tuomas laid a circle of wood in the centre and held the torch to it until it caught. Then he took his drum and walked around the entire area, beating and chanting. She watched the circle rise into the air and seal itself overhead.

"Not staying outside this time?" he asked in surprise.

"Your company is one which I enjoy," she replied with a small smile. Water dripped from her hairline and she brushed it off.

Tuomas smiled. His tail flicked – at exactly the same time as hers.

"Come on," he said, beckoning Aki over. "Lumi, can you keep watch while I get him to sleep?"

She nodded, stared out at the tundra as Tuomas led the little boy inside. She walked as far away as she could, so the fire's heat couldn't touch her.

The night opened around her like a flower. It was a land of contrasts: shadows and highlights lay stark against each other, playing off their neighbours in a never-ending dance. Even in the low light, the snow shone; deep blues and purples swirled amid the blackness of the sky. Were it not for the rip, raining fear as much as *taika*, it might have been as perfect a scene as nature could create.

She heard Aki and Tuomas whispering, and turned her ears to listen.

"Where are we going?"

"Not too far. It's called the Northern Edge of the World. I've been there a few times. Your mother took me during the Long Dark."

"Didn't you fall off?"

"No. It's not an edge like a cliff. That's just what it's called."

"Oh. Why are we going there?"

"Because we've got a job to do. I'll tell you more about it later, when we arrive. But for now, I need you to behave and let me concentrate. It's going to be alright. Lumi and I won't let anything happen to you. There's no reason to be scared."

"I'm not scared," said Aki sleepily. "This is what it was like before. Me, Mama, and Uncle Kari. Just us." He yawned. "You're like him, you know. Uncle Kari."

She heard Tuomas's breathing change.

"How so?"

"You're nice. You look after me, and after Mama."

Tuomas hesitated. "Well... thanks."

"He and Mama told me stories about when you came down from the sky, and walked into the south," Aki continued. "He knew a lot of stories. One was about nasty mages who would pull off people's skins and wear them like coats, but it was always just a trick. Do you know that one?"

"Uh... something like it."

"He talked about you a lot. He said that he and Mama were there when you were born. They knew you would be a mage, but they went away. I think Uncle Kari wanted to bring you, though. So you could be my friend..."

His voice trailed into another yawn. She turned around, watched Tuomas's silhouette through the tarp. He was sitting with his knees drawn up, one hand stroking Aki's hair.

"Go to sleep now," he said quietly.

The next few moments were silent. Then Tuomas added another log to the fire and climbed back outside. He walked straight past her and took hold of the rim of the sleigh.

"I know he means well," he muttered. "So did Lilja, when she said it. But..."

He touched his chest, then frowned, glanced down as his fingers touched the fox carving around his neck. His ears drooped.

"I can't really believe Kari used to be a good man," he said. "He was going to cut out my heart."

"I cannot claim to have watched him too closely," she admitted. "But on the mountain, I held one of his souls. There was morality in him, once."

Tuomas turned around. His eyes glistened with unshed tears. Behind them, she saw the glow of the Spirit within: pure gold, brighter than ever before. It wove so tightly and beautifully with his human form that she could barely tell where one ended and the other began.

More water dripped from her fingertips. She winced as she felt it sliding over her skin, but didn't allow it to hurt her.

"Could that have worked?" Tuomas asked. "Him taking my power, I mean?"

"I see no reason why not," she said. "Mages have used demons before, to take the *taika* of other mages. But none had ever attempted it with a Spirit."

"Of course," Tuomas said bitterly. "Before me, there were no other Spirits just walking about, were there?"

He rubbed his face. She took hold of his hands and pulled them down.

"Tell me why you are afraid," she said, as soft as she could.

Tuomas swallowed. "Don't you know? We're going to the Deathlands. And Kari is in the Deathlands – one of the Earth Spirits told me."

She shook her head. "He cannot harm you anymore, Tuomas. You need not fear him. And there is no need to fear the Horse-Riding One, either."

Tuomas smirked. "Says the one who prides herself on being terrifying."

"Only when it is deserved," she replied, and sent a wave of Lights around the two of them.

Her own energy pushed against her form, desperate to break free and transform the sky green. But it was more than the simple longing to be uncontained, to trail the souls in her wake. She fancied that, had she a human heart, this is what it might feel like to break. Such darkness shrouded her; no amount of power and grace could quell it. Her poor brother, so weak and yet so perfect in this imperfect body… If only he knew…

Tuomas fingered the fox head again, pressed his frostbitten stumps over the points of the ears.

"Are you sure we'll be safe out here?" he asked.

"Certain," she replied.

"In that case, I'll cross through the fire and check on Lilja, before we go into the World Below."

"Do you think that wise?"

"Why not? She doesn't know the Silver One is calling off the trolls."

"And what of the boy?" She brandished her arm at the tent. "What will you tell Lilja in regard to her son?"

"That he's safe, which is true," replied Tuomas. "Lumi, I just want to make sure she's alright. She wasn't holding up too well when she left."

She sighed, flicked her tail and shot a jet of blue across the snow.

"Fine. I shall remain here and mind Aki. But first…" She reached out a hand. "Will you dance with me?"

Tuomas blinked. He looked at her, then at the sky.

"Dance?" he repeated. "But I thought you couldn't go back into the World Above."

"Not yet, that is true. Even when I defended you in your dream, spoke with my mother, it was still here," she replied, spitting out mention of the Moon Spirit like a dart. "But I am still the White Fox One."

Tuomas smiled. "Fox fires."

He wove his fingers with hers. She let her head roll back, her hair billow like a snowstorm. The aurora spilled from every inch of her skin, enveloped them, lifted them off the ground. It wasn't by much – only a few feet – but after so long spent walking and running, it felt like the whole sky had opened beneath her.

She cartwheeled and dived, pulling Tuomas at her side. As she moved, his own tail swept about, sent sparks flickering from the end.

Her body came apart, twisted into a thousand shapes. She sensed he wanted to do the same, forsake his cage of flesh and bone, let the flames and light inside free as he had long ago... but it was not possible. He was trapped by life itself, by mortality, by everything else he held equally dear.

That hurt more than she was expecting. She felt it, so deeply, that water rained from her face and became a flurry of snowflakes.

If only he knew.

Chapter Sixteen

Tuomas had lost all sense of time when Lumi set him down on the snow. He gasped for breath, held onto the sleigh as he found his balance. All things considered, it hadn't been long since he had last danced with her, but in a way, it felt like an eternity.

"Why has it left me so tired?" he asked. "It never did before."

"We are not in the World Above," she replied. "We are not… home."

It was a simple answer, but her voice was edged with sadness, like a sheen of meltwater over an icicle.

Tuomas frowned. "Lumi, are you alright?"

She drew her shoulders back. "Perfectly. Are you sure you feel able to go to Lilja?"

"Yes." He glanced at the tent. "I don't want to go through that fire, though. It will wake Aki."

"What makes you think you need a fire?" Lumi asked. "You *are* the fire."

"What?"

"I have seen you creating flames. Do the same now."

"Will that work?"

"It should. Try."

Tuomas bit his lip nervously, winced when he gnawed the dry skin. But then he shrugged, cupped his hands and stared at them, so intensely that he thought his eyes might pop out.

His heart fluttered, but he didn't fight it; allowed himself to reach deep into his *taika*. The hair on his arms stood on end, heat grew across his whole body, he smelled flowers and tasted lingonberry. If he concentrated hard enough, it was no longer winter, but the height of summer: the Long Day, when the Sun Spirit wheeled across the tundra and never set...

A fire sprang to life against his skin. He nursed it, willed it to grow. Lumi moved away, but her eyes glowed with pride.

Tuomas beamed. "I can do it! I thought last time was just a fluke!"

"Not in the least," smiled Lumi. "You have control, remember that. This is not something you are merely bending. This *is* you. This is who you are, Red Fox One."

Her words rang inside him, truer than anything he had heard before. In a heartbeat, he recalled all the magical feats he had achieved so far: pulling Lumi out of the sky, splitting the avalanche, holding his hand into the fire... They had been terrifying, but now, there was only exhilaration. This was as natural and perfect as walking, breathing... Perhaps even more so.

It was freedom.

"Alright," he whispered. "Wish me luck."

Before he could lose his nerve, he chanted, matched the staccato flickering of the flames. He brought himself higher, forcing the *taika* to stay contained; it welled up around him like a rising tide of delicious heat. He thought of Lilja, wherever she might be, of the fire which she would have woken in her shelter.

His hands transformed into an inferno. He flung it at his feet, swept it over his body. It surrounded him, swallowed him...

The crisp night air transformed into something more humid. He smelled roasting meat, musty reindeer fur, the herbs from a pot of tea.

He opened his eyes. He was standing in a new tent, face to face with Lilja.

She recoiled in shock, waved the knife she had been eating with. But then she realised who it was and instead grabbed the front of his coat.

"What are you doing here?" she barked as she pulled him out of the embers. Then she brandished a bowl of sautéed reindeer. "I was having my dinner."

"Sorry." Tuomas brushed the ash off his clothes and drum. "I came to check on you."

"Why? What about Aki? I told you to look after him."

"He's fine. I'm not staying for long."

"Who's watching him if not you?"

"Lumi."

Lilja cocked an eyebrow. "She didn't strike me as the type to like children."

"Well, don't worry, he's safe and everything's alright," said Tuomas.

He pushed the flap aside and poked his head out of the tent. Several others were dotted nearby, along with some sleighs and older reindeer which hadn't joined the migration because their teeth were too rotten. He recognised the patterns on their harnesses: Einfjall and Poro.

"You've got everyone?" he asked.

"Yes. We're only thirty miles outside of Poro, though," replied Lilja.

Tuomas turned his eyes to the sky. Even though it was only late afternoon, most of the stars were already out, and he quickly took note of their position. After some quick mental calculations, he knew exactly where Lilja had pitched the camp.

The rip seemed to leer at him where he stood. He drew back inside so he couldn't see it.

Lilja crawled over, peered at him.

"Do you know your eyes are glowing?"

156

Tuomas blinked. He grabbed a pot of water from the fireside and peered into it. Sure enough, though his irises were still blue, there was a faint golden sheen around their edges, like a ring of Sunlight.

His breath shook and he fell onto his backside. Lilja came straight after him and took hold of his hands. She gasped when she touched him.

"By the Spirits," she whispered. "You're so warm."

"I'm fine," Tuomas said, but his voice shook. His entire body was fluttering; he felt as though his skin was the only thing keeping him from flying everywhere at once. It was so hot, the *taika* so alive…

He snatched a cup made from a hollowed-out birch burl, dipped it into the water and drank it all in two gulps.

"I'm fine," he said again.

Lilja didn't move. "Are you sure?"

He nodded. To his relief, Lilja didn't press him and instead retreated back to her side of the fire. She picked up her bowl and carried on eating, lifting the meat to her mouth on the flat edge of her smallest knife. The handle, like everything she owned, was carved with an extraordinary level of detail. Around her fingers, Tuomas could see individual tree branches etched into the antler.

"Have you had food?" she asked.

"I'll eat when I get back, thanks," said Tuomas.

"Are you at the Mustafjord yet?"

"No, still several days' walk away, providing it's still frozen enough to hold the herd. If you head due east from here, you should meet the others. Then everyone can go the rest of the way together."

Lilja nodded. "Is that seriously all you came to tell me?"

Tuomas swallowed. He knew it would be a bad idea to mention where he was taking Aki.

"I wanted to let you know that the Moon Spirit sent the trolls, to kill all the mages except me. She wants to force me to go back and be her son."

Lilja stopped chewing and stared at him.

"But it's all sorted now," Tuomas continued. "Lumi got me away from her, and she told me the Moon Spirit will call off the trolls. The mages will be safe, but I still think it's best to be careful. I trust Lumi, but not *her*. And they might still come after the reindeer."

"Good point," said Lilja. "Only Sunlight can stop a troll. Are there just the three of them that we saw at Anaar?"

"I think so."

She nodded to herself, but her cheeks were ashen, and she stared into the fire as she finished off her meal. She was a woman of little emotion and few words, but Tuomas had learned how to read her, and the fear on her face was as clear as day.

He swallowed anxiously, then spoke again.

"Listen, Lilja... Sigurd came to speak with me. About Aki."

Lilja froze. "What about Aki? Sigurd knows you know?"

"Yes. But he hasn't mentioned anything to Alda or Elin. He still wants to be friends with you."

"Easier said than done."

"That's what I told him."

"What happened between us was a long time ago," Lilja muttered. "But we have our own priorities and lives now. It's better for everyone if they remain separate. Fewer people will be hurt that way."

Tuomas licked his lips and nodded. "I just wanted to tell you, so you can prepare yourself for it. He'll probably want to talk to you when we all get to Akerfjorden."

"I'm so excited," said Lilja sarcastically. "But thank you. I don't know what will happen to me and Aki after all this, but I trust the Spirits to point us in the right direction."

If we're all still alive after all this, Tuomas thought.

Right on cue, he felt the air ripple around him, thrumming with torn magic and the restless silent cries of the damaged realms. He winced as it battered against the *taika* inside him. Lilja sensed it too, because she shuddered and put her knife back into its sheath.

After a long uncomfortable moment, it resided, but the two of them shared a concerned glance. No words were needed – enough had been said already to know how serious this was.

"So," Lilja muttered, "I have a conversation with my old lover to look forward to when we reach Akerfjorden. I'm surprised he didn't swear you to secrecy."

"He did," Tuomas admitted. "But I said I wouldn't talk about it with anyone who didn't already know. So that's you and Elin."

Lilja smirked at his ingenuity. "Any word out of her yet?"

Tuomas's expression dropped. "No. She's really angry with me. And Mihka is, too. I found him in the forest at the base of the mountains."

"What?" Lilja leaned forward in alarm. "And he was alive?"

"He played dead," Tuomas explained. "He's got hypothermia and frostbite – he'll be lucky if he keeps his hands and feet. But he's furious. He's blaming me for what happened to his father."

Lilja's eyes flickered over him. "And you believe that, don't you?"

Tuomas shifted uncomfortably. "I know Lumi was the one who ended up trapping them, ripping the sky... but I didn't help."

"No, you didn't. But it's not your fault that the draugars were looking for you. It's not your fault that Sisu tried to attack Aki. *That's* what made them drag him under the water."

Tuomas shook his head. "Lumi told him to lay off me. But he won't. He'll never forgive me for the part I played."

"Then he's childish, but we knew that from day one, didn't we?" said Lilja.

She reached for the woodpile and went to toss another log on the fire, but stopped. A low groan sounded from outside.

The hairs on the back of Tuomas's neck prickled. The sound swept straight through him.

The two of them jumped to their feet and bolted through the flap. Tuomas tore his bow off his shoulder.

The moaning hadn't gone away. It might have been mistaken for wind, if only there had been any. Those on watch duty had heard it too; they peered in every direction, arrows drawn. Others emerged from the neighbouring shelters, some making the sign of the hand.

When they saw Tuomas, they gasped; many lowered their heads and took off their hats.

"Son of the Sun!"

"What's he doing here?"

"How did he get here?"

"Be quiet!" Lilja snapped.

Tuomas ignored them; let his eyes dart around, trying to pick up any sign of movement. There was only darkness... but something was close. He could sense it, like a physical pressure on his chest.

"I don't like this," he whispered to Lilja.

"Me, neither."

"You've made a circle, haven't you?"

She shot him a pointed look. "Of course I have. Can't you feel it?"

He could: it was several feet behind Lilja's tent and stretched all around the camp. A second one surrounded the reindeer. It was difficult to see in the low light, but when Tuomas relaxed his eyes, he spotted it: a faint rippling in the air, as though he were looking through the thinnest skin of water.

His breath froze as he exhaled; all he heard was his own frantic heartbeat. This felt horribly similar to when he had been outside Einfjall, and Kari's demon had come running towards him...

More than ever, he hoped it was just a wolf. Greylegs were never welcome in the tundra, but they would be better than anything else.

"There!" one of the watchmen shouted.

Tuomas staggered back in horror. A great black shadow tore itself out of the very earth, then lumbered towards them. Moonlight glinted off its ice-laced body, and in its hand flashed a huge flint blade.

"You were supposed to call them off!" Tuomas shouted at the Silver One.

She didn't respond. And the troll was coming closer.

Chapter Seventeen

The reindeer panicked, bellowing and rolling their eyes in terror. The troll threw them a glance, but didn't make a grab for any; instead, it picked up its pace and ran at the tents. With a savage grunt, it flung itself forward.

To Tuomas's relief, the shield held.

"Shoot it!" Lilja yelled.

She and Tuomas nocked their bows. Immediately, everyone gathered in the centre of the circle and sent a rain of arrows into the air. They passed cleanly through the barrier, as though it wasn't there. The troll covered its face with one arm and the flint tips embedded into its mossy coat. It didn't even flinch with pain.

"Elin, I wish you were here," Tuomas muttered as he loosed another. On the Einfjall mountain, she had vanquished Kari's demon with just one well-placed shot…

"This isn't working!" one of the watchers cried.

Tuomas slipped his bow onto his shoulder. He went to reach for his drum, but then paused, looked at his hands. He had made fire. Lumi had said he could create Sunlight, too…

There was no choice, no time. He needed to try.

His tail lashed furiously as he concentrated. Flames erupted from the fur; those around him drew back in fright. He didn't let them distract him, focused on drawing his energy into his palms. His heart hammered, the *taika* swirled so much, he thought he might vomit. The hole in the sky was pulling at him – the harder he fought, the deeper it drove, until he could scarcely keep his feet on the ground…

The fire flared in his hands. He went to throw it, when a woman beside him released one more shot.

What happened next would have astounded him if it wasn't over so quickly.

The troll fixed its eyes on the arrow as it soared closer. Then it reached out, and just as the head broke through the circle, grabbed it. The entire shield trembled violently; Tuomas felt it shudder, like a sheet of ice cracking around his ribs.

Lilja cried out from the pressure. She ran forward to close the hole, hammer raised above her drum. But before she could strike, the troll forced one hand across the barrier, using the arrow like an anchor, and drove its fist into her.

She flew back with a scream of pain, and landed with her arm beneath her body, followed by a loud crack. She didn't move.

"No!" Tuomas yelled.

The troll stared at Lilja, its mouth twisting into a leering grin. It pushed its other arm through the hole, working its way closer. The circle splintered, scarcely keeping its shape.

Tuomas's head spun; his chest felt like it was going to cave in from the amount of *taika* it was holding. He couldn't let that thing get to Lilja…

Panic and desperation filled his blood. Barely thinking, he jumped between her and the troll. He gathered all his power, felt the fire on his shoulders, through his hair, in his hands… and with a scream which tore at his lungs, hit his drum.

A blinding light exploded in front of him. His feet left the ground, then he came down on his back, too stunned to move. Overhead, all he saw were stars. His heart stung as though he had been stabbed.

Had the troll hit him as well? Was he dead?

He blinked hard, sat up as fast as he could. His vision swam; he groped blindly for his drum, ready to strike it again. But then he looked straight ahead, and dropped the hammer.

The circle was still in place, and the troll was there, both arms through the gap and reaching for Lilja. But it didn't move a muscle; every wrinkle in its face was petrified and its black eyes were grey and blind.

It had turned to stone.

Tuomas stared at his hands. Just beneath his flesh, there was a faint golden glow, brighter than that of flame. It was hotter than anything he had felt before.

Sunlight.

"I did it," he gasped.

He looked around. Everyone was whispering, gaping at him; several rubbed their knuckles into their eyes, blinded. A couple of watchers recovered themselves and moved toward the troll. One warily held out his bow and tapped the creature's hand. Sure enough, it didn't move.

"I think it's dead," he said.

Tuomas suddenly remembered Lilja. Trembling with adrenaline, he crawled to her side – if the troll truly was petrified, then he could inspect it later.

The snow around Lilja was spattered with blood. Amazingly, she was still breathing, but the damage made his stomach roll. The troll's rough hand had slashed from her jaw up to her ear; ripped straight through her clothes and left a smaller wound on her shoulder. But worst of all was her right arm, splayed at an unnatural angle under her back. Tuomas didn't need to look twice to know it was broken.

"Lilja?" he said shakily. "Lilja, can you hear me?"

The muscles in her face tightened, then she groaned.

"What happened?"

"You were hit. Just stay there," Tuomas replied. He looked up. "Can someone lend a hand, please?"

The herders were huddled together in fright – he could only imagine what the spectacle must have looked like from where they stood. After a few long moments, an older woman approached. She bowed her head.

"Thank you," Tuomas said, trying to keep his voice steady. "Everyone else, please bring me some warm water, blankets, and as many spare strips of hide and sinew as you can. And a straight piece of wood, for a splint."

A couple of people went to their tents and began bringing out supplies. Tuomas returned to Lilja. A clammy sweat had broken out on her face and she gasped for breath as the true extent of the pain set in.

"What do you need me to do, Red Fox One?" asked the woman.

"Lift her while I pull her arm free," Tuomas replied. He shrugged out of his coat to give himself more room to move. Then he took a leather pouch from his belt and eased it between Lilja's teeth.

"Bite down on that," he instructed. "This is going to hurt. I'm sorry."

Lilja nodded to show she was ready. The woman raised her, and as soon as the weight was off her arm, Tuomas eased it from under her back. Lilja shrieked and let out a stream of curses.

He tried not to wince at the sight. It looked like the limb of a ragdoll cast aside by a child. While no bone had come through her skin, it was a horrifying injury.

A man hurried over with the materials. Tuomas muttered thanks and slid a blanket under Lilja's shoulders as carefully as he could. He kept her arm, however, out on the snow. He needed to set the bones, and for that, it would be best if she was numb.

She spat the pouch out to speak to him.

"Do you know what you're doing?"

"Henrik talked me through it. And I've had reindeer with broken legs before," Tuomas said, hoping there wouldn't be much difference. He held the pouch at her mouth again. "Put that back in so you don't bite your tongue."

A pot of steaming water was brought. He dipped a cloth into it and wiped the blood from around her cuts. There were no herbs to make a poultice, so he took some reindeer skin, cut it into a strip with his knife, and wound it around her jaw. The gash on her shoulder wasn't as deep; he simply cleaned it and then tied her coat back into place.

He could almost hear Henrik behind him.

"Work fast, boy. When you're weak, cold does more damage than bleeding out."

Lilja's head lolled. Her eyelids fluttered, cheeks becoming paler by the moment.

"Stay awake," Tuomas urged. "Lilja? Stay awake."

He knew the dangers of falling asleep after taking a blow to the head. Once, when he was younger, a girl of his age had hit her temple on a rock while playing by the Mustafjord. A slumber swept in, from which nobody could wake her. Henrik had said it was a coma; that her souls had retreated too deeply into her body. A week later, she died.

Tuomas pushed the memory away so he wouldn't panic, and tapped Lilja's face as hard as he dared. She moaned in protest. That wasn't the best response, but at least she was still conscious.

He grasped the piece of wood. She couldn't wait any longer.

"Think about Aki, Lilja," he said. "He's waiting for you. You need to meet him in Akerfjorden, remember? It's very important."

He gently prodded along her swollen skin. After a mercifully short time, he found the break.

He took a deep breath, and pushed the bones back together.

Lilja howled. The woman quickly grabbed her shoulders and restrained her while Tuomas lined up the splint. Then he wound the rest of the reindeer skin and sinews around it as fast as he could.

Lilja gasped for air. She pulled the pouch out of her mouth with her unharmed hand and glared at Tuomas.

"You're lucky I like you, boy," she snarled.

Despite everything, Tuomas couldn't help smiling.

He used the rest of the reindeer skin to make a sling. Then he got to his feet, thanked the woman, and called for more help. Two of the strongest men lifted Lilja off the ground. She cried as they moved her back into her tent.

Now she was out of sight, Tuomas rocked back on his heels and turned his face skywards. He let out a long sigh of relief, but it was cut off when he noticed the Moon Spirit in his periphery.

Rage turned his blood to fire. He gripped his drum, tempted to chant himself into a trance and confront her. If she thought he would go back to her after this, breaking her word, she had another thing coming…

But he stopped himself. If he did that, he might make her angry, and then she could make the entire journey even harder for him. And he needed to return to Aki, catch some rest before they carried on to the Northern Edge.

He closed his eyes. How was he supposed to sleep, or do anything to relax?

The watchers were gathering around the troll. There was more confidence in their gait now they were sure it was dead. Tuomas pulled his coat back on and walked over to check it for himself.

"You did that," said the woman who had helped him with Lilja. "You threw Sunlight at it…"

"Good," Tuomas replied. "That was what I was trying to do."

Her mouth opened in awe. "Thank you, Son of the Sun. Thank you so much…"

"Tuomas," he said softly, then turned to the troll and carefully ran a hand over it. In many respects, it looked no different to the way it had when alive, but the wicked gleam had vanished from its beady eyes. He regarded the blade, still clutched in one giant fist, shuddered at the keenness of the edge. It could have chopped down an entire tree in a single swipe.

He imagined that same blade buried in Enska and Aino's stomachs, slick with their blood. Had it been quick? Was this the same one which had killed them?

He gritted his teeth. No, he couldn't think about that, not now. Distraction wasn't an option.

Without a word, he took his drum again and set about laying a new circle, to replace Lilja's fractured one. He struck the skin with a steady beat, forcing the *taika* into his footprints so a protective shell formed in his wake. After several minutes, he completed it, and swept the air with his fingers to ensure it would hold.

"Stay away from the edge," he warned. "Barriers are always weaker on the inside."

"Alright," said the woman. "Will we be safe now?"

"Yes."

"What about Lilja?"

"I'll check on her," said Tuomas. "Listen, everyone, I can't stay for long. But you need to head due east from here and meet the others. Take Lilja in a sleigh and make sure she drinks, even if she doesn't eat anything."

"Why can't you stay?"

"I was only meant to be here for a few minutes."

"But what if the trolls come again?" an elderly man protested.

"If you move as fast as you can, you should reach the Mustafjord in another day," Tuomas replied. "Trolls can't move in the Sunlight, but travel after dusk if you have to. Don't stop, don't waste any time."

He quietly excused himself, then headed to Lilja's tent. The men had placed her in her sleeping sack. To his relief, she was breathing easier and colour had returned to her cheeks.

"How are you feeling?" he asked.

"I'll live," she groaned. "I suppose I should be thanking you."

"Don't mention it," Tuomas said. "You would have done the same for me."

"Maybe," said Lilja, with a hint of a grin. "What happened to the troll? I saw it... it was petrified again."

"I did that. I threw Sunlight at it. Don't ask me how."

"Well done, boy. You're really coming into your power now, aren't you?"

Tuomas grimaced. "I suppose I am," he said, then inspected his hands again. They looked like normal pink flesh now, just crossed with teeth marks and the occasional spot of blood.

"I don't understand," he muttered. "Lumi said the Silver One was going to call them off."

"Well, it seems Lumi was wrong," Lilja said tartly. "You should have gotten out of here as soon as that thing showed up."

A firm note crept into her voice, but Tuomas noticed that beneath it lay panic. He saw through the gruffness at once. She had feared him getting hurt, and not just because he was one of the few mages left, or even because he was the Son of the Sun. It was because she cared.

He reminded himself, this was the woman who had delivered him as an infant, fought her brother's influence to attack him, trusted him with her deepest, darkest secrets. She had let him get close when she pushed all others away. He might have only known her for one winter, but their paths had been entwined from the beginning.

"Will you be able to manage?" he asked.

"It takes more than this to keep me down," replied Lilja. "Don't worry. I'll still make a circle; I'll just ask someone else to hold the drum for me while I beat it. Cumbersome, but not impossible."

"Make sure you keep warm," said Tuomas.

"I will," Lilja drawled, but not spitefully. "You'd best get back. It's not that I don't trust the White Fox One with Aki, but I'd just rest happier knowing you're with him as well."

Tuomas nodded. Then Lilja suddenly threw her head back against the furs with an anguished growl.

"I wish my father were here," she whispered, and breathed through a sob before it could consume her. "It's strange... I lived apart from him for years, and I missed him, but I coped. It felt nothing like this."

"Because you knew you could always go back and see him whenever you wanted, within reason," said Tuomas.

Lilja turned her eyes on him.

"Would it surprise you if I told you I miss Kari as well?"

Tuomas swallowed. "No. He was your brother."

Lilja didn't blink. "My whole life, I spent more time in his company than anyone else's. He was like Enska: always wanted to help people – and he gave it all up for me, because he knew I needed the most help of all. But he never stopped dreaming of great things, of everything he'd sacrificed for me. And those dreams sowed the seeds of what he became. But now, he's gone... and my father, and my mother died when I was born... Aki's the only family I have left."

She reached out with her uninjured arm and grasped Tuomas's hand.

"I know you're still frightened of him. You'll always carry those scars, in more ways than one. But I wanted you to know that."

Tuomas hesitated. Even as she spoke, he could still feel the blade cutting through his exposed chest, catch the carrion-stench of the demon on the air. His memory flashed with Kari peeling Paavo's skin off his face... It had been an illusion, but it had seemed so real...

"And I know I didn't tell you this earlier, and I should have," Lilja continued, "but thank you, Tuomas. Thank you for bringing my baby back to me."

Her tone was so sincere, his heart shuddered. For so long, he had felt the consequences of his rash actions; they were all anybody had let him know about. Amidst all that turmoil and pain, to hear those two simple words were like the first sense of warmth after winter.

"You're welcome," he said earnestly. Then he cleared his throat, brushed down the front of his coat. His fingers tapped against the fox carving.

"Is there anything else you need before I go?" he asked.

Lilja blinked slowly, and her eyes became warm. For a moment, he thought she might lose control at last and burst into tears. But she didn't; she just sighed.

"No. Tell Aki I love him, and I'll see him soon."

"I will," Tuomas promised.

He bit his tongue to keep himself from telling her the whole truth. The convoy would likely join the others in a little over twenty-four hours. His quest could take up to a week. He hoped she wouldn't be stupid enough to come after them when she learned why he and Aki were missing. With any luck, by then, one gateway would be closed.

"Take it easy," he said quietly. "And no matter what happens, stay strong."

"You too," she said. "Thank you. Go in peace."

"Stay in peace."

He swept a hand over his drum, then faced the fire. The *taika* swelled within like a flower opening to the light. He grasped it, pulled an image of his camp into his mind, let it envelop him and twist around his souls. When it reached a crescendo, he moved forward, sank his shoes into the hot embers, and surrendered to the flames.

When he took another step, it was onto his own sleeping sack. Aki was curled up on the other side of the tent, nose twitching as he dreamed.

Chapter Eighteen

Tuomas stumbled through the flap, into the snow. His foot had no sooner come down when Lumi grasped his shoulders.

"What happened?" she asked. "I felt the energy shifting."

"What *didn't* happen?" Tuomas muttered, and told her everything.

Her eyes widened as she listened; her tail flicked back and forth, the aurora turning crimson at the edges. Then she turned around and flung a blast of Light at the Moon Spirit. It didn't break through to the World Above, but it lit up the sky like an inferno.

Tuomas moved away. She was shaking with fury.

"Let me out of this circle!" she hissed.

Tuomas beat his drum and opened a gap for her. As soon as she was through, she burst into a green and red flash and shot upwards. He watched in horror as she blazed across the night. The power behind her movements made the gash sway like a cobweb in the wind; stardust showered onto the snow. Tuomas's reindeer snorted in alarm and he stroked its neck to calm it.

After several long minutes, Lumi drifted down and took her human form again. Her eyes were the colour of blood.

Tuomas quickly let her through the barrier.

"Did you go to the World Above?" he asked carefully.

Lumi shook her head. "I cannot while the rip lies open, remember?"

"But you spoke to her?"

"Yes. She says she *did* order the trolls to stop."

"And you believe her?"

"This is just as surprising to me as it will be to you, but yes, I do. There was sincerity when she answered me. She is afraid."

Tuomas stared at her, then at the Moon Spirit, hanging there with half her face hidden. As soon as he focused on her, she let out a pulse of silver light.

"She does not have complete control over them," Lumi continued. "She awoke them, gave them their instructions, and now cannot restrain them. She can only hinder them a little; that is why we have not seen them since they appeared at Anaar."

"But they're still coming after us," said Tuomas darkly. He looked at the sky again, read the stars to discern their position. "Lilja and the caretakers are only about twenty miles away. I dealt with one of them, but where are the other two?"

"I cannot say," replied Lumi. "I am unable to see the entire World Between unless I am outside it, looking down from my normal place."

Tuomas gave a frustrated sigh. "So what do we do?"

"Be cautious and move swiftly," Lumi said. "You really should rest."

"I'm not tired. Not now."

"You should still try. I will watch through the night; I have no need to sleep."

Tuomas knew she was right, but he shook his head. He snatched a handful of virgin snow and placed it in his mouth. It immediately turned to water and he swallowed it, gasped with relief as it cooled his throat.

Lumi watched him, not blinking. She glanced at her fingers, then at Tuomas's. Her irises returned to an ethereal turquoise as the anger left her.

"You said you managed to create Sunlight?" she asked. "You petrified the troll?"

"Yes, but I don't know if I could do it again. I was trying, and nothing worked; I just panicked. I didn't have control at all."

Lumi hesitated.

"I can… try to help you," she offered.

Tuomas blinked. "Won't it hurt you?"

"Not if we are careful," she replied. "I will show you how I do it. Observe."

She brought her hands in front of her as though she were holding an invisible ball. The air between her palms rippled, then transformed into a spinning sphere of dancing Lights.

Tuomas stared at it in wonder. "Wow."

"This will run deeper than the *taika* you have used before," Lumi said. "Mages may learn to go into trance, and the stronger ones may learn to travel through fire or send out shockwaves. But this is beyond the power of any human. Reach to the Spirit that you are. Draw it to the surface. Let yourself be liberate."

She pressed her palms together and snuffed out the aurora.

Tuomas copied her movement, cupped his hands as he had done when trying to summon the fire. He dived within himself, into his heart, to where his souls lay wrapped around each other: one a star, the other a Sun.

Something flickered in the air. He risked a glance. A couple of sparks appeared, but nothing more.

"Go deeper," Lumi urged.

He flexed his fingers, closed his eyes in concentration. He felt himself hit the edge of his *taika*, and then his souls starting to twist, like he was working a muscle which he'd never

175

known he had. It protested against the sudden onslaught, but he pressed on, until heat started to gather and prickle his skin... hotter than before: the hottest flame there was...

He inched one eye open and was instantly blinded. A tiny ball of white light was hovering there. Lumi had disappeared; he spotted the tip of one ear behind the tent as she concealed herself.

The tension hit breaking point. Pain coursed through his heart; Tuomas yelped and his knees buckled. The sphere of light fizzled out like a dying ember.

Lumi stepped back into the open. He hung his head in defeat.

"That was awful," he growled. "I told you, I can't control it."

"You will," she assured. "That will come."

"It hurts," he said, clutching his chest. "Why is it so hard? If I'm a Spirit, that means I'm older than even the oldest of souls. It shouldn't matter that I'm in a human body. Why can't I do it?"

"Your life-soul is your Spirit. Your body-soul is like any other."

"So my body-soul is holding me back from doing it properly?"

"It appears so."

Tuomas snarled. "Then what chance have I got?"

Frustration overcame him and he drove a fist into the snow. It was shallower than he was expecting and his knuckles crashed into a rock. He checked for blood, found none.

Lumi waited until he was calm before offering her hand. He took it and she pulled him to his feet.

"Do not give up," she said. "Keep practising. You –"

She broke off, spun around. Her ears shot forward.

"What is it?" Tuomas hissed.

"Someone is coming."

"A troll?"

Tuomas listened as hard as he could. Sure enough, he heard something: quiet at first, but growing louder with every moment. At first, he thought it was stone limbs knocking together; waited to hear the awful groan which portended the monsters' arrival.

But it didn't come. Instead, he recognised bells, and a soft clicking sound: reindeer tendons.

A glow appeared in the darkness. Tuomas watched as it grew into a flaming torch. He spotted a sleigh, pulled by a single bull. He walked close to the barrier, squinted, trying to figure out who was driving.

His mouth fell open.

"Elin?"

She drew closer, held the torch beside her face so he could see. Yes, it was her.

Tuomas hurriedly hit the drum, opened the circle wide enough for her to urge the reindeer inside.

"What are you doing here?" he cried.

"I followed you," said Elin. "It's lucky it hasn't snowed in ages; I might have lost your trail otherwise. But then I saw a flash... that was you, wasn't it?"

She clambered out of the sleigh, lowered her head in Lumi's direction. Then she faced Tuomas. Her eyes were hollow with uncertainty; she looked as though she was going to cry.

"I'm sorry," she said. "I know I've been horrible to you. This was the time when you needed friends the most, and I turned my back on you. I was scared and angry, and... Well, I want to make it up to you. You saved my life; you didn't have

177

to do that. You *shouldn't* have done it, but you did anyway. And you did the same for Mihka, even though he pushed you away."

"You do realise how dangerous it was for you to come after us like that, in the dark?" Lumi chided.

Tuomas held out a hand, asking her to be quiet.

"But what about... the other thing?" he whispered. "Aki? Your father?"

Elin's eyes flickered to the tent. "He's in there?"

"Yes. Alseep."

"Why did you take him? The elders wouldn't say."

Tuomas gnawed on the inside of his cheek. He could tell her apology was sincere, even though her face was still chiselled by the struggle to understand.

"So he can set the trapped souls free."

Elin swallowed. "Really? You're going to save them?"

"*He* is going to save them. I'm just taking him there. And then I have to close the gateway to the World Below."

"You mean, the Northern Edge of the World?"

"Yes. It has to be done," said Tuomas. "Elin, listen, this will be dangerous. I'm going with Aki across the Night River, into the Deathlands."

He watched Elin to gauge her reaction. She drew in a nervous breath, but then she steeled herself.

"Fine."

Tuomas only just held back a small smile. He knew she was strong, but it was comforting that it would still take a lot to frighten her.

"This is very ill-advised," Lumi warned. "There is nothing you will be able to do to help."

"Please let me come with you," said Elin. "You might need another bow."

Tuomas glanced at Lumi. "That's a good point. She's a better shot than me."

Lumi raised her chin and flattened her ears. "Arrows have no effect on the trolls. You know that."

"If she wants to come, she should be allowed the choice," said Tuomas. "Anyway, you said yourself it was dangerous to follow us in the dark. I don't think it's a good idea for her to go back now, not until dawn."

"I'm not going back," Elin maintained. "Please, Tuomas, Lumi. I'm sorry. This is the only thing I can think to do. Don't go on without me."

Tuomas toyed with the fox carving. There was such honesty in her eyes, and a desperation which struck him to his core.

He stepped forward and hugged her. She put her arms around his shoulders, grasped handfuls of his coat.

"Thank you," he whispered into her ear.

Lumi watched them, the corner of her mouth turned up in a sad smile. Then she walked away and stood at the edge of the circle, staring out into the tundra.

Chapter Nineteen

Tuomas barely felt as though he had closed his eyes before Lumi awoke him, bending into the tent for just long enough to shake his wrist. Then she shot back outside and waited as he roused Elin.

She started rolling her sleeping sack. Tuomas gave her a tentative smile. A part of him had thought he'd dreamed that she had come after him.

He crawled to where Aki was lying, on the other side of the fire. The little boy hadn't moved all night; he was still in the same position Tuomas had left him. Elin watched uneasily as he patted Aki's shoulder.

"Time to get up," he said.

Aki groaned. "I don't want to."

"Well, you have to. We've got a busy day ahead."

"But I'm still tired!"

"You can sleep in the sleigh if you want. But I need to take down the shelter, so come on."

Tuomas slid his shoes onto his feet and tied them. As he worked, Aki's eyes rose and settled on Elin. He hunched his shoulders, trying to make himself smaller.

"Why's she here?" he whispered. "She doesn't like me."

"Elin's come to keep us company. She's a friend," Tuomas replied, then glanced over his shoulder at her. "Aren't you?"

Elin pursed her lips, but nodded.

Tuomas led Aki outside, wrapped him in a blanket in the sleigh, then helped Elin strip the tarp off the tent. They folded it, split the load, and strapped the reindeer into position.

The sky was still dark, but the blackness of night had faded slightly to a deep blue, as dawn inched closer. Seeing the light returning earlier and earlier surprised Tuomas. It was far from the first time he had witnessed it, but this winter had seemed so long, it felt strange that nature could continue in the same old way. It was over two months since the solstice now – in another one, the spring equinox would arrive; day and night would be equal. And after that, the Sun would outshine the Moon, until there was no such thing as darkness.

He went to climb into his sleigh, but paused. Aki had curled up on one of the skins and gone back to sleep.

Elin gazed down at him with a tight expression.

"See?" Tuomas said under his breath. "He's fine. Harmless."

"You're... good with him," Elin admitted. "Better than I could be."

"You should try. Give him a chance. None of this is his fault," Tuomas whispered. "I don't want to disturb him. Can I ride with you?"

Elin nodded woodenly. She dragged her reindeer in front of Tuomas's, then tied a long length of rope between its harness and the back of the sleigh, so they would walk in a line. As she worked, Lumi sank into her fox form, leapt in beside Aki, and buried herself under the furs.

Tuomas broke the circle, and when all was ready, they set off into the north west. Another twenty miles, and they would reach the Northern Edge of the World.

The Sun Spirit spilled over the tundra behind them and transformed the snow into a sea of glittering gold. A few lonely clouds streaked across the rip like purple ribbons, but they would soon burn away. A cold day lay ahead.

Soon, they climbed a gentle hill, and Tuomas steered the reindeer along the top of the ridge. He threw a glance to his left, where a large lake sat in the distance. A few jagged sheets of ice still clung to its banks here and there, but the majority had melted into crisp blue water, dotted by floating bergs.

Tuomas shivered when he saw it. This was the Nordjarvi: the place where the draugars had lured Aki away from Lilja, and where she had later accidentally shoved a torch into his face.

But the longer he looked at it, the more his souls settled. The last time he had been here, the surface was shrouded with thick mist, snaking its tendrils everywhere, in an attempt to find the strongest *taika*. Even the Spirit of the Lake seemed to have left. But now, he spotted patches of greenery poking through the snow on the edges; sensed life and normality returning. There was nothing terrible about this place, save for the memory.

"What's the matter?" Elin asked.

"Nothing," Tuomas said quickly. "Just thinking."

He tossed a glance over his shoulder to check on Aki. He was still asleep, mouth open and mumbling to himself. Even being this close to the Nordjarvi didn't disturb him.

Elin peered at him as well, and shook her head.

"He doesn't look anything like my father. He's all Lilja."

"I know. Is it any wonder why nobody's guessed?"

"You really haven't told anyone else?"

"No. It's not my business. And like I said, I found out the truth at the same time as you. I just didn't realise you were behind that bush."

Elin turned to Tuomas. "Would you have told me?"

132

He sighed. "I don't know. I would have wanted to, but... even if Lilja hadn't sworn me to secrecy, I understood her reasons. She wanted to protect everyone. And... I would have wanted to protect you, too."

Elin worked her mouth, brows knotting together. Then she cleared her throat and dug into a pouch for some reindeer jerky. She offered a strip to Tuomas, wedged another between her teeth, and put the rest back.

"For when he wakes up," she said softly.

Tuomas smiled, then gave the rope a snap to encourage the reindeer to go faster.

"I really am glad you're here," he admitted. "It felt strange, heading off without you. Even though there's not really much you can do."

"I can shoot us dinner," Elin replied, with a hint of a smirk. "I'm glad I'm here, too. I had a battle with the elders, trying to get away. Birkir refused. But I argued enough, and I suppose they knew I'd gone with you in the past."

"Well, at least we only have two trolls to worry about now," Tuomas said. "I went through the fire to check on Lilja, and one attacked us. But I managed to fight it off."

"How? Did you make a shockwave?"

"No. I... made Sunlight. It turned to stone."

Elin's eyes widened. "Was that the flash I saw, just before I arrived last night?"

"That was me practising. Badly. I did better when I *wasn't* trying. That seems to be the story of my life, doesn't it?"

He took a bite out of the jerky, more aggressively than he meant to. After he'd swallowed, he leaned over the side of the sleigh and grabbed a handful of snow. It began to melt before he even had a chance to put it in his mouth.

"Did you see Mihka before you came?" he asked.

"Yes," said Elin. "He's doing fine. Well... as fine as he can. He's in a lot of pain."

Tuomas winced. "I can imagine. He'll be lucky to walk again after that. But at least he'll live."

Elin bit her lip. "Was it true? What he said about you dooming the souls?"

"Yes and no," Tuomas said, with another glance in the direction of the Nordjarvi. "I made a bargain with the draugars, that they could feed off me forever if they let all the souls go, and they agreed. But then Lumi came and saved me, voided the bargain. She mentioned, after Mihka left, that she could only protect me and whoever was closest."

"Me and Aki," Elin finished. "And that's what tore the Worlds? When she went after you?"

"Yes."

"And you did all that for me? You never would have thought to sacrifice yourself, if they hadn't taken me, would you?"

Tuomas swallowed. "I don't know what I would have done. Did they hurt you? The draugars?"

Elin sucked in a breath. "I can't remember a lot of it. There was water in my lungs, I was drowning... then the next thing I knew, I woke up on the beach. And you had *this*."

She motioned at his tail, lying between them on the seat. Then she twisted so she was facing him better.

Tuomas looked at her. He could hardly believe she had been sick now: her cheeks were healthy and ruddy, and the shine had returned to her hair. Her fringe sat across her brow in a straight black line – he supposed Alda had trimmed the ends not too long ago.

"You're different," she said quietly. "Your eyes... There's light in them. And your skin, too."

Tuomas glanced at his hands. He hadn't noticed it before, but sure enough, there was a faint golden glow under his flesh.

"Are my eyes… still blue?" he asked cautiously.

Elin nodded. "It's just around the edges."

Her attention shifted up, to his ears. She pulled off a mitten and tentatively lifted her hand. Tuomas stayed still as her fingers brushed through the red fur. Her mouth opened in wonder.

"You're so warm," she said.

Tuomas didn't speak, just carried on watching her as she moved down the ears, felt how they disappeared into his hair. But beneath the awe, her anger was gone, and her expression was the same as it had been from the beginning.

His mouth dried as the heel of her palm brushed his cheek. It was calloused from cold and the hard life of the Northlands, yet so alive and gentle.

She let go of him and took another quick bite of jerky. Tuomas collected himself, picked up the rope and turned his eyes forward, as the Nordjarvi vanished behind them.

The Sun Spirit was past her midday point when they finally drew close to the Northern Edge. The snowbanks which Tuomas had been forced to blast through last time had melted to shapeless lumps, and the sleighs carried on with ease. The ground dipped, and in the middle of it lay a huge lake: the largest in all the tundra.

Tuomas could have cried with relief. Even from here, he could tell the surface was still frozen.

Elin pulled the reindeer to a halt on the bank. While she bound its rope to an exposed boulder, Tuomas surveyed the surface. It was slick with a layer of water, and streaked by white and grey patches which made his stomach twist with nerves. The darker areas were where the ice was thinner. They would have to place each step carefully to avoid falling through.

He approached Aki and shook him awake.

"Alright, you really do need to get up now."

Aki looked around and gasped.

"Wow!" he cried. "Is this the Northern Edge of the World?"

"It sure is," said Tuomas. "Now, listen, we need to walk across the lake, alright?"

At that, Aki's eyes widened and he pressed himself against the furs. He leaned against Lumi and she gave an indignant bark.

"I don't want to," he whimpered.

Tuomas took hold of his hands.

"Aki," he said softly, "I promise that nothing is going to happen. There isn't anything in that lake except fish. Your mother would say the same. Please come with me."

Aki's lip quivered and he threw himself into Tuomas's arms.

"Don't let go of me," he begged. "Don't let them come back for me!"

"I won't," Tuomas promised. "Come on, now. Be brave. You can do this."

He lifted Aki onto the ground and grasped his wrist. Then he pulled off his coat and tossed it to Elin.

"Can you get Lumi, please?" he asked. "Make sure she's completely covered."

Elin nodded and held the coat so Lumi could dart under it. Tuomas fetched some birch bark and twigs from his sleigh. When all was ready, they stepped onto the ice.

It immediately moved beneath them; a groan sounded deep below the surface, like the yawn of a giant creature.

"Spread out," Elin said.

They did, but Aki kept tight hold of Tuomas. He fixed his eyes downwards so he could watch for cracks. Rumbles sounded at every moment. The lake was waking up after the long winter, and making its impatience known.

Eventually, after what felt like an eternity, they reached the hole in the middle. While Elin picked her way closer, Tuomas arranged the wood into a conical structure and stuffed it with bark.

He went to strike a flint, but stopped himself – there was no point anymore. Instead, he focused on his *taika*, waited until he tasted it, like fresh berries, and flicked his hand.

A flame shot from his fingers and caught the tinder.

Aki and Elin gaped at him.

"How did you do that?" Elin asked.

"He's a Spirit," Aki replied, but he couldn't keep his own shock out of his voice. Tuomas wasn't surprised. Aside from the caretakers with Lilja, they were the first people who had seen him do something like that.

"Alright," he said. "Elin, I don't know how long we'll be. Can you mind the reindeer?"

She narrowed her eyes. "No. I'm coming with you."

Tuomas snarled. "Elin –"

"*No.* I've come this far. Anyway, I've always wanted to see the World Below. I suppose it's fitting that I get my chance when it's the last time it will ever be open."

Lumi growled under the coat, but Elin ignored her and glared at Tuomas.

He gripped his hammer. He had a mind to beat the drum and bind her legs so she couldn't follow, but he chased that thought away. Hadn't he, just last night, defended her right to make her own choices?

"Fine," he said tightly.

Lumi barked again.

"She'll be fine," Tuomas snapped, then turned back to Elin. "But I don't want you coming across the River."

"What River?" Aki asked, but Tuomas shushed him.

"Tough," said Elin.

"No... you haven't seen that place. Just stay with the Earth Spirits, in the caves. You'll be safe with them."

"Who cares about safety? I've been in worse positions than crossing a river."

"It's not just any river, and you know it."

"And I also know that I'm coming with you."

"Elin!" Tuomas cried. He stepped closer and grasped her arm. "Just stop! Please! I don't want you to get hurt again... I can't risk you getting stuck there!"

His ferocity shocked her, but she shrugged it off just as quickly.

"Well, I'm not letting you get stuck there, either. And who says we're even going to get stuck? I'm here now, and I'm with you every step of the way. I owe you that much, and you're my friend. So shut up and accept it!"

Her eyes were harder than rock, blazing in the cold light.

Tuomas tried not to blink, but the longer he looked at her, the more his resolve faded. The aloofness and tension of the last few weeks meant nothing in the end – he had risked everything to save her. He hadn't really understood why, except for the simple reason that he cared for her.

His shoulders sagged in defeat.

"Alright," he said. "Are you ready?"

Elin didn't move. "When you are."

Lumi growled again, but softer than before. He could tell she had realised Elin was too stubborn to stand down.

Without another word, he spun a circle around the hole, held his drum over the fire. He kept it there until the skin became tight on the frame, then began to beat.

He started slow, closed his eyes, drew his *taika* into a chant. He didn't try to harness it or push it into something it didn't want to be. Warmth spread through him as he forced it through the ice, deep – deeper than it could possibly extend. He called to the Earth Spirits, to the Great Bear, to the ravaged fabric of the Worlds, asked it to part just enough to let him enter one more time.

He felt the edge, where the Below and Between touched, willed them to open.

The black depths of the hole glowed. The light grew, pushed itself up like a bubble. But no ghostly white reindeer leapt across this time. The boundary was too fickle, the connection too weak. The two realms were clinging to each other by a thread.

Tuomas hurriedly tied his drum to his belt. He grabbed Aki's hand, nodded at Elin, and they jumped.

Chapter Twenty

There was no water, only air, whistling past Tuomas's ears. The three of them tumbled into darkness, Aki clinging to him in fright. Elin was screaming, too.

"It's alright, don't panic!" he shouted, but they were falling too fast, and the wind whipped his words away.

A layer of dense cloud appeared below. They passed through it, and for a moment, the surroundings turned completely grey. Then it thinned, and they emerged above an autumnal forest stretching in all directions. Everything was dark – it was night here: the opposite of the World Between. Some trees still boasted the fiery reds and golds of stubborn leaves, while others stood bare and skeletal. Lakes were scattered here and there, looking like nothing more than puddles from so high up. One lay directly beneath them, and Tuomas spotted the boat in the centre.

"Brace!" he yelled, and they crashed down.

Elin cried out and almost dropped Lumi. She quickly wriggled from under the coat. As soon as she was free, she shook herself, sending the colours of the aurora bristling over her fur like electricity. Then she slowly began to change, her features becoming more humanlike, until she had returned to her human form.

"Is anyone hurt?" Tuomas asked.

Aki shook his head nervously. Elin did the same.

Tuomas glanced around to get his bearings, and a stone of horror dropped through him.

Despite the autumnal colours, the leaves had lost their vibrancy, and the soil looked like it was laced with ash. Most of the bark on the trees had turned black, as though scorched by fire. Everywhere was silent – not even the call of a bird or the clicking of a reindeer's knees could be heard. The air held an unnatural taste, of something more than decay, but of sheer nothingness. It was creeping closer: a disease spreading through the great tree which held everything together. The roots had taken the infection first; now it was only a matter of time before it moved up the trunk and branches.

"No…" Tuomas breathed.

Elin saw it too and held a hand to her mouth.

"That's what the broken Worlds are doing?" she gasped.

"It's fading," Tuomas said. "It's worse than I thought. We don't have much time."

His eyes filled with tears. Seeing so much life vanishing was a blade in his gut. To the people, just because something wasn't like them didn't lessen its value – every tree, animal, and herb had as much right to life as any child. Prey might be eaten and wood burned, but eventually, all returned to the earth, and gave back everything they had taken.

Without another word, he and Elin picked up the oars in the bottom of the boat and rowed. Aki's eyes grew huge and he pointed at the bank.

"Who's that?"

It was behind him, but Tuomas didn't need to look to know what he meant.

"One of the Earth Spirits," he said. "Don't worry, they're our friends."

"Friends?" Aki repeated, a note of hope in his voice.

The keel ran against the ground and Tuomas jumped out. Sure enough, he was met by a being made entirely of autumn leaves. Ripe cloudberries and blueberries ran down its front in an array of patterns; dry grass and long reeds cascaded from its head like hair. Its clothes whispered as a breeze swept against them.

Elin and Aki each snatched one of Tuomas's arms and stared at the Spirit in amazement.

"Tuomas Sun-Soul," it said. "So you have returned."

"To do the right thing this time," he replied.

He bowed his head; the others followed suit. The Spirit regarded them with eyes like cold stars.

"You caused much grief when you last walked upon this ground," it said. "You and the White Fox One, both. Tell me why you are here."

"You already know."

"Yes. But I wish to ensure you do, and that you will complete it."

Tuomas licked his lips, looked at Aki. There was no way he could stall anymore.

"I'm going to shut the gateway. But before I do, we're going to the Deathlands, to free the trapped souls."

He didn't have to wait long before Aki turned on him in alarm.

"The Deathlands?" he squeaked.

"The Great Bear Spirit told us we had to," said Tuomas, as gently as he could. But Aki's eyes filled with fearful tears and he shook his head.

"No! No, no, no! I don't want to go there! Nobody goes there!"

"We can. We're the only ones who can, because we've died and come back to life in the same body. It's an honour."

Tuomas tried to make himself sound more confident than he felt. His anxiety about the Night River had been hard enough before, but now he was here, in the World Below, so close to it…

"Aki," he said, "do you remember how the Great Bear saved your mother?"

Aki nodded.

"Well, it wanted to save *you*, as well. Because this is a job you need to do, with me. You're going to be the best mage ever. And all mages have to go through a test. So just think of it like that. And you won't be alone; I won't leave you. Alright?"

Aki whimpered, brought his hands to his face and wept.

Then, to Tuomas's surprise, Elin approached and took Aki's shoulders.

"You can do it," she said. "You're strong."

Aki stopped crying and stared at her, shocked that she was even touching him. He glanced nervously at Tuomas.

"See?" Tuomas said. "I told you she was a friend."

Aki hesitated for a moment, then sniffed back a sob and put his arms around Elin. She froze, and Tuomas thought she might push him off. But instead, she patted him uncertainly on the head.

Lumi's eyes sparkled bright green at the sight. Tuomas smiled, and turned back to the Earth Spirit.

"You have my word that I'll see things through this time," he said. "I'm so sorry for what I did; it was disrespectful and ignorant."

The Spirit's expression softened.

"Luckily, there is still time to act. You have not squandered your last chance yet."

"Thank you," Tuomas said humbly. "I know I don't deserve your forgiveness. But I won't let you down."

He glanced at himself. In circumstances like this, it was best to leave an offering, to appease an upset Spirit. But it

needed to be something of value, or which could be valuable –
like the antler he had left on Anaar, which would have made a
perfect utensil. He considered cutting his hair again, or spilling
his blood, but something told him that wasn't enough. Once he
returned from the Deathlands, he would complete the very task
he had been reborn for. These Spirits, whom he had harmed and
insulted so much, deserved an offering equal to such an act.

With a heavy heart, he untied all three of his knives from
his belt. He had made each one with Paavo almost ten years ago:
sat with his brother for days, chipping them away from flint,
fitting them to antler handles, carving them with circles and
lines. They were even more familiar to his touch than Henrik's
drum. They were a part of him, of Paavo.

He braced himself and laid them at the Spirit's feet.

"I hope you will accept," he said tightly.

The Spirit regarded the blades, then swept them up in a
single graceful motion and attached them to its own belt.

"I do accept, on behalf of the Earth Spirits, Red Fox
One," it said.

Tuomas bit back the pain of seeing his precious knives
gone forever. It was awful to not feel their weight around his
hips. To distract himself, he returned to the boat and snatched
his coat.

"Now, I shall take you to the Night River," the Spirit
continued. "The Deathlands are not under our dominion. We
can lead you as far as the bank, but it is the Ferry Spirit who
must allow you further."

"The Ferry Spirit?" Tuomas repeated.

"I know of her," Lumi said from behind him. "She is
similar to the Spirit of Passage. But darker."

Tuomas bit his lip. "You're not giving me much
confidence, Lumi."

"You will need your courage," said the Spirit. "I will give you one further warning: it will not be an easy place for you to set foot. The far shore is unlike anywhere you know, and the Horse-Riding One is as formless in nature as your sister. They are opposite sides of the same face, she and he."

Tuomas shared a glance with Lumi. As usual, her snowy expression was unreadable, but the flash of cool turquoise in her eyes confirmed everything. Tuomas might be her equal: of the Sun as she was of the Moon – but the Spirit of Death was something which transcended time. According to the fireside tales, he was even older than her, and it was only by the grace of her position that she'd been able to take the ancestors into her Lights. All Spirits were unspeakably powerful, but after the Great Bear, this one was probably the strongest of them all.

The Spirit beckoned them. Aki snatched Tuomas's wrist in fright, but allowed himself to be led. As they passed a tree, Tuomas held out a hand to touch the blackened bark. His fingers fell straight through, as though it wasn't even there.

He could feel the damage more than ever here: the *taika* seeping through the cracks like sand. For the first time, it seemed a physical pain. The realms were truly hurt: an animal with a crippling injury, moving towards a slow but certain death.

"Is it reversable?" he asked.

"In time. The faster you act, the faster it heals."

"I didn't realise it was this bad."

"It is, sadly, a common trait among humans," the Earth Spirit said sadly. "To not realise the extent of tragedy until it is upon you."

They walked for what felt like miles, before finally reaching a cave mouth, flanked on either side by flaming torches. Multiple dark doorways gaped along the passageway. Tuomas kept his eyes on the Spirit, so he wouldn't lose it in the winding maze. He supposed it would take an entire lifetime to try and map the full extent of the underground tunnels, and even then, they would carry on shifting and growing, like a tree's roots through decades.

Eventually, after descending a slope which seemed deeper than any other before it, they reached a single shaft. A ghostly light was emanating from it, brighter than the Moon yet dimmer than the Sun, cold and warm in the same instance.

Tuomas's stomach flipped. It had been in a completely different part of the caves, but this was the light which had last led him to the River.

Fear mounted in his blood. Everything in him screamed to turn away and run as far from this place as he could.

Aki clutched him so hard, he lost the feeling in his fingers.

"I'm scared," he whimpered.

"Me, too," Elin admitted.

Tuomas wanted to reassure them, but he couldn't. The words turned to ash in his mouth. It took all his energy just to keep moving forward.

Suddenly, his feet sank into something soft.

He looked down. The rocky ground had transformed to grey dust. It was between sand and snow, rising and falling in dunes and dips beneath a sky blacker than any other. No stars shone and no wind blew. The silence was absolute.

Lumi appeared beside him. Just like in the World Between, she balanced atop the powder as though she carried no weight at all. She was deathly still, her eyes changing all different colours.

The Earth Spirit faced them.

"This is where I must leave you," it said. "We have come to the borders of our domain, and you must carry on alone. But we will be here to wait for your return."

Tuomas swallowed his fear for long enough to give a respectful nod. Then the Spirit strode past them, back into the tunnel, and disappeared.

Elin sucked in a breath and grasped his hand.

"I don't like this," she whispered.

"I know," said Tuomas. He kept his voice low, terrified at the prospect of disturbing the awful calm.

"I'm scared!" Aki said again. "Please don't go any closer!"

"We have to," Tuomas replied.

Even Lumi looked perturbed. Their presence was akin to the first footprint pressed into a perfect sheet of virgin snow at the start of winter. Once there, it would never go away.

"I have not been here before," she said. "This is the furthest from the World Above I have ever come."

Tuomas gritted his teeth. The worst thing to do was to stay still – he felt that the longer he remained there, the more he would lose his nerve.

"Let's go," he said. "The sooner it's done, the sooner we can leave."

With that, he walked forward, kept his eyes straight ahead. Aki clung to him and shook with terror. Every movement was laborious. Even their breathing was something new to this place.

Then the Night River appeared. It raged one moment and was still the next, white with foam and then moving over deep dark patches. When they reached the bank, the water drew away as though it were alive.

Tuomas felt sick just looking at it. He peered across, but saw nothing. The River stretched too far, merging seamlessly with the black sky, so he couldn't tell where one ended and the other began.

Then his heart leapt. A boat was coming towards them out of the darkness.

Chapter Twenty-One

The prow cut through the water, not even swaying when a wave battered the sides. The movement was so steady and slick, it didn't look real. The mere sight sent shivers through Tuomas's body.

A tall and skinny figure was standing at the back of the boat, a long pole in its hands, which it used to push the vessel forwards. Like the Earth Spirits, it was dressed in garments of leaves. But where the Earth Spirits' clothes were bright and elaborate, this one's were dark and shabby, with decaying grasses and patches of fungus. The Spirit they covered took the shape of an old woman, her back hunched and skin loose, yet there wasn't a wrinkle or liver spot in sight – as though she was a youngster who had aged overnight, and the body was still adjusting to the sudden change.

She drew the boat close, but far enough away that they couldn't step inside. She regarded them with dark eyes, set so deeply in her face, it seemed they were looking out from the very back of an empty head.

Aki scurried behind Tuomas and grabbed hold of his tail in fright.

"Only souls come here, to the shore of the Deathlands," said the Ferry Spirit. "You are not souls. You are still bound in bodies, Tuomas Sun-Soul, Aki Wandering-Soul and Elin of Einfjall. You are not dead. And you, White Fox One, are not among the living or the dead."

It took all Tuomas's resolve not to bolt like a terrified calf. Her voice reminded him of cobwebs and rotting things beneath the forest floor. If he was this anxious standing before *her*, how was he going to manage the Spirit of Death?

"Aki and I have been sent by the Great Bear," he said, hating how loud he sounded in the eerie silence. "We've come to free the children and adults who were killed by the draugars. They must be separated, and Aki is the only one who can do that."

The Ferry Spirit switched her pole to the other hand and leaned closer.

"I am well aware of them. I carried them across here, entwined with each other. The draugars caused harm and spread chaos."

"I know," said Tuomas carefully, "but the kids and the others – Sisu, Paavo – they're innocent. They don't need to be bound."

The Spirit shrugged. "Innocent, guilty. Decent, wicked. It is not my position to judge deeds, only to carry the dead. Which you are not."

Lumi suddenly stepped forward.

"They may not be dead now," she said, "but all three have crossed the threshold, Ferry One. I brought them back from the edge myself. I forced my brother's souls back into his body, and saved both the boy and the girl. They have all returned to life. And they have a task to complete."

The Ferry Spirit stared at her for a horribly long moment. "So that is why you are here, White Fox One. I did wonder why. It is to right your own wrongs. Most unbecoming of a Spirit like yourself."

Lumi's ears twisted. "My brother is also a Spirit, simply bound in human form. He made mistakes too."

"And we're both here to make up for it," Tuomas added quickly, sensing Lumi's growing anger. "We're going to close the gateways. But first, we need to speak with the Horse-Riding One. Please take us across. The Great Bear has ordered it."

The Ferry Spirit fixed her eyes on him. They pierced right down to his souls, and he trembled under her unblinking gaze. He could feel her testing his *taika*, feeling deep inside him for the truth.

Beside him, Elin slipped her hand into his. She was shaking.

The Spirit drew herself up tall.

"None have come across here who were not dead," she said. "Yet I sense there is something different about the three of you. What the White Fox One says is correct. You have been in the grasp of death, and returned from it. So I will strike a compromise. I shall take you in my boat, but I will not bring you back. That will be your responsibility."

Tuomas bristled with alarm. "But I need to close the gateway! What if we can't get back?"

"Of course you can get back," replied the Spirit. "I simply will not be the one to bring you. Do you accept?"

Tuomas threw a glance at Lumi. She looked reserved, but gave a tiny nod. If that was her response, then he knew this was probably the best offer they could hope for.

He went to step aside so Lumi could get in the boat first, but a sudden movement from the Ferry Spirit made him turn. She had held up a grey hand.

"No, Tuomas Sun-Soul. The White Fox One must remain here."

"What?" Tuomas cried. "Why?"

"Because she is a true Spirit, not alive nor dead, and never to be alive or dead. You and your friends have a special condition, and the order of the Great Bear. But not your sister. She must stay."

Panic wrapped itself around Tuomas's chest. Go into the Deathlands without Lumi? She was more than capable of taking care of herself, but the idea of leaving her behind tore at him like claws.

Lumi's ears twitched, but she lowered her head in submission.

"If that is your bidding, Ferry One, I will honour it," she said.

"Lumi!" Tuomas hissed.

"This is not my domain – I must respect and defer to the Spirits who govern it," she replied firmly. "The Horse-Riding One would never trespass on me in the World Above, so I extend the same courtesy to him. Besides, this was never my mission. You and Aki must do this; I am only here to help you close the gateways."

The Ferry Spirit moved the boat closer. Now only a short stretch of black water stood between the prow and their feet.

Tuomas turned to Elin. Her face was almost as white as Lumi's.

"You don't have to come."

His words snapped her out of it like a spark catching dry tinder.

"What did I say before we jumped?" she snapped. "I'm with you every step of the way. You don't need to ask me. Of course I'm coming."

Before Tuomas could speak again, she strode past him and leapt the short distance into the boat. It wobbled under her weight, but the Spirit counterbalanced it perfectly.

Tuomas shot Lumi an apologetic grimace, but she only motioned for him to follow Elin. So, holding his breath to keep himself from shaking, he lifted Aki over the water, then followed. Aki grasped him around the waist and held him so tightly, he thought his ribs might crack.

Without another sound, the Ferry Spirit turned the boat and pushed off. The River churned at the movement, each wave and ripple merging with its neighbour, as though it was a giant liquid lung drawing breath in and out.

Tuomas looked over his shoulder at Lumi. Already she seemed so far away: a single glowing white figure among miles of monochrome desert – and it suddenly struck him that he'd just crossed a barrier which even she was powerless to save him from.

The boat moved steadily on. The only sound came from the Ferry Spirit's pole as it tapped against the side. Tuomas, Aki and Elin sat close together, not daring to even breathe loudly.

The darkness was universal, wrapping around them like a shroud. The water stretched on without end, until Tuomas couldn't tell which direction they were travelling in anymore. Sometimes it seemed more like they were floating across an ocean. There was no horizon line, no currents... and then suddenly swells would appear from nowhere, raging around the boat but never touching it.

Through it all, the Ferry Spirit kept straight and perfectly balanced. Tuomas wondered if her feet were actually fused to the vessel, and it was actually an extension of her own form.

He glanced at the water. It flowed similar to the rivers he knew in the World Between, yet there was something unnervingly delicate about it, as though it was liquid fused with mist. It was too dark to see into the depths, but every now and then, a flash of solidness broke the surface.

"What is that?" he asked quietly.

"The knives of men and the needles of women," replied the Ferry Spirit.

Now she said it, Tuomas could recognise the objects. They moved as though they had no weight at all, poking their sharp edges into the air.

"Why are they here?"

"Sometimes, when a human dies, so do their belongings, if they are not passed down through the generations and become forgotten. Then they appear here, in the Night River."

"Why?"

"You ask a lot of questions, Son of the Sun," the Ferry Spirit snapped, but then she carried on. "You humans are the only living things who make tools, and also the only ones who can truly choose to be decent or wicked. Save for the draugars, the only souls which may be bound in the Deathlands lived their last lives as a human.

"So to have your weapons here is a fitting part of the cycle: they act as a line of defence against those who chose evil in life. If those bound souls should ever get free of their prisons, they would not be able to cross here. They would be wounded, and ensnared in the nets below the surface. Then I would simply haul them in and take them back."

Tuomas and Elin glanced at each other. It was a clever solution, but still frightened them.

A grey mist suddenly appeared ahead. Aki saw it and his face flashed with horror.

"No!" he cried. "Don't! I want to go back! Mama!"

Tuomas wrapped his arms around him.

"It's alright," he assured. "It's safe. Nothing's going to hurt you."

"There are no draugars in that, Aki Wandering-Soul," said the Ferry Spirit. "You may be calm."

Hearing it from her, Aki quietened, but his muscles remained sprung tight. Tears cascaded over his scars.

Elin waited for a swell to lower, then carefully moved so she was sitting on Aki's other side. It was a small gesture, but Tuomas gave her a smile.

The Ferry Spirit steered towards the mist and passed through without a moment's hesitation. It grew brighter, until it was a brilliant white. Only the water remained black – the boat was floating in an abyss of light. Then a bank appeared on the horizon, equally white, bare of any detail. Tuomas could only tell it was solid by the faint shadows which fell on it.

The vessel drew to a halt. Not needing to be told, Tuomas jumped across, followed closely by Elin and Aki.

He turned to thank the Spirit, but she had already moved the boat out of reach. The glints of blades and needles peeked out of the water in front of her. True to her promise, she had brought them across, but would not be taking them back.

"I wish you luck in your errand," she said, "and in returning to the Earth Spirits' forest."

Without another word, she pushed hard on the pole, spinning the boat away from them completely. Then she manoeuvred it back through the churning water and disappeared.

Aki pressed himself so tightly against Tuomas's side, he almost pulled him over. Tuomas held onto him and tried to stop himself from trembling.

There was absolutely nothing here. How could such emptiness exist? It reminded him of something a child might draw in the snow: all lines and simplicity; no depth to anything. Even the air he breathed seemed different than normal: thin, hollow.

Elin's hand twitched, and Tuomas immediately knew she was desperate to get her bow ready.

"No need," he said, nodding at her quiver of arrows. "There shouldn't be anything which can hurt us."

She didn't look convinced. "What makes you so sure?"

"If this place is anything like the Lights, it's formless. And all the wicked souls are locked away, remember?"

A chill passed through him as he said those words. Somewhere, out there in the Deathlands, was Kari.

He let go of Aki with one hand and touched his chest. Fear clamped around him like a wolf's jaws. It turned his blood to fire, locked his jaw, pressed his throat until he thought he might suffocate. And all his enemies were so close, all those who had tried to tear out his heart and consume his power...

"So, what do we do now?" Elin asked.

"I suppose we just start walking," Tuomas said. "We're bound to end up somewhere eventually."

"What if we get lost?" whimpered Aki.

"We'll just come back to the River. It's the only black thing here; I'm sure we'll find it easily enough."

"But what about the Horse-Riding One? What if we can't find him?"

Tuomas flattened his ears nervously. The Spirit of Death probably knew they were there already.

He moved forwards into the endless light. Elin followed close behind him, then moved to his side and took his other hand. Their shoes made no noise on the ground – it didn't even feel like any kind of stone or grass. It just *was*. A disorientating thought swam through Tuomas's mind: that they weren't actually walking on anything, and were just suspended in oblivion.

Souls began to appear: flickering orbs, both transparent and solid at the same time. They drifted by, danced around each other; some drew close and spun about the three of them like moths.

Elin's mouth fell open.

"I didn't think they would look so beautiful," she whispered.

Despite the situation, Tuomas couldn't hold back a smile. He told himself that this place was a haven first and a prison second: these souls were no different to those in the World Above. They just hadn't taken their place up there in the sky yet, or had chosen to wait here before returning to new life.

"They seem happy," he noted as he watched them move. "Just as happy as with Lumi."

Aki extended a hand towards one of the souls. It fluttered away, leaving a stream of light in its wake.

"Were any of these in Uncle Kari?"

Tuomas swallowed. "I don't think so."

Aki turned to him, but before he could say anything else, his eyes widened and he leapt back.

"What is it?" Tuomas asked.

He spun around, in the direction Aki was staring, and gasped in fright.

The Spirit of Death was standing in front of them.

Chapter Twenty-Two

"Red Fox One," the Spirit said. "I thought you would come."

Fright froze Tuomas to the spot. The voice was deeper than even Henrik's had been. Elin snatched his hand so tightly, his knuckles cracked.

True to his title, the Spirit was seated atop a huge horse, yet the animal and rider were all clearly the same entity. No features were visible where the face should be; it was just a black shape, as though it had been cut out of the whiteness with a knife. Around the edges, the same wispy flow as the River swam and writhed like hair in water. It brought to mind how Lumi's Lights moved, and Tuomas remembered how he had imagined both of them as equal rivers, each flowing through the roots and branches which bound everything together.

He suddenly realised he hadn't shown any respect since arriving. He lowered his head, dragging Elin and Aki down with him.

"Thank you for coming to us, Horse-Riding One," he said in a small voice.

The Spirit leaned forwards a little. The horse tossed his head, sending a hazy mane whipping through the air.

"Why do you tremble, Son of the Sun? There are far worse things than myself. You have faced many of them already."

"Do you mean the trolls? The draugars?"

"Yes, and I dare say your own sister is more terrible than I have ever been."

"Then why am I afraid of you?" he asked.

"Your fear is not of me, only directed at me," replied the Spirit. "It is the human part of you – of all of you – which makes you feel such terror. But *you* are beyond that, Red Fox One. You are of us, too."

He began to circle them, featureless face always turned in their direction. Elin kept hold of Tuomas's hand.

"I know why you are come," the Spirit continued. "The Great Bear sent the draugars to me, combined with the souls of those they had stolen. And now it has charged you to separate them."

There were no eyes, but Tuomas could tell the focus had shifted to Aki. The little boy squirmed and hunched his shoulders.

"I want Mama," he whispered. "Tuomas, I don't want to!"

"It's going to be alright," Tuomas assured. "We've come this far. We can do this. *You* can do this. You're going to be the best mage ever, remember?"

Aki started to cry. Tuomas pulled him into a hug and glanced at the Spirit.

"Can't *I* do it?" he asked. "I know the Great Bear said it needed to be him, but…"

"No," said the Horse-Riding One. "You know the consequences of defying the Great Bear, Son of the Sun."

Tuomas thought fast. "Then can I at least stay with him? Please?"

The Spirit cocked both his humanlike head and horse head to the side in eerie synchronisation.

"I will allow that. But there is one more thing I must tell you. In order to use *taika* so intensely in a domain as formless as this, you must harness it from the depths of your souls. To do that, I will lead you through layers of truths, to the one at the very core of your beings. You will see things unknown to you, and they may not be pleasant to bear."

Aki shuddered and wiped his tears on his sleeve.

"Will it hurt?"

"Not in body," replied the Spirit. He stopped circling and the horse pawed at the ground. "In addition, Son of the Sun, I understood that the Ferry One has refused to help you back across the Night River. But you must return to close the gateway. I will personally reverse the direction of the weapons in the water, so they cannot prevent you from leaving the Deathlands. But for this, I ask a price. An offering."

Tuomas glanced over himself. "I gave my knives to the Earth Spirits…"

The human figure atop the horse's back leaned forward. "Your drum."

Tuomas balked. One hand flew to the instrument at his belt. Could he dare refuse?

But to be without this drum… Henrik's drum… He might not have made the instrument, but it was a part of him, a connection to all he had gone through…

He shuddered at the memory of Paavo throwing Lilja's old drum into the fire. She had turned feral, shrieked like a dying animal…

"Can't I give you something else?" he asked carefully.

"No," the Spirit said.

"But if I don't have it, how am I supposed to go into a trance and use my *taika*?"

"You do not need it. I sense the strength in you. You are a Spirit, Red Fox One; the Spirit of the Flames. Your power need not be directed by the physical anymore."

"But –"

"No. You have heard my offer. Do you accept?"

It wasn't a question.

Tuomas's heart hammered as his fingers fleeted over the drumskin. He recalled Henrik passing it to him on the morning he'd left Akerfjorden; thought of how familiar the weight had become in his hands. He had split an avalanche with it, survived the draugars with it, become a mage to its beat…

"Alright," he said.

"Tuomas, are you sure?" Elin whispered in his ear.

"I have to," he replied, equally quiet, though he knew the Spirit could hear every word.

Elin opened her mouth to protest, but Tuomas locked eyes with her, and she saw the raging emotion in them. So she gave a tiny nod and moved away.

Biting his lip so hard that he almost drew blood, he untied the leather thong which bound the drum to his belt. He looked at it fondly, caressed the symbols. Then he held it out and lowered his head.

The Horse-Riding One didn't move, but the drum lifted from Tuomas's hands. It hung between them and slowly began to disintegrate. First went the wooden frame, leaving the stretched skin hanging free; then it crinkled and split from the outside, like a crumbling log in the centre of a fire.

Tuomas grasped Aki tightly.

"Do not let go of me," he breathed.

The *taika* inside him pulsed and strained. He crashed to his knees. Elin grabbed his shoulders, but he barely felt her. She was somewhere far away; her voice sounded as though she was calling for him underwater.

The reindeer disappeared, then the huts, the hunters, the swirls for Lumi's Lights…

Tuomas screamed. It felt like his souls were going to rip apart.

The symbol of the Great Bear at the centre shattered, and the drum was gone.

The *taika* overwhelmed him. His eyes rolled shut, and then he fell, Aki beside him.

He spiralled down, then up, felt himself come apart and stitch back together again. The *taika* had wound everything too close and too tight. Inside his chest, his life-soul and body-soul whipped around each other, stinging like the bites of a million mosquitos. He couldn't find his form.

It was pain beyond pain.

The Spirit of Death had been wrong. He needed the drum. He wasn't strong enough to survive without it. And now it was gone...

Then, suddenly, it all started to recede.

He felt like a cup full of water, the contents slowly dripping out – no, being *drawn* out. The *taika* was settling; his souls coming to rest. Aki's hand was in his. And he sensed the Horse-Riding One, galloping in a circle, pulling the little boy's power free and spinning it into a rope. The rope became a lasso, entwined with the Spirit...

Tuomas opened his eyes to the deepest trance he had ever entered.

He wasn't formless, like he had been before, but stood in his own body. The white coat covered his torso, and Aki was there too, equally solid.

They were standing in the middle of a village. All the snow was gone, and the tundra was ablaze with colourful heathers and saxifrages. The Sun Spirit hadn't long set, and people thronged around the central fire pit, heaping logs into it for the evening. Behind the turf huts stood an enormous single mountain.

At the sight of it, Tuomas shuddered. No matter that it wasn't covered in ice; he would always recognise that place.

"Where are we?" Aki whispered.

"Einfjall," replied Tuomas. "This is Elin's home."

The laughter of children sounded. Near a wooden drying rack, laden with strips of reindeer meat, stood a group of boys and girls. They had stuck an antler into the ground and were taking turns to throw a lasso over it. All of them, as was the Einfjall custom, had a fringe cut across their brows, and their tunics were decorated with the symbol of the mountain.

"Can I play with them?" Aki asked hopefully.

At that moment, a woman walked past Tuomas, and her arm slipped straight through his body. She was carrying a drum.

"Aino?" he blurted. "Aino! It's me!"

She didn't turn around. At once, Tuomas understood.

"This isn't real," he said. "It's just part of the trance."

"How?" Aki frowned. "I can see them fine!"

"I know, but they're just shadows of things which have already happened."

He looked again at Aino. She was younger than he remembered.

Then, with a sneaking suspicion, his gaze returned to the children, and he drew in a gasp. Among them was a girl with brown eyes and raven black hair, tied into a braid. She was only about four years old, but her features were unmistakable.

It was Elin.

Movement sounded in the hut behind them, and a door opened. A woman stepped outside, inspecting a handful of bone needles as she walked away. Her clothes were embroidered with the reindeer head of Poro.

Aki gave a joyful gasp.

"Mama!" he cried, and went to run forward, but Tuomas kept tight hold of him.

Yes, it was Lilja, but like Elin and Aino, she was about ten years younger – eighteen at most. She still had her long sandy hair, strong build, crisp intelligent eyes. But there was a lightness to them which Tuomas had rarely seen, and when he glanced at her throat, there was no scar there.

This was long before Kari had made his demon. Before Aki was even born.

Right on cue, Sigurd stepped out of the hut, followed Lilja into the shadows. Tuomas and Aki hurried after them.

Out of sight, at the edge of the village, stood Lilja's sleigh and a couple of reindeer, tethered to a boulder. Beside it was a tent. She drew aside the flap.

"Kari?"

There was no answer.

"Is he still up on the mountain?" Sigurd asked.

"It seems so," replied Lilja. "Who knows when he'll be back? I've known him go into trance for hours."

Sigurd nodded, licked his lips. His eyes hadn't left her.

"Thank you for making that poultice for Alda," he said.

"You're welcome. Just tell her to rest her leg, and have Aino check up on her. And thank her for these, when she wakes up."

Lilja brandished the needles, then dropped them into a pouch on her belt. As she was tying it shut, Sigurd stepped close to her. He turned her around, raised a hand to her cheek. She didn't back away, but nerves fleeted across her face.

"You shouldn't," she said. "Someone might see."

"No, they won't," whispered Sigurd.

"It's wrong. You're married. You have a child already."

"Nothing will happen. Let me thank you for everything, Lilja. Just once."

He bent his head and kissed her.

Tuomas's mouth went dry. He tightened his grip on Aki as Sigurd gently pushed Lilja into the tent.

He blinked, and the scenery changed. Einfjall was gone; there was snow on the open tundra and the Sun Spirit hung low against the horizon. It was just after the end of the Long Dark. The same tent stood before them, but lit from the inside, and Tuomas could see two silhouettes against the tarp. One was a woman; even in profile, he knew it was Lilja. She was crying.

"I can't do it!"

"Yes, you can! Push! One more time!"

Terror froze Tuomas's heart. He knew that voice.

"Uncle Kari?" Aki whispered.

"Don't move," Tuomas breathed. He touched his chest, thought of the scar there, the knife, the demon leaning over him...

"Push, Lilja!" Kari ordered.

She let out a scream that echoed across the land. Then, a few seconds later, came the wail of an infant.

"It's a boy!" said Kari happily. "Lilja, look! It's a little boy!"

There was the motion of Kari cutting something, then he handed her a tiny bundle wrapped in a blanket. He threw his head back and exhaled with relief.

"It's a good thing we delivered that *shining one* in Akerfjorden," he laughed. "I might never have known what to do otherwise! Well done, Lilja. Are you alright? Can I fetch you anything?"

"No..." she panted, all her attention on the baby. "Hello, Aki."

Tuomas looked at Aki. His face had drained of blood, and he stared at the image of his family, mouth agape.

"That's me?" he asked in a tiny voice. "And my papa is Elin's papa?"

Tuomas gritted his teeth nervously.

"Yes."

The Sun Spirit rose, wheeled overhead with impossible speed. The tent disappeared, snow came and vanished, so fast that Tuomas could barely keep track of how often it changed. The very landscape shifted into something new: what he knew were hills became mountains, lakes dried up, rivers changed their courses like snakes writhing across the earth. And all the time, he and Aki rose up, into the sky, through the barrier to the World Above.

There were people down there, but fewer than he knew, all clustered in the north. The end of the Mustafjord was nothing but forest. Akerfjorden didn't exist yet.

Tuomas and Aki spun through the celestial labyrinth. The Sun and Moon Spirits hung on opposite sides, one golden, the other silver. Each held a Spirit in their light: a red fox and a white fox.

My sweet, beloved son, the Moon Spirit whispered into the silence. *You are everything I wished for. Such warmth, such beauty.*

Tuomas's couldn't believe what he was seeing. As she spoke, the Red Fox One shone like the brightest star. But it wasn't in fear or suspicion, or anything *he* had felt whenever he'd faced the Silver One. It was contentment, happiness, on a level which stunned him to the core.

Let me never part from you, Mother, was the reply, as warm and glowing as a fire.

Time spun around them. Far below, the World Between cycled through its seasons, but up here, nothing changed. Except for one day, when the white fox – Lumi – drifted over.

It is a lie, brother, she whispered, so insidiously that it turned Tuomas's stomach.

No, this entity wasn't Lumi. There was none of the gentleness and patience which he knew she had learned. This was more like the Spirit he'd pulled out of the sky, who had attacked Mihka, terrified generations of men and women. He sensed her pride, her iciness, colder than the darkest winter. Not an inch of humanity surrounded her.

What do you mean? the Red Fox One asked.

You are not the child of the Silver One, she replied. *I am. You are of the Sun Spirit.*

Tuomas sensed a pulse of hot alarm in the air.

How can you know such things?

The Golden One told me. The Silver One coveted you over me, so she switched us. Your mother raised me regardless, because she is a Spirit of brightness, not of darkness, like my mother. It is all a lie. She wants only what you represent, what she can never know. Heed me; I tell the truth!

The Red Fox One twisted around himself. At the same time, Tuomas felt the same Spirit moving inside his chest. He winced.

"Tuomas?" Aki whimpered. "Have you got a tummy ache?"

"No…" he gasped. "Just keep quiet, Aki, I need to listen…"

How can the Spirit of the Flames belong with anyone else but the greatest fire of all? continued the White Fox One. *You must get away from her. Punish her, for both of us!*

217

The stars shifted. Was it by days, or years? It was impossible to tell. In any case, the Sun Spirit reached her height, and the World Between basked in the glory of midsummer.

I do not wish to be with you any longer, Silver One, the Red Fox One was growling.

The Moon reached for him with her spidery fingers. As she touched him, Tuomas sensed them also stroking across his own skin: desperate, horrified.

No, my dear! I need you! I have cared for you and nurtured you! You owe everything you are to me!

And it is all lies!

My Golden sister told you?

No. She who is my equal told me.

The White Fox One? That selfish, cruel little girl! She seeks only to hurt me, sweet thing! Do not listen to her!

She spoke truth! You stole me from my mother! cried the Red Fox One. *She is the Daughter of the Moon, and I am the Son of the Sun! Admit it!*

The Silver One's invisible voice broke with sorrow. *My dear son...*

Admit it!

Tuomas spun around as the White Fox One appeared. There was such hatred in her movements; the aurora flashed bright red.

You could not bear the thought of me, but you will know me, she snarled. *You will never have him again! You will never steal him, or whisper lies to keep him near you! Let him return to the Golden One!*

What purpose will this serve? the Moon Spirit spat at her. *To spite me, hurt me?*

Precisely, Mother, replied the White Fox One. Her words were like perfect snowflakes, icicles so sharp they became daggers.

She sprang forward and seized the Red Fox One. The Moon Spirit tried to pull him back, but he fought against her.

Help me, sister! he shrieked.

The fabric of the realms trembled as equal powers clashed and wrenched around each other. Tuomas panicked; this had been exactly what it felt like just a few months ago, when he'd pulled away from Lumi and tore the hole in the sky...

I cannot free you from her! cried the White Fox One. *You must jump!*

Keep me from her!

Always, she replied coldly. *I would save you a thousand times.*

She yanked him out of the Silver One's grasp.

There was a blinding flash – Tuomas and Aki spun away. He saw the Red Fox One plummeting towards the World Between: a drop of pure Sunlight. He became the orb of a life-soul and shot into a hut in the middle of a human village. Immediately afterwards, a newborn baby wailed.

Tuomas stared at the White Fox One in horror. All this time, he had believed he'd chosen to leave the World Above to get away from the Moon Spirit. But that had only been half the story.

Lumi had convinced him to do it. That devious whispered truth was what had started *everything*.

The surroundings dripped away like a sheet of melting ice, until all that was left was whiteness. Tuomas and Aki clung to each other, shaken, unable to move. Then solid ground appeared underneath them, and they opened their eyes.

Chapter Twenty-Three

Tuomas gasped for breath. His mind spun; his body felt leaden, as though it had been filled with stones. His souls were still hovering somewhere above him, unsettled.

Elin's face appeared. He tried to focus on her, but she was too blurred...

"Are you hurt?" she was asking. "Tuomas? Can you hear me?"

He couldn't move his mouth. Where even was his mouth? He tried to raise a hand, to feel for it, and accidentally smacked himself in the nose.

"Take your time," said the Horse-Riding One. "You travelled deeper than any mage has ever dared."

Tuomas turned his head and spotted Aki. He rolled over, checked him as best he could.

"Are you alright?" he slurred.

"Mmm," Aki groaned.

Tuomas let his lungs fill with air, then eased himself into a sitting position. Elin wrapped an arm around his back to help.

"What did you see?" she asked.

He rested against her weakly and shook his head.

"Lumi. She..."

He stopped himself. He needed to collect his thoughts. And the first who he needed to speak to was his sister herself.

His sister, who had convinced him to jump out of the sky...

Elin suddenly stared at him.

"Your eyes," she said. "They've changed colour."

"What?"

"They're not blue anymore; they're like Lumi's. But not green... Yellow. Like fire."

Tuomas touched his cheeks, and paused in alarm when he saw his fingers. The faint glow he had noticed in the sleigh had intensified. Now, it was as though every hair on his body was brushed with golden light. And his heart felt warm behind his ribs, warmer than it could possibly be...

"You grow, Son of the Sun," said the Horse-Riding One. "Do you see now? No living thing can know life before first undergoing a death. This has been yours."

"And mine," Aki muttered, with a clarity which stunned Tuomas. He looked straight at Elin.

"You're my sister," he whispered.

Elin stiffened. "I... well... Half-sister."

For a long moment, Aki didn't react. But then a smile broke across his face, creased the scars on his cheeks. Tuomas hadn't seen him so happy since the time when he'd been reunited with his mother.

The Spirit of Death approached. In his hands was a lasso, shimmering as though it was made from stardust. But it was something more formidable than that: pure *taika*. The same as Tuomas had seen in the trance.

"I told you that uncomfortable truths would come," the Spirit said. "Now you both know your origins. And while you drifted through it all, I have twisted your power with my own."

He leaned down, took hold of Aki and pulled him to his feet. He waited until the little boy was able to stand, then passed him the rope.

"Are you ready?" he asked.

Aki trembled, but nodded.

Without another word, the Horse-Riding One raised his arms. At once, a swathe of mist bloomed forward. It curled around them, feeling and creeping with a mind of its own. Aki drew in a fearful breath.

"You can do it," Tuomas urged.

Aki looked over his shoulder.

Tuomas was struck by how like Lilja he was. Not only in appearance anymore, but in strength. There was a hardness to his eyes which hadn't been there before; the empty air sang with his *taika* and the rope glowed in his hands. Tuomas remembered detecting it when he'd been with the draugars: so simple, yet so bold: the open tundra, laughter, the feeling of his mother's arms.

Lilja and Kari hadn't been exaggerating, and it was no surprise that the monsters had targeted him. He might be a child, but he was so powerful.

Souls began to appear in the mist. Around each one hung a black stain, and as soon as he saw it, Tuomas sensed decay and darkness from between the Worlds. Elin grasped him tighter.

"Are those the souls which were stolen?" she whispered.

He nodded. "And the draugars."

Aki reached for his power as though he'd been doing it all his life, then threw the lasso.

It landed around the souls, and with a single tug, the misty coils were broken. The black marks disappeared like ash being washed away, floated aimlessly in the air. The Spirit of Death pulled the fractured draugars out of reach, one by one, until all were free. Then he bound them in his lap.

"Perfect," he said. He took the rope from Aki and broke it in two.

Aki gasped as the *taika* shot back into him, but recovered and hurried to Tuomas. The souls drifted after him, and Tuomas felt an overwhelming sense of relief emanating from them, as though heavy rocks had been lifted away. There were no features besides their light, but Tuomas caught a sense of the last people they had been: Eevi, Sisu… and Paavo.

His heart wrenched as his brother drew close. He extended a hand, but just as in the trance, he couldn't touch it. It was a thing not of the physical.

Paavo's soul pulsed pure white, and disappeared into the air.

"Where did it go?" asked Elin.

"They are free from the draugars now," replied the Horse-Riding One. "Most of them wish to remain here for their rest. But that one heads to your sister, Son of the Sun."

Tuomas staggered to his feet. Elin kept hold of him until she was sure he could take his own weight. Then he bowed to the Spirit.

"Thank you."

"There is no gratitude for me, Red Fox One. Are you still afraid?"

"No."

"Then my work is done. Do you see? Your fear was never for me, or for my realm, or even death itself. It is no better or worse than that which you have already known. Your fear was for the *living deaths*, and what they would force you to confront. For a human, that is the worst prospect of all. And a part of you is still human, Tuomas Sun-Soul."

A shudder passed through Tuomas's body. The words struck a chord in him deeper than he had ever thought possible. It was exactly how he felt, condensed into simple speech: the whirlwind of pain which had engulfed him and not let him rest.

"I will never forget this," he said softly.

The Spirit let out a small laugh; so quiet, he thought he might have imagined it.

"I know. Now, the three of you must leave this place. Close the gateway you opened so long ago."

Tuomas nodded, but paused when Aki took hold of his hand. He glanced at the little boy, at his crisp blue eyes. So like Lilja's. So much like…

"Wait," he said. "If I may, there's one more thing I'd like to do."

The Horse-Riding One cocked both of his heads. "And what is that?"

Tuomas took a deep breath. "I want to ask you to free Kari's soul."

Silence hung between them. Tuomas stood his ground, tried to find something to focus on in the pitch-black face, but there weren't even contours to suggest a nose or cheekbones.

"The wicked mage?" the Spirit said. "I bound him at the behest of the Great Bear."

"I know," Tuomas said carefully. "But he wasn't always wicked."

"He committed unspeakable and unnatural acts."

"He also saved lives, and gave up all his hopes and dreams for others."

Elin came to Tuomas's side.

"Are you sure this is a good idea?" she whispered. "He's evil."

"He *was*. For a short while," Tuomas argued. "But not always."

The Horse-Riding One took a step closer. The mane waved in a wind which Tuomas couldn't feel.

"Come with me."

Tuomas blinked. There was a warmth to the voice which he hadn't heard before. It almost sounded like satisfaction. But he didn't pause to question it; he needed to act fast, before he could convince himself this wasn't the right thing to do.

He let go of Aki and followed the Spirit across the empty white land. There was no way to mark the distance; each step felt like a mile while scarcely moving. But soon, something loomed out of the void.

It was a cairn of pale rocks, similar to the one which had imprisoned Kari while alive in the Earth Spirit caves. But this time, there was no man inside, only a shining soul.

Even from where he stood, Tuomas could sense the remnants of Kari's life, like the faint taste of berries washed in water. They pushed into his mind and took shape there: love and loyalty to Lilja and Aki, the desire to help as many as possible… and how that wish had twisted against itself to form something dark and arrogant.

"If evil comes into existence, it lies in the hearts of humans," said the Horse-Riding One. "You shall never find an evil tree, or an evil animal. Even the predators of your realm – the wolves and eagles and bears – they only make their kills to survive, to feed their young. Never with an agenda. That is why I ensure those souls which go to humans who choose such a path… they do not leave here. The life-soul may pass on to a new being, but the body-soul remains under my watch."

The Spirit drew closer, and laid one of his hands on Tuomas's shoulder.

"This is your choice, Son of the Sun," he continued. "The draugars, your enemies across eternity, are contained with me. This is your enemy across this lifetime. Will you have him remain here, too?"

Tuomas licked his lips, then shook his head.

"No."

With that, the Spirit raised a hoof and kicked the cairn. It fell apart, sending stones and *taika* spilling across the ground.

The soul inside rose slowly, as though unsure. Tuomas swept his tail nervously as it floated close to him. If he squinted, he almost fancied he could see it taking the shape of Kari's face. That face which had leered over him, haunted his nightmares...

He lowered his head – not in forgiveness, but acceptance.

The soul let out a pulse of light, then danced into the sky and across the Night River.

"You knew I'd do this, didn't you?" Tuomas asked quietly.

"I knew it was a possibility, and one which I hoped you would take," said the Horse-Riding One. "Things, events, people, Spirits... very few are as they seem. Accompanying the boy here to free those souls was not the only reason the Great Bear sent *you* to me, Son of the Sun."

Tuomas blinked, and touched his chest.

"It was to free myself," he realised.

Without another word, the Spirit let go of him, turned with a flick of the tail. Tuomas watched as he trotted away, growing smaller and more blurred, until he vanished.

Tuomas, Aki and Elin stood alone in the middle of the abyss.

Overcome, he fell to his knees and wept. Elin ran over and put her arms around him. Aki wormed between them as best he could. None of them spoke, just held each other, and bent their heads as a plethora of souls drifted around them like butterflies.

Chapter Twenty-Four

Tuomas didn't know how long they stayed there. There was no sense of time, of existence, save for the touch of Elin and Aki. He focused on their breathing, the sound of their heartbeats, deafening in the empty silence.

Soon enough, he managed to pull his sobs under control, and got to his feet. Elin didn't let go of him for a moment.

"Are you alright?" she asked.

He nodded, wiped his cheeks on his coat sleeve. The white fur, so pure and spotless, looked almost dull now, against his shimmering skin. It was similar to how Lumi's body glistened, like the light hitting a million snowflakes.

His stomach clenched. What was he supposed to think of her now, knowing what he did?

He needed to speak to her.

"Come on," he muttered. "We'd better get back."

They walked in the direction they had first come from. Tuomas squinted as he placed each step. The whiteness wasn't blinding, but the sheer lack of any landmarks made his head spin.

After a while, a black smudge appeared on the horizon. They stumbled towards it, and reached the bank of the Night River. The Ferry Spirit was nowhere to be seen – but, as promised by the Horse-Riding One, the glints of knives and needles were all pointing the other way.

"Look!" Elin said.

Tuomas peered in the direction she was pointing. Far away, on what he assumed was the other side of the River, a dancing aurora filled the sky.

"It's your sister," said Aki with a small smile. "She's showing us how to get back."

Tuomas pursed his lips at the sight.

"How are we supposed to get there?" Elin asked.

Tuomas glanced up and down the shore, but found no similar vessels to the one which had brought them across. He reached for his drum, to try and split the water like he had with the avalanche. But his hand just knocked against an empty belt.

His heart sank.

"I think we'll have to swim."

Aki grabbed his wrist frantically. "I can't swim!"

"It will be alright, I won't let you sink," Tuomas promised. "Just keep tight hold of me and you'll be fine. Do you trust me?"

Aki gazed at him, eyes wide with fear. But then he nodded.

Tuomas grasped his hand, took a deep breath, and leapt into the River.

It was deeper than he'd thought; his feet didn't touch the bottom, and when he opened his eyes to look, all he saw was blackness. He kicked towards the surface, found Elin beside him, clutching her arrows so they wouldn't be swept away.

"Get on my back!" he snapped at Aki, then reached for Elin. Water had taken her away once before; he wasn't going to lose her the same way again.

"Just go towards Lumi!" he said.

They began to move. The River felt thick, as though they were trying to swim through mud. Aki's weight pushed Tuomas down and he spat out a mouthful of water. It tasted rank, like something which had flowed through a grave.

A current wrapped itself around their ankles. Feeling it, Elin hauled Tuomas away before it could pull them under. The threatening glints of the weapons passed inches from their faces. Amazingly, every time they brought their arms down to paddle past, the needles and knives shifted at the last moment, so not a single point pierced their skin.

Tuomas glanced at a particularly intimidating blade and sent silent thanks to the Spirit of Death. It was no wonder the Ferry Spirit had said they were used to block any rogue souls from escaping. If the weapons had been left facing the other direction, there was no way the three of them could have gotten through.

The waves began to rise. It was slow at first, but then they towered overhead. Tuomas switched his grip from Elin's hand to her wrist, so they couldn't be ripped apart.

"Hold on tight, Aki!" he gasped.

He tried to keep his eyes on Lumi's glow, but it still seemed miles away, and he was tiring…

Something snagged his foot. He yelped in shock and stopped dead in the water.

"What is it?" spluttered Elin.

Tuomas tried to kick himself free, but the thing had wound around him fast.

"I think it's one of the Ferry Spirit's nets!" he said.

Elin pulled a knife from her belt and dived. He felt her hand on his ankle, followed by the jagged sawing pressure of her blade. After several long moments, the net drifted free, and Elin reappeared.

"Thanks," he coughed.

"Thank me later!" Elin snapped, and took his wrist again. "Come on!"

She had hardly finished speaking when a massive wave slammed over them.

They cartwheeled though the water, surrounded by darkness, cut here and there by the flashes of needles. The current snatched at them like invisible hands.

Tuomas almost panicked – it felt so much like a hundred slimy fingers, pulling his flesh, trying to tear it apart in search of his *taika*…

He managed to get control before he let out any precious breath. There were no draugars here.

He pulled Aki close and tried to find his bearings, but he couldn't tell which way was up or down. He opened his eyes, found himself floating in eternal night.

A small knife drifted past him. Even though the current was raging, it was still, pointing steadfastly in the same direction.

Tuomas looked at it, then a needle next to it. That was aimed the same way.

He didn't waste a moment and kicked, pulling Elin behind him. Their heads finally broke the surface.

"Follow the weapons!" he wheezed. "They're pointing towards the bank!"

Elin was too exhausted to reply. They swam as hard as they could. Aki's arms tightened around Tuomas's shoulders.

"I'm scared!" he cried.

Tuomas didn't have the strength to comfort him. It took all his focus to just stay above the waves.

Then the water dipped, and relief filled his heart. The grey shore was within sight. And standing at the edge, blazing white and green, was Lumi.

It gave him and Elin a final burst of energy. The ashy sand appeared under their knees.

Halfway out of the River, Tuomas collapsed, trembling all over. Aki climbed off his back, fell beside him. Lumi drew the Lights into herself, then a group of Earth Spirits ran forward and lifted Tuomas into their arms. He noticed more of them carrying Elin and Aki, both gasping for breath.

The last thing he saw before his eyes closed was Lumi, walking beside him, and water cascading down her face.

Chapter Twenty-Five

The Earth Spirits took the three of them back into the caves, with her bringing up the rear. She allowed them to lead the way, winding down tunnel after tunnel, until they arrived in a huge underground chamber. The floor was covered with spongy moss and autumn leaves, but she didn't sink into it, just walked over the top with no weight. Torches lit carvings and paintings on the high stone walls. Her eyes lingered over one depicting the Great Bear Spirit. It stretched from floor to ceiling, painted in so many white dots, it would have taken an entire human lifetime to count them all.

Tuomas, Aki and Elin were laid upon some white reindeer skins beside a fire in the centre of the cavern. Then the Earth Spirits swept their hands over the three of them, and all the moisture of the Night River evaporated, until they were completely dry. Finally, the one who had greeted them raised its arms, and an array of food appeared.

Thank you, she said.

The task is complete, replied the Earth Spirit, and tapped its belt, where Tuomas's knives hung. *Allow them to awaken, regain their strength, then leave this place, White Fox One. There is still much to be done.*

The Spirits took their leave, and she headed to a spot against the wall furthest from the flames. Her tail swept the ground and sent a wave of green and purple towards the ceiling.

She looked at it wistfully. Soon, she would be back in the World Above, able to fill the sky with these wonderful colours. The souls would swarm around her again, as they had for so long.

She recalled the one which had approached her from the Deathlands. She had known, in that moment, that Aki had done his job. She had greeted it, held it close, told it that she would be with it soon. But it hadn't appeared worried, or even insisted on remaining with her. Its focus had all been for Tuomas.

Then she had realised who the soul had belonged to: his brother, Paavo.

She watched Tuomas as he lay there, ears twitching in his sleep. He was aglow, as though a fire burned just beneath his human flesh. The power radiating from him was incredible: truly a match for her own now. It stunned her how he was able to still function in that body. How long could it be before his lungs were overcome and heart stopped beating?

She felt the vibrations of the tiny invisible aspects which made everything around her. Like in the World Between, it was trembling; she could sense the magic seeping through the cracks as the realms bent and warped in a way they were never meant to. But down here, it was stronger. The roots of the great tree were decaying first; she had seen it the moment they had leapt across the gateway. It would continue until she and Tuomas completed their tasks.

She tried to reassure herself. The end was in sight now. Just a few more moments – nothing against the eternity she knew – and it would be half-done. Then it was her turn.

More water formed on her chest. The end...

Tuomas rubbed his face wearily and sat up. She twitched, wanting to approach him, but she didn't dare. The flames were still burning strongly, and it was too hot for her.

Water streamed along her arms. She flicked it away, and it transformed into snowflakes.

The movement caught Tuomas's attention. She stiffened as his eyes settled on her. Yellows and golds were chasing each other through his irises.

"Well done," she said. "They are free."

"Paavo left. Did he come to you?"

"Yes. I sent him to await me with the others in the World Above. As I did with… the other one. I am proud of you."

Tuomas didn't move. She surveyed him without so much as a twitch, but inside, confusion pulled at her. She had seen him look upon her with fear, care, even love… but never like this.

Then, she sensed the tangle of thoughts in his mind, read them as though they were her own. She glanced at the mural on the wall behind him: the Sun and Moon Spirits, with two foxes beneath them.

"You know what I saw, don't you?" Tuomas asked. "I *was* happy with the Silver One. And you convinced me to pull away from her."

She sighed. There was no point in denying it.

"Perhaps we should speak somewhere a little more private," she said, then turned down the nearest tunnel. Tuomas staggered after her. She cast a faint trail of Lights as she walked, then dryly reminded herself that he wouldn't need them to follow. His eyes were not those of a human anymore.

They emerged into the neighbouring chamber. It was smaller than the other one, and completely dark, but the two of them glowed so brightly that it didn't matter. The aurora drifted overhead and wound itself about the stalactites on the ceiling.

"What happened to your drum?" she asked.

"The Horse-Riding One asked for it as an offering," said Tuomas. His voice rang heavy with sadness. "Lumi… why did you do that? There was no need to, was there? Everything would have been fine if I'd stayed with the Silver One."

"It was a long time ago," she said tightly.

"I was happy," Tuomas argued. "Why did you do it?"

"I was angry."

"That's it?"

"Do you doubt my impulsiveness?"

"No. I've seen it too often," Tuomas said coolly.

She didn't blink. "Are you afraid of me?"

"No, I'm not," he replied. "But I'm disappointed. You started all of this."

"How do you arrive at that conclusion?"

"If you hadn't done that, I never would have jumped out of the sky. The Great Mage never would have been born, the Northern Edge never opened, the draugars never unleashed. All that, because you were *angry?*"

She flattened her ears. "I had no foresight of such things."

"What does that matter?" snapped Tuomas. "You still did it!"

"The Spirit of the Winter Winds lays snow upon the mountaintops. If she chooses to lay more than normal, an avalanche occurs and an entire woodland dies. Do you think the Spirit of the Trees feels emotion because of that loss? No. He rebuilds. Such is the cycle of life and death."

"You can't use that as an excuse, Lumi," said Tuomas. "That's natural. Nothing either of us has ever done has been natural. If it was, you wouldn't be standing here, and there wouldn't be a massive gash in the sky."

Her hands curled into fists and the Lights took on a red tint. But before she could argue, defeat settled over her like a film of creeping ice. He was right. She was only contesting him

235

because to be prideful and rash was her first response. But if being among him this winter had taught her anything, it was that a Spirit could be more. He was living proof of it: an eternal, formless, uncontainable entity… somehow contained in a body which felt and loved.

"How could you have done that?" Tuomas demanded. "This is all your fault!"

"Fault has no place among Spirits. It was one occurrence which led to others."

"And nothing more? Can't you see how much that knowledge hurts me?"

"She stole you. Even your own mother warned you against listening to her!"

"Yes, my mother, who told *you* the truth. And *you* were the one who chose to act on it, set up this feud between them. I know my mother missed me, but she was still kind to you! You were the one who told me it's better to endure than to sacrifice, but that's what you did from the start! Everything I've been through was because you couldn't bear to see the Moon Spirit happy with me!"

He spat the words out like darts. She heard the betrayal and disbelief in them, as though they were physically pressing against her. But the next ones were so cold, it almost sounded like herself from long ago.

"Would it shock you if I told you I wasn't surprised, though? This is *you*, after all. The Spirit who rips out the souls of innocents to teach them a lesson."

"And the Spirit who ripped out *your* soul in order to save it from oblivion," she snarled back. "How dare you speak like that to me!"

Tuomas didn't flinch. "I will speak to you as your equal, White Fox One."

Her anger transformed the Lights blood red. She went to rush forward and pin him against the wall, terrorise and intimidate him... but her feet refused to move.

Hadn't she made things terrible enough for him already? Hadn't he been the one to tell her that she need not resort to cruelty? And, with more weight than the words his breath formed, did she not sense his pain? It struck her deeper than she believed was possible: a raw, uncontained *human* pain.

Whatever she did in these next few precious moments would define how he would see her for the rest of time.

She closed her eyes, lowered her hands, let the aurora return to its cool greens and blues.

"I did not wish to hurt you," she said. "I wished only to hurt my mother, avenge myself upon her. What was so awful about *me*, that made her cast me away? Perhaps that was the very thing which gave me the potential for such coldness, Tuomas. I only wanted you to be happy, where you belonged, with the Golden One. I wanted to give you the choice neither of us ever had."

As she spoke, water covered her skin. It fell from her hair, ears, face, arms... her starry dress clung to her as though she had leapt into the Night River. There was such warmth welling inside her. It ached to behold it, burned as it pushed against the snowy form she stood in. It took all her focus not to fall to her knees. Never had she felt it this strong... such love for her sibling...

Then she gasped. More water flowed down her cheeks – but this time, it came from her eyes. She was *crying*.

So human. Such a perfect fusion of the mortal and immortal. If only he knew...

It was time he knew.

"You must listen to me," she said. "I have something to tell you. Something I decided not to reveal until you returned from the Deathlands. It is inescapable; you would have found out sooner or later, so it is best you hear it from me."

Anxiety darkened Tuomas's face. He reached to his neck and toyed with the bone fox head which hung there.

"Go ahead," he said. Still, his voice was so guarded, so saturated with anguish. The sound tore through her as none other ever had.

"You are to close this gateway. I am to close the tear in the sky. But there is one more price to pay. When both are closed, there is nothing to keep you in the World Between. When I ascend, you must come with me. And you will never return."

Tuomas blinked, then frowned, then staggered backwards until he hit the wall. His ears flattened against his scalp, and behind him, sparks flickered at the tip of his tail.

"*What?*" he blurted. "Are you saying I'm going to die?"

She gave a single forlorn nod.

"It is the decision of the Great Bear, not me. You were only allowed to be reborn so you could close the Northern Edge. You cannot be of two forms any longer – of human and Spirit at the same time. It will risk all this being repeated in another life."

Tuomas stared at her in disbelief.

"No… It can't be!"

"It is. I am so sorry."

Tuomas's brows suddenly lowered and he slammed his palm against the tip of a low-hanging stalactite.

"How is that fair?" he snapped. "I'm doing what was asked of me! And this is my reward? I'm only fifteen!"

"You are much older than that."

"The *Spirit* is, but *I'm* not! I have a life! I have Akerfjorden and Lilja and Elin..."

His voice broke and tears dropped onto his coat.

"Why does it have to be now?" he cried. "Why not in another fifty years? Why can't I have my life?"

She raised a hand towards him. "Look at yourself. This body will not hold you for much longer."

"This is wrong, Lumi! It's not fair, and it's wrong! How can you just stand there? Didn't you even try to defend me?"

"It is not my decision, and there is nothing I can do to prevent it. The Great Bear governs us all. Tuomas, you have been into the World Above. Never mind the Golden One and Silver One; you have been at peace there, with *me*. Why are you afraid?"

"With you?" Tuomas repeated. "How can I be at peace there now, knowing what I know?"

She gasped as though he had driven a blade through her belly.

"Please, listen to me. I am sorry, for everything I have brought down upon you. Do not fear me. Please... I would not have you be afraid of me. Not now, not ever again. I would never hurt you!"

"I'm not scared of dying," Tuomas snarled. "You and the Horse-Riding One have seen to that. And a part of me wants to go back there, be free from all this. But *you've* never been alive... not like me. You don't know..."

A gentle breeze drifted through the caves from somewhere far away, lifted the fine white strands of her hair.

"I may not have ever experienced life as you would," she said slowly, "but I do know. I have listened to the stories of souls, more times than anyone could count, since the very first night I threw my Lights across the sky. And you brought me down here. You showed me what it is to feel emotions. Even as they pain me, I will always be grateful for that."

Tuomas put a hand against the wall to steady himself. Deep within the fur on his tail, a tiny flame burned.

"I should stay," he protested. "I need to protect the people. I'm Akerfjorden's mage now. Who else is going to help them?"

"Another will come. They always do," she replied. "You must return with me, Tuomas, let the Spirit of Passage take your souls and deliver them into my Lights. It is the only way."

Tuomas shook his head, but she could tell it was no longer in defiance. It was defeat.

He had been raised among the people, who revered nature and took comfort from its cycle never being broken. Death was simply a state which one needed to pass through before they returned as new life. To know he would never come back as a tree, or an animal, or another human? That must be among the worst things for a mortal to bear.

Tuomas sank to the floor. She approached him. With every step, she felt his *taika*, roaring like an inferno just behind his flesh. But it didn't hurt her, like normal fire. It was the Spirit within him, speaking to the Spirit within her.

"This is not what I wanted for you," she said. "The Great Bear allows you to make your choice about returning to the Silver One. But no matter what happens, I shall be with you. And the soul which was Paavo awaits you, too. It wishes not to be reborn until it sees you again."

She tentatively touched his shoulder, but he pulled away.

"Don't."

"Tuomas…"

"No. I need you to leave me alone for a while, Lumi. And please don't tell anyone what you've told me."

"You have my word."

"I just… I don't know if I can leave. I want to stay." He paused, drew in a shaking breath. "I want to stay with Elin."

She closed her eyes. She didn't need to remind him that such a thing was impossible. She could tell from the despair in his voice that he knew well enough. And she knew that if she also had a human heart, it would be breaking for him.

Chapter Twenty-Six

When Tuomas returned to the other cavern, he found Elin and Aki awake, and tucking into the food which had been left. Elin looked up, wiped some cloudberry juice from her lips.

"There you are! I was wondering where you'd gone."

"Sorry. I was talking with Lumi," replied Tuomas

"Spirit stuff?"

"You could say that."

He seated himself on the opposite side of the hearth, grasped a birch burl cup and filled it with tea. Aki crawled over and laid his head against his chest.

"I did it, Tuomas!" he beamed. "I got rid of the draugars! Mama was right, I am going to be the best mage ever, aren't I? Hey, what's the matter? You've been crying."

Tuomas quickly shook his head. "No, I haven't. I'm just tired."

"Didn't you sleep well? I did. I haven't slept that good in my whole life! I didn't even have any dreams. Did you have dreams, Elin?"

She swallowed a piece of ptarmigan meat. "Not really."

"I'm glad you're my sister," Aki carried on, with a wide smile. "Why didn't you like me, if you knew you were my sister?"

Elin hesitated, glanced between him and Tuomas. Tuomas shook his head and she took a hurried swig of tea.

"I just… was scared," she said in the end.

Tuomas shrugged. That was accurate enough.

Aki stuffed a salmon cake into his mouth and gazed around at the paintings on the walls.

"This is so pretty!" he exclaimed. "Look! There's the Great Bear Spirit! Is that really how big it is?"

"Bigger," said Tuomas. "This is where your mother and I stayed, last time we came here together. There weren't as many... empty areas, though."

Elin recognised his meaning immediately.

"When do we need to leave?" she asked.

"As soon as possible."

They finished the rest of their meal in silence, eating until their bellies could bear no more. Then they tidied themselves and walked into the tunnel. For a moment, Tuomas worried about getting lost, but he found himself remembering the way, and the light from his body transformed the stony walls orange.

Elin's hand knocked against his. Before he could think too much about it, he took hold of her.

Tears threatened to fall, but he blinked hard to keep them at bay. He had only just repaired his friendship with her. How could he turn away now, when she was one of the few people left who cared?

They emerged back into the forest. The air was heavy with autumnal dampness, and the sky was dark, with the promise of dawn lingering in the east. Lumi waited beside a crumbling tree, and behind her stood a crowd of Earth Spirits – more than Tuomas had ever seen. They extended in every direction, all around the lake: a mass of leaves and nuts and mushrooms in human shape. Here and there, white reindeer stood among them, crowned with antlers so spectacular, no beast in the World Between would have been able to bear them.

Elin bowed so low, her arrows almost fell out of her quiver. Aki did the same.

"I'm sorry," Tuomas said, as loud as he could. "I was selfish, and stupid, and you were the ones who paid the price. But now I will set things right. I promise."

The Spirit closest to him stepped forward. It was the one to whom he had given his knives. His heart wrenched at the sight of them on its belt. Until a few hours ago, he might have comforted himself with the idea that he could always make more, and a new drum as well. But not now.

Empty realisation stabbed through him. No more knives or drum... even his blue eyes were gone. Was there anything left of who he had been?

"You are forgiven, Red Fox One," the Spirit said. "We bid you farewell, all of you. Let your work be done."

Lumi came to Tuomas's side. He hesitated when she looked at him – he was about to perform the feat which was his reason for living.

"What do I do?" he whispered. "I've never left this World under my own power before."

"Think of the World Between, in the greatest detail as you can manage," she replied. "Do not just see it, but feel it, smell it. Your *taika* will do the rest. And then, on the way out, close the gateway."

She extended her hands to Elin and Aki.

"I shall take you both back. Tuomas, follow us."

"Won't the Sun Spirit be up?" Elin asked nervously.

"Day is coming here. It will be ending there," said Lumi.

As soon as they were holding onto her, she rose into the air. Aki shrieked, but in no time at all, the three of them were swallowed by the clouds. Tuomas sensed them pass through the Northern Edge, like a drop falling into a lake.

He took a deep breath, then closed his eyes. It felt so strange to not be working magic with a drum. He ached for its weight, for the motion of bringing the hammer down on the skin... but then the Spirit of Death's truth floated before him.

He didn't need it. The drum was not his weapon, nor his shield. It was only a channel. None of his power laid inside it, only inside himself.

He drew the Northlands into his mind: the melting snow, blue skies, the brown stripes which laced the papery bark of birch trees; the warbling yelps of a territorial ptarmigan. He felt the growing warmth of the Sun Spirit on his skin. The aroma of sautéed reindeer drifted by his nose. The boughs whispered to each other as they swayed in the breeze, shaking off their feathery ice crystals as spring came rolling in...

His souls began to loosen and his *taika* stretched out like roots searching for water. It was majestic, a fire spreading through his muscles, along every blood vessel, until he felt nothing but heat and light.

His feet left the ground.

His heart beat frantically, but he kept his concentration, focused as hard as he could on the image of the World Between. It was coming closer...

The air became crisper as the dampness of autumn faded away. He spiralled through the opening. As he passed it, he grasped the sides – with both hands and *taika* – and pulled it together. He spun his power as though it were an ethereal thread, closed the gate, bound it shut like the stitches over a wound.

The effort wrenched at his souls. Splitting the avalanche had been nothing compared to this. He was moving entire Worlds with a feeble human body...

The last tear in the gateway closed.

He flew into the air, then came down hard, flat on his back. All the breath was knocked from his lungs. He lay gasping, face crumpled in pain.

"Tuomas?"

Elin's voice drifted towards him. She was close, but still sounded a million miles away.

He eased his eyes open to a dusky sky, fast turning to twilight. Beneath him was the ice of the Northern Edge. And at his side, where the entrance should have been, now there was only regular lake water in the middle of the hole.

He had done it.

Chapter Twenty-Seven

Elin helped Tuomas to his feet. As soon as he was standing, Aki hugged him. He patted the little boy's head, then glanced around to get his bearings.

To his relief, the reindeer were unharmed, still tethered to the boulder where they had left them. He knew no wolves would have come this far north, but in any case, that would have been the last thing they needed.

Now they were back in the World Between, everything was reversed once again. The autumnal trees had reverted to the snowy boughs of early spring, and the last of the light was fading. Overhead, the rip stretched from north to south. It didn't seem to have grown, but the sight still came as a shock to Tuomas. He had forgotten how jarring it was. He tasted it: a strong metallic edge, like blood and rotten things, fading to pure nothingness. Never mind that one gateway was closed, the second wound still lay open.

Lumi looked at it too, and the cascade of *taika* reflected in her eyes.

"Well done. You did your part," she muttered. "It is my turn next."

"Not now," Tuomas argued. "Please. It's lasted for this long. Let's get Aki and Elin back to Akerfjorden first."

She read the meaning behind his words at once. It wasn't just about leaving his friends stranded in the middle of the tundra. If they caught up with the convoy, it would give him the chance to bid farewell.

Water flowed from her eyes.

"To Akerfjorden," she said, barely audible.

Aki grasped Tuomas's hand as they walked back across the ice. Only Lumi moved unhindered by the thin patches, and soon reached the bank. Tuomas held out his free arm to keep his balance. The fur on the bottom of his shoes gave a wonderful grip on snow, but the meltwater saturated them.

After several nerve-wracking moments, he stepped onto solid ground and ushered Aki towards the sleighs.

"Alright, in we go," he said.

"Silence!" Lumi hissed suddenly. Her ears swirled and a ball of Lights formed around her hand.

Then Tuomas heard it too: a long, low groan.

"Oh, no," he breathed.

Elin looked at him, and silent realisation passed between them. She whipped an arrow onto her bow, held it ready to draw. Tuomas ran to the sleigh and grabbed his own. But even as he nocked it, dread settled around his heart. What good would arrows do?

On the hill in front of the lake, the earth heaved, and the troll flung itself into the air. It came sliding down the slope like a boulder, its blade glinting viciously in the twilight. Its mouth was smeared with blood and pale tufts of reindeer fur.

Lumi flung a jet of green at the giant. She struck it in the stomach and knocked it back a little. At once, Tuomas and Elin loosed their arrows. His embedded uselessly in the troll's chest, but Elin's pierced its eye with perfect accuracy.

It fell to its knees so heavily, the ground shook.

"Tuomas, now!" Lumi snapped, leaping behind the sleighs for cover. The reindeer tried to bolt, but the rope pulled tight.

Tuomas shouldered his bow, held out his hands as she'd shown him, and reached for his *taika*. Warmth welled between his palms, fire sputtered, transformed into a ball of white light. But it was no larger than a berry, and sputtered out as soon as he tried to throw it. His chest stung... it was too much power; his body couldn't contain it...

He panicked. The troll was coming straight at them, arrow still protruding from its eye.

"It's not working!" he shouted. "Run!"

Elin didn't argue. She grabbed Aki, then cut the reindeers' ropes with one of her knives. The animals bolted. The troll snatched at them, but they jumped over the stony hand and disappeared into the tundra. Snarling in frustration, the monster instead slammed its fist onto the closest sleigh and crushed it to splinters.

Tuomas, Lumi, Elin and Aki broke into a sprint. He didn't even know how they could escape. There were no trees or bushes this deep in the north, nothing to hide behind. And without sleighs or skis, they wouldn't get far.

He needed to do something...

He tried to summon the Sunlight again. But no matter how hard he pushed, nothing happened except a flash of pitiful sparks. And each time, he cried out in pain; it felt like somebody was forcing needles into his heart. It was too much for his human flesh to stand...

In desperation, he looked at the Moon Spirit.

"Help us!" he screamed. "Call it off! Please!"

"She cannot!" Lumi replied.

The troll roared – a sound which made the hairs on Tuomas's arms stand on end. He didn't dare look back. He could hear it crashing after them, the earth groaning under each massive foot. Its angry bellows filled his ears.

Then it flung itself forward and snatched Aki by the legs.

The little boy screamed as it raised him off the ground, dangling him upside down. Dark blood dripped from its blinded eye.

"Help!" Aki wailed. "Tuomas!"

Lumi conjured a massive aurora and hurled it into the troll's face. It recoiled with a howl, but still didn't let go. Elin drew another arrow, but she didn't shoot. It was too risky – if she misjudged it by an inch, Aki would be the one hit.

Horror wrapped around Tuomas's throat like a rope. Henrik had been restrained just like this. All the troll needed to do now was grab Aki's arms and pull...

"*Mama!*" Aki screamed.

There was no time.

Tuomas ran forwards, hands apart. As his tail swept the snow, fire erupted around the fur, until a trail of flame followed him, but he scarcely felt it. Beyond his own fear, anger surrounded him as he drew his power from deeper than he even thought he could bear. He closed his eyes; heat grew, spread through him...

The troll roared, and Aki shrieked.

For a horrible moment, Tuomas thought he was dead. But then he looked up and noticed the little boy sprawled in the snow at the monster's feet, shaken, but in one piece. The troll, however, was groaning in pain.

Tuomas gasped. He had definitely released Sunlight, but not as much as last time. Half the creature's body was petrified, its already-grey skin frozen into stone. However, somehow, it was still alive.

Ignoring the pain in his chest, he dashed to Aki, hauled him upright, and ran. With every step, more fire flew from his tail, entwined with Lumi's aurora.

The troll growled, and Tuomas thought it might come after them again. But when he looked over his shoulder, he was stunned to see it lumbering away, dragging the stony half of its body in a dead weight. The blast of Sunlight must have hurt it too much to carry on. Then it dropped down and melted into the rocks of the tundra, as though it were water rather than solid earth.

It wasn't enough to make him stop, though. They carried on running until they couldn't anymore. A stitch grew in Tuomas's side, but he ignored it and turned to Aki. He checked him over, but to his relief, there were no wounds.

"Are you hurt?" he asked.

"No…" Aki whimpered, shaking like a leaf.

Lumi was ringing wet and panting with pain, but the Sunlight didn't appear to have hurt her too badly. She flung off the beads of water and they burst into a cloud of snowflakes.

"Nice shot," Tuomas said to Elin.

She managed a tight smile.

"See? It's a good thing I decided to come after you."

Lumi's ears twitched and she looked into the tundra. It stretched around them for miles: a massive expanse of patchy snow and soft rolling hillocks. But in the distance, there was a faint silhouette, accompanied by bells and the clicking of reindeer tendons.

A sleigh.

Tuomas let out a huge breath and almost fell over with relief. There were two men sitting in it, a flaming torch between them. At the side trotted the reindeer Elin had cut loose, lassos around their necks. The men must have caught them as they ran past.

"Elin! Tuomas!" one of the figures called. "Is that you?"

Tuomas's solace turned to ice. It was Sigurd.

He, Elin and Aki all glanced at each other.

"Is that my papa?" Aki asked.

Tuomas gripped his arms. "Not a word. I mean it."

Aki opened his mouth to question him, but Tuomas gave him such a firm look that he fell silent. Elin shouldered her bow and ran to the sleigh. Sigurd halted the reindeer, leapt out and met her halfway, enfolding her in a massive hug.

"Thank the Spirits! We've been looking all over for you!" he cried. "What was all that noise? Don't tell me one of those monsters was here! You could have been killed! Elin, your mother and I were worried sick! What were you thinking, sneaking off like that?"

"We're fine," Elin assured.

He went to say something else, then peered past her, and his expression changed into pure shock. Tuomas wasn't sure what had stunned Sigurd more: his own glowing skin and eyes, or Aki standing right next to him.

Sigurd let go of Elin and bowed. Tuomas grimaced, but Lumi only drew her shoulders back and flicked her tail again. The other man in the sleigh also lowered his head; when he straightened up, Tuomas recognised him at once.

"Aslak?"

"Nice to see you," he replied guardedly. "You look…"

"Don't start," Tuomas said. "Why did you come after us?"

"For Elin," Sigurd said, brandishing his hands at her. "You and I are going to have a serious talk, young lady. You're lucky you didn't get killed!"

"Well, I didn't," Elin replied. "Anyway, the trolls were only going after mages. It wouldn't have hurt me."

"I don't care about that!" snapped Sigurd. "Spring is the most dangerous season, and you rode out here by yourself!"

"Sigurd," Tuomas interrupted, "she saved our lives just now. I know it wasn't the best idea for her to come, but she did."

Sigurd's face darkened. Tuomas could tell he wanted to continue the argument, but a greater part of him knew better than to contest a Spirit. Tuomas recognised the expression and fought the urge to flinch. In these circumstances, it was in his favour.

Instead, Sigurd bundled Elin towards the sleigh.

"Get in," he said. "There will be time for talking on the way back. I don't want to stay here, especially not if there's a troll nearby."

"Did you come from Akerfjorden?" asked Tuomas.

"No," said Aslak. "The others only just reached the Mustafjord before we left to find you. And Lilja's arrived, with the winter caretakers; she got attacked by one, too. By the time we catch up with them now, they'll probably all have reached the village. Now, where are your sleighs? Five people aren't going to fit in this one."

Tuomas pointed in the direction of the lake. At once, Aslak climbed in beside Elin, snapped the reindeer rope, and they shot over the snow to pick them up.

Tuomas put a hand on Aki's shoulder and watched Sigurd nervously. Sure enough, Aki didn't say a word, but Tuomas could tell he was looking at his father, waiting for him to do something.

Sigurd squirmed, eyes darting everywhere, unsure where to focus. Then he cleared his throat and turned away.

Aki's lip trembled. He took a step forward, but Tuomas bent in front of him and blocked his path.

"Don't," he whispered.

"He doesn't like me," Aki mumbled sadly, and tears rolled over his scars.

A short time later, Aslak and Elin returned with the one surviving sleigh and tied it together with Sigurd's. They moved all the camping equipment and supplies into Elin's, and Aslak perched on top of the hides while the three youngsters clambered aboard the other one. Then Sigurd himself jumped on the runners and rode at the back. As they moved off, Lumi sprinted parallel to them in her fox form, Lights streaming behind her.

Tuomas watched her. His own tail had done that just now, but it had been the other kind of fire. With every day that passed, he was becoming more and more like her.

Aki pressed close to him, and Tuomas pulled a blanket up to his chin so he wouldn't feel the cold. He had stopped crying, but the lines of tears were still visible in the flickering torchlight. Tuomas stroked his hair the way Lilja did, and soon the little boy fell fast asleep.

He turned his attention to the sky. Behind the cascading shower of the rip, thousands of stars twinkled, like snowflakes which had frozen mid-fall. He traced the constellations, found the Great Bear Spirit. He could feel its gaze on him, all-knowing, yet revealing nothing.

Why did the plan have to be like this? It was so unfair.

He closed his eyes to keep himself from weeping, and rested his cheek atop Aki's head.

"Are they asleep?" Sigurd whispered.

Tuomas heard Elin moving forward to check him. He didn't move. It sounded as though Sigurd wanted to talk about something without him.

"I think so," Elin replied. "Thank you for coming to find us. I'm sorry for running off. I thought Birkir had told you."

"He did, the next morning. And then we came straight after you. How do you think your mother and I felt, finding you gone? It was like the draugars all over again; I thought I'd lost you!"

"I know. I really am sorry. I didn't mean to hurt you. I just... I hurt *him*, Father. And it was killing something inside me."

There was such pain in her voice, Tuomas almost gave up the farce and hugged her. But he kept quiet and still, and listened.

"Well, I'm just glad you're not hurt," said Sigurd, softer now. "Do you have any idea how lucky you were? How did you get rid of that thing, anyway?"

"Tuomas did it," replied Elin. "He... made Sunlight in his hands, and it turned the troll to stone. Half of it, anyway."

"*Sunlight?*" Sigurd repeated. "By the Spirits. Lilja mentioned he'd done that when he went to her. I didn't believe it."

"Well, he did."

"I suppose we can add that to avalanche-splitting, then."

Tuomas heard Elin rubbing her hands together.

"Father, listen... I know about Lilja and Aki."

Sigurd adjusted his weight on the runners.

"What about them?"

There was silence, but Tuomas felt Elin twisting to look around at him. Then Sigurd sighed in defeat.

"How long have you known?" he asked.

"Since the night I got dragged under the water. I heard Lilja talking about it."

"To whom? Tuomas? It couldn't have been anyone else. Why didn't he tell me you knew?"

"It doesn't matter," snapped Elin, careful to keep quiet so Aslak wouldn't overhear. "Let's just accept that the four of us know: you, me, Tuomas, and Lilja. We need to let things be. It can't go on like this, trying to hide it from each other. And… I've spent a bit of time with Aki now. He's a good kid, and down there, he saved all the souls. He's not wicked, Father. He's just a little boy."

Sigurd made a choked sound, as though he was trying not to cry.

"What must you think of me?" he whimpered. "I went behind your back, and Alda's back. You were only little, Elin; just four years old. I thought nothing would come of it. I was weak and stupid, and I'm so sorry."

"It's alright," Elin said gently.

"If your mother finds out about this, it will destroy us."

"I know. But that's exactly why Lilja kept it quiet. Why she ran off. She left everything behind for *us*. For… the greater good."

"The greater good? We were worth that much?"

"I don't know. I might not understand it, but I forgive you. I forgive Lilja, too. And Aki doesn't deserve any blame. You're still my father, and I still love you."

Sigurd sniffled, and Tuomas heard him lean forward to kiss his daughter on the cheek.

Chapter Twenty-Eight

They rode for hours, until the reindeer began to tire, then stopped to catch a couple of hours' sleep. After erecting the tents and throwing down some lichen for the animals, Tuomas carried Aki inside and tucked him in a sleeping sack. The little boy didn't stir, still too tired from his fright with the troll.

"Tuomas, can you lay a circle?" asked Aslak.

Tuomas hesitated. He wasn't sure he would be able to manage it without a drum. But he decided it was best to try, so he walked into the open and held his hands before him.

"Come on," he muttered to himself. "It's no different to all the other times you've done it. Just focus."

He grasped his *taika*, drew it close, until the taste of lingonberry and the heat of summer overpowered him. He began to walk, clapping with each step, as though he were beating a drum. Sure enough, he felt the energy forming behind him, like a sheet of the clearest ice, twisting and knotting high into the air. When he had completed a circle around the camp, it fused together into a perfect dome.

He sighed with relief.

"I'll keep watch," Sigurd offered. "You both go and get some rest."

Aslak nodded and ducked into the smaller tent. Tuomas headed for the other one, but as he passed Sigurd, their eyes met. No words were said, but knowledge hung between them like the ringing of a bell. Then Tuomas crawled through the flap and tied it shut behind him.

Elin was sitting on her sleeping sack, oiling her bow with a strip of reindeer fat. The wood gleamed in the firelight.

"What's the matter?" she whispered.

"Nothing," Tuomas replied as he removed his coat.

She leaned forward. "Remember when you were the one calling *me* a liar?"

Tuomas tore his eyes away from her and stared at the fire. Desperate for distraction, he thrust his hand into it and let the flames wrap themselves around his fingers.

He couldn't bear to tell her…

"Nothing's ever going to be the same, Elin," he said eventually.

"I know," she nodded. "But it's a good thing, right? The Northern Edge is closed now. You know, it was even more amazing than I thought it would be. And the Earth Spirits… Until Lumi, I'd never seen Spirits with my own eyes, or souls. Thank you so much for letting me come with you."

Tuomas smirked. "*Letting* you? You didn't give me a choice!"

Elin shrugged. "Would you expect any less?" she quipped. "I suppose what I'm trying to say is, thanks for not trying to push me away when I did come with you."

Tuomas felt his ears twisting as he regarded her. Her hair was tangled from the swim across the Night River, and her cheeks had filled out; the ravages of the soul plague were a distant memory. The light reflected in her eyes, turned them into a flickering haze of gold. Was that what his eyes looked like now?

He recalled the image of her as a little girl, playing with the antlers in an Einfjall from eleven years ago.

Despair dragged itself through his veins like mud.

"Come away with me."

Elin blinked. "Away? To where?"

"Anywhere," said Tuomas. "A place where nobody will know who I am, with no Spirits or burdens. I've done my part; I've closed the Northern Edge. Now Lumi just needs to close the rip in the sky."

Even as the words spilled out of his mouth, he knew they were pointless; when he heard them, they crumbled and fell like something dead.

Elin put down her bow, crawled to his side and took hold of his hands. His short fingers wrapped around her long ones, and he realised for the first time how her skin was calloused from the strain of drawing arrows, dry and chapped by the long cold winter; yet ending in nails which seemed more adult than he remembered.

"You can't leave," she said gently. "You're the only one who can make Sunlight, the only one who can stop the trolls. If you ran away, they would kill the mages. Niina, Lilja, Aki…"

Her gaze fleeted towards the little boy, and he turned over in his sleep.

Tuomas watched him until he was still. Aki was so young, with his whole life ahead of him, and already he'd endured so much. It would probably be enough to stand as his mage test. But even if it was, what awaited him now, in these shifting new Worlds? How could he ever take up a mantle which Tuomas and Lumi had broken?

"The mages don't even have all their *taika* anymore," Tuomas muttered. "Even if the rip closes, I don't know if they'll ever be able to connect to the Spirits again. See, that's what I mean. Everything's changing, and I don't know if it's for the better."

"The Great Bear Spirit will know," Elin assured.

"I don't want to talk about the Bear right now."

He sighed, then pulled a hand free and held it to his chest. Of all the powers he had, he wanted nothing more than to do what Lumi could: reach through and rip out that shining life-soul.

Why did it have to come into him? Why not some other person, at some other time? Why couldn't he have just lived a normal life with Paavo, and never clung onto the stupid dreams of being a mage?

Tears trickled down his cheeks. He drew his knees to his chest and hid his face. He didn't sob, just let the grief pour from him, like a river finally breaking free of its icy prison. With every breath, he felt heavier than before, as though he were the one who had been petrified.

"Listen, Tuomas," Elin said. "I wanted to tell you I'm proud of you, for what you did in the Deathlands. Asking for Kari's soul to be released. I don't know how you did that."

Tuomas sniffed, turned to look at her again. Her eyes shone with respect – though not the kind he had seen from so many others, which spoke only of trembling awe. This was the same kind of respect Lilja had given him: friend to friend, soul gazing into soul.

"The same way you've accepted Aki," he replied. "And me."

Elin bit her lip, then shuffled closer than she ever had before, put her arm around his back, and rested her head on his shoulder.

She didn't need to draw close to the tent to hear the conversation. She just stood on the other side of the barrier, ears turned in her brother's direction, and listened to the pain in his voice as he spoke to Elin. In the firelight, she could see the two of them sitting side by side.

The sight made her ears droop, and her entire body became slick with water. There was so much of it… never had she felt his anguish so deeply. It raced through her mind in a stream of formless thought: the same invisible matter which made her and him and every single Spirit. It was greater than death, greater than fear. It was the taste of a summer berry turned sour, a cloud across an open sky, a night without stars.

Tuomas wept. As his tears fell, so did her own. She wasn't sure if it could truly be real… It was impossible for a Spirit to cry. Yet he did. And now, somehow, so did she.

When he had first pulled her out of the sky, forced her to take the human form she had once hated so much, had he also given her a piece of his own humanity?

Slowly, yet certainly, she realised what needed to be done.

She turned around and moved away from the camp.

"Spirit, where are you going?" Sigurd called after her, but she ignored him. She let her fox paws fade; the fur broke apart until she was a sheet of green and blue Lights, sweeping over the tundra like a blanket. Then she rose as high into the sky as she could and reached out for the Great Bear Spirit.

It appeared from clouds and stardust and empty air, so large that she felt its vibrations in everything around her. It looked at her through the thin skin of the Worlds, the cleft hanging between them.

I come to you, White Fox One, it said, in a voice like the faintest breeze and strongest thunder, both at the same time.

I wish for an audience, she said meekly, *with you, and the Silver One.*

The Bear regarded her. *I know your intention. I will allow this.*

She waited, until the Moon Spirit drew close. Since the incident on Anaar, her face had been slowly waning. Another few days, and she would turn away from the Northlands, and bask in her own darkness.

Have you come to give me further grief, White Fox One?

No.

She sensed the Silver One's confusion.

No? Where is your coldness, your cruelty? What is this I see? Such foolish human emotion!

Precisely, Mother.

She swept her aurora about herself, let it extend as wide as she could, until the snow below blazed under its glow. And as she moved, she allowed all her defences to fall away, for the first time in her long and wild existence.

Look upon me, she said. *I am weak, but not in a way you might know. I cry. I feel. I love, like a human. I am Lumi: that name which my brother gave me. It is with this name that I admit to my wrongs, Silver One. He has shown me what it is to be human, and to be repentant. I am sorry for all I have done.*

The Silver One didn't reply. Her shock rattled the stars.

You are apologising to me? After all this time?

Yes, she replied. *My brother forced me to take form, and that has forced me to see. I hurt you, and him. And if I had not done so, all of this would never have happened.*

She spread herself thinner, held nothing at bay. Mere months ago, she never would have let them witness such vulnerability. Even now, a part of her protested, clung to the idea which had been spun for so long. She was a winter Spirit, light among darkness, vicious as the harshest blizzard. She was the flame which burned cold, which made humans lower their heads and draw back in fear…

She let it all go.

See me, as I see, she whispered. *I am sorry.*

Her mother hung silent and still, as though time had stopped and lost its meaning. Her pale light stroked over her like spiderwebs, mingled with her own aurora. They were so similar, so freezing…

I accept this, daughter, replied the Silver One. *And I thank you.*

Do you forgive me? she asked.

I likely shall. Your honesty touches me. You have done what no other of our kind has ever fathomed. To still be intact through it all is a testament to your own strength, not just my son's.

She bit back an impulsive remark, and instead lowered herself before the Moon Spirit. It wasn't about keeping Tuomas away, or trying to save him. It was about choice, and acceptance, and nothing less.

He is the son of both of you, she said. *And I am the daughter of both of you. We are both simply the fox fires.*

The Great Bear wrapped itself around her.

And so, you have both descended to the core of your beings, White Fox One.

She looked at it, deep into the eyes which transcended existence.

This was your riddle, she realised. *All things must come to an end. The choice of how will be his. That is what you told me, in the World Below.*

The Bear shone every colour of the rainbow.

It is what I am, it whispered. *What else do you wish to say?*

She pulled her Lights back towards herself and faced the Moon Spirit.

I beg you to try and call off the trolls again, she said. *Please.*

I am unable to control them, White Fox One. You know I have failed. Only the glow of my sister will stop them now, and they will never appear while she shines.

Then can you not convene with the Golden One? There must be a way. I have put aside my feud; can you do the same? Please, do not let the mages die for this, especially not Aki. That little boy has suffered too much to have his life ended so soon.

I concur, said the Great Bear. *I bade you to do whatever you must to amend this, Silver One. Your task is not yet complete. Do it.*

The Moon Spirit shone in assent. *I shall.*

And, White Fox One, I have heard the despair from your brother, now you have told him the truth, the Bear continued. *When the tear between the World Above and Between is mended, I shall ensure that all taika is restored to the mages. They will be able to connect with Spirits again, travel through fire, send out their shockwaves, bind with chants... all shall be as it has always been.*

Except that he will be here with us, she said sadly.

He will be home, the Silver One insisted. *He will be with his family.*

The Lights dimmed until they were barely visible.

This is where I will understand in the way you never can, Mother. He loves. That part will always remain, even up here, until the Worlds stop turning.

The Great Bear Spirit surveyed her without a sound. She spun away so she wouldn't have to feel its gaze upon her, and sank back onto the tundra. Water dripped off her fingers, transformed to snowflakes as soon as they met the air. The aurora twisted into feet and she stood upon them.

She looked down in shock. For the first time, the snow gave way under her. She took a few uncertain steps, and left a trail. It was faint, but it was there.

Chapter Twenty-Nine

The stars spun overhead into a pink dawn as the two sleighs moved south-east. The thawing ground sparkled beneath the emerging Sun Spirit, tree branches drifted in a breeze too high up for Tuomas to feel. Every now and then came soft whumps as snow fell from them.

When the light truly broke the horizon, Lumi approached in her fox form. Tuomas didn't waste a moment before lifting his coat. She jumped onto his lap and he covered her.

They travelled hard, for several days, the mountains rearing in the distance against a sky of crisp baby blue. After passing the forest where Tuomas had found Mihka, they reached a dried riverbed and turned down it, following the natural road it had left embedded into the earth. The sleighs bumped violently over the uneven ground, but the reindeer kept their balance and were not fazed.

Tuomas's bull knew this route; it was the traditional one which the Akerfjorden herders used on the migration. This winter was the first in recent memory when they hadn't walked along it.

Eventually, the old river opened its mouth, and Tuomas almost cried with joy. Two huge walls of solid rock towered towards the sky on either side, their sheer faces fringed by hardy trees and the thin cascades of waterfalls. And between them, still frozen solid, was the Mustafjord.

The Moon Spirit was reduced to a tiny sliver in the sky, so Aslak lit a torch. Without needing to be told, everybody

266

exited the sleighs and helped to guide the reindeer onto the fjord.

Tuomas took Aki's hand and pulled him away. Lumi lingered ahead, sweeping her tail so the aurora could cast some light. In its shimmery green radiance, Tuomas spotted the grey patches and carefully stepped around them. The ice was still firm, but it groaned under their weight, and he could tell by the feel of it that it was thinning rapidly. In another few weeks, it would be gone completely, and where they were walking now would be an open body of water.

It was only when they rounded a bend that Tuomas finally allowed himself to relax. The far bank was still miles away, but he could make out the welcome glow of fires and silhouettes of turf huts. Reindeer bells filled the air, and the forest heaved with the dark shapes of the herd.

At long last, the end was in sight.

The ice became firmer, so they jumped back into the sleighs for the final stretch. After another gruelling hour, they reached Akerfjorden.

Tuomas gazed across the village. The place seemed smaller than he remembered. It was the first time he had seen it since they had left on the migration, almost two months ago. And while he'd previously spent whole summers at the coast without coming back, this felt as though he had been gone for a lifetime.

From the looks of things, the others hadn't long arrived themselves. The Akerfjorden villagers stood by their own shelters, making offerings to those from Einfjall and Poro to stay. The faint aromas of cooking meat were only just starting to drift into the air.

Voices carried on the wind as the sleighs were spotted, and a crowd gathered at the bank. Lumi drew level with Tuomas. They shared a glance, but didn't speak.

To distract himself, Tuomas helped Sigurd and Elin push the runners onto solid ground, then freed the reindeer so Aslak could take them to the forest.

He turned to face the people. Several at the front staggered away in awe when they saw his shining skin and yellow eyes.

"Son of the Sun…"

"Great Mage…"

"Red Fox One…"

Maiken appeared and took a few tentative steps towards him. Her jaw was slack. Then she removed her hat and bent so deeply that her hair touched the ground.

In one fluid motion, everybody else followed suit. Tuomas's heart pounded as heads were lowered, torches brought towards the snow, until he and Lumi were the only ones standing. Even Elin, Sigurd and Aki bowed.

After several long moments, Maiken and the other elders straightened up.

"Welcome back," she smiled. "Did you do what you needed to?"

Tuomas nodded, and motioned to Aki. "The gateway is shut. And all the souls which were taken are free, thanks to him."

Anssi's face lit up and he brushed a tear from his eye.

"Thank you, little one," he smiled at Aki.

Aki shot an uncertain look at Tuomas.

"You did it," he insisted. "You can say, *you're welcome. It's alright.*"

"Uh… you're welcome," mumbled Aki, but he still shuffled behind Tuomas and tried to hide.

"Is everybody alright?" Tuomas asked.

"Absolutely fine," replied Birkir. "We didn't run into any trolls, thank the Spirits. We're all just very tired."

"Us, too," Elin admitted.

She barely had time to finish before Alda barrelled through the crowd and ran into her. Sigurd hurried over too and the three of them embraced.

Aki peeked around Tuomas's hip with a forlorn expression. However, he didn't have to wait long. A couple of people parted, and Lilja appeared.

"Aki," she said.

A grin split Aki's face.

"Mama!"

He shot towards her. Several men drew back, trying to keep distance from him, but he ignored them and threw himself against Lilja's stomach. She fell to her knees and clutched him, sobbing into his shoulder. The wound on her face was scabbed over and her arm was still in a sling, but Tuomas noticed it had been freshly bandaged – he presumed by Niina.

Then she looked straight at him.

"Why in the name of all the Spirits didn't you tell me you'd taken him?" she demanded. "I almost had a heart attack when I found him gone!"

"It wasn't my idea," Tuomas replied. "The Great Bear told me you weren't to know."

At that, everyone within earshot gasped. Some even bowed again. But Lilja only blinked, and cool acceptance swept over her face. She was the only other person in the entire gathering who had connected with the Great Bear Spirit.

"Fair enough," she said tightly. She stood up, took Aki's hand. "Baby, come on. You need to get warm."

Without another word, she led him away. As inconspicuously as he could, Tuomas watched Sigurd. Both he and Elin were peering over Alda's head, watching as the two of them disappeared into a hut at the very edge of the village.

"You should get warm, too," said Maiken, then cleared her throat as she realised the absurdity of such a statement. "Well... in any case, you know where you're going, don't you, Tuomas?"

He gave a curt nod.

As the crowd began to dissipate, he trudged the familiar routes between the huts. A couple of them were still unclaimed, and his breath caught in his throat when he spotted Henrik's. Even from where he stood, he could just about pick up the phantom smell of dried herbs and strong tea.

He braced himself, turned around. Directly across the way was his old shelter: the one he had shared with Paavo for as long as he could remember. The door was closed; no fire was lit inside. The last time he had laid eyes on it, his brother had been alive.

A hand appeared on his arm, and he knew it was Elin without even needing to look.

"I'm sorry," she whispered.

Tuomas bit his lip, raised his own hand to hers and grasped it.

"I want you and your parents to stay in there," he said. "Unless Alda's already found somewhere else, that is."

Sigurd overheard him. "Are you sure?"

"Of course I'm sure," Tuomas replied. Nevertheless, he swallowed hard to keep himself from crying.

"You're with us, aren't you?" Elin asked. "Or are you going to Lilja?"

"Lilja will probably want her own company. You know that."

"So you're staying with us."

"Yes, yes, fine."

He kept his eyes down so he couldn't look into hers. Just feeling her fingers through his coat was difficult. He was back now; there was nothing between him and the gash floating over his head. How was he going to tell her he wouldn't see this snow melt, or eat with her, ever again?

"You get settled in," he said. "I need to make sure Lumi's alright."

Before Elin could question him, he hurried away, towards the faint green glow hovering at the bank of the fjord. It didn't surprise him to see his sister alone. Nobody trusted or knew her well enough to linger too close.

"It will be daylight soon," he muttered. "You need to shelter."

"And where do you propose I do that? The huts will be too warm."

Tuomas thought quickly, and his attention strayed to one of the food stores close to the treeline. It was built off the ground so no animals could get at the contents, and held no openings – even the gaps between the logs were packed with mud to keep out wind and snow.

"Will you be alright in there?" he asked.

Lumi looked at it, nodded. Tuomas walked to it, climbed the ladder and shouldered the door open. He crawled inside to check it would be safe, and Lumi followed him, settling against some bags of dried meat and berries.

He went to exit, but she grasped his wrist. Her hand was so wet, beads of water dripped over the fur on Tuomas's sleeve.

"Wait."

"What is it?" he asked. "I've got things to do. People who I need to… see."

Lumi didn't let go. "Will you hear me, for a moment?"

Tuomas hesitated. A part of him still just wanted to run as far and fast as he could. But her expression stunned him; through the sheen of moisture, there was hardly a semblance of the aloof and dangerous Spirit which he had first seen in the Long Dark.

With a sigh, he turned to face her.

"So, what happens now? I've done my part."

"Yes, you have. You did it beautifully. I shall do the same. I will take you up there with me, and the Spirit of Passage will come."

"And then it's all over," said Tuomas, with a glance at his hands. The flesh felt so real, so warm. He had left it several times while in trance, basked in the freedom of floating without form. But what would it be like to be stripped of the physical forever?

"What about the trolls?" he asked. "Two of them are still out there. They'll come for the mages. Just because we're here doesn't mean it's safe. It won't be safe for months."

"I spoke with the Silver One, on the journey," Lumi said. "I apologised."

Tuomas stared at her. He couldn't believe his ears.

"You *apologised? To her?*"

"I have owned my mistakes, as you have owned yours," she continued. "The Silver One may not be able to control the trolls, but I asked her to work with the Golden One. Together, our mothers will be strong enough to defeat them. I trust in that."

"Our mothers?" Tuomas repeated, aghast.

"It may take me some time to grow used to the idea, but I will not keep you from the Moon Spirit again," said Lumi. "I will not poison you against her, and I will not encourage discord between her and the Sun. She is dark and cold and cruel, but so am I, and yet I have made this so. Because of you, my brother."

Once again, water flowed from her, dripped onto the floor. The sight made Tuomas's heart race.

"Did I hurt you? When I made the Sunlight, I mean?"

"A little. It was not strong enough to deal excessive damage."

"I know," he said sourly. "It wasn't even enough to kill the troll."

"Do not chastise yourself for that," she replied. "Tuomas, listen to me. Can you forgive me for what I did? It was so long ago, and I know that is no excuse, but I do not wish for you to hate me."

Tuomas shook his head. "I don't hate you. It takes a lot for me to hate someone. Another lesson I've learned this winter, so it seems."

"So it seems," she agreed. "You are not the same as you were when you pulled me out of the sky."

Tuomas scoffed and gestured to his tail. "Well, that's a surprise."

"That is the least of it," said Lumi. "You were like me. So angry, so sharp. Now, you speak differently, walk differently. You are a man."

"And not a moment too soon, before I die."

"It will not hurt. I will ensure it. And then we will dance through the sky forever. You will see Paavo again, your human parents."

"Until they come back to give new life," murmured Tuomas. "I'll never be able to do that. Ever."

He wiped at his eyes with his spare hand. "I know this isn't your idea, Lumi. But you're the only one here who knows. And I do forgive you. Or accept it… whatever you want to call it. You're not the same as you were, either. So I suppose the best thing to do is finish what we started, and try to move on from this point."

She smiled. "To move on, and go home."

Tuomas swallowed. Home… it was such a strange word. And yet, hadn't he felt so at home when he had allowed her to lift him into the sky? Before he'd pulled away from her, and opened the first fissure which would lead to the fabric of the Worlds tearing apart?

Lumi's face changed again. Her emotionless exterior fell away, and she moved forward, wrapped her arms around him.

He didn't even hesitate before he embraced her back. Gone were the times when he had been terrified of her. He couldn't even find it to be angry at her anymore; there was too little time. Just like when he had bound her into this form, she felt unbelievably light, as though if he held her too tightly, his hands would break straight through her like a thin sheet of ice. She was colder than snow – yet there was also a shred of warmth there which he had never sensed in her before.

"One more day," he whispered. "Give me that much. Please."

She nodded. "One more day."

Chapter Thirty

Once all the shelters had been claimed and the reindeer fed with the lichen from the islands, everyone gathered around the central fire pit. It needed to be enlarged to accommodate those from Poro and Einfjall, and dinner was hardly the grand feast which had heralded the start of the migration, but nobody complained. The journey had been too long, too hard, too wracked with anxiety. Many children were struggling to stay awake before the food was even served.

Silence fell when Tuomas joined them. He sighed and plucked at the fur on the reindeer skin covering the log. It was the place he had always sat; his neighbours had seen him perch on it for over a decade.

"I'm still me," he said half-heartedly, then accepted a bowl of sautéed reindeer and blood pancake. He tried to force away the idea of how deliciously Paavo would have cooked it, and instead focused on the taste and texture.

This was his last meal. When the Sun Spirit rose in just a few hours, it would be the final time he would watch her from the World Between. Forever.

His stomach twisted and writhed as though he had swallowed a worm. He wanted to tell everybody, remind them how much of an honour it had been to live among them. Could he really just slip away with no true goodbye?

No, he thought. It was better to bid farewell in his own way, quietly, so they couldn't try to prevent it. That would only make things harder.

Niina approached. Beside her was Mihka, one arm slung over her shoulders for balance. He hobbled with each step, shoes untied to accommodate the thick bandages around his feet. His hands were uncovered now, but still hidden under mittens.

Tuomas watched, expecting Niina to seat him near Anssi and Maiken. But, to his shock, she instead brought him to Tuomas and lowered him onto the log.

Tuomas stared at Niina questioningly. Had it been her idea to put them together? But when he caught her eye, she just shot him a wink and hurried to collect her own helping of food. She was pale with exhaustion and her red hair was thin, but a newfound confidence shone in her face, and Tuomas smiled. She had been so afraid of being the lone mage, and yet she had managed it perfectly.

Stellan passed Mihka a bowl of meat. He gave a nod of thanks, then pulled two small knives from his belt. He passed one to Tuomas.

"I noticed you lost yours," he muttered.

Tuomas hesitated for a moment before he took it.

"Thank you."

Mihka raised his brows and lifted some food to his mouth on the flat edge of his own knife. His hand shook with the effort, but he managed.

"How are you feeling?" Tuomas asked quietly.

"As well as I can be," replied Mihka. "Niina did a good job."

"Will you... well, how's your frostbite?"

In answer, Mihka removed a mitten with his teeth. All four of his fingers had been amputated. The skin itself was stitched and flushed red, but appeared to be healing well.

276

"Niina had to take two off the other hand, as well," he said forlornly. "And half my left foot, and all the toes on my right. More might have to go. She's keeping an eye on it."

Tuomas grimaced and he glanced at his own fingers, with their stumpy missing tips. Both of them had been extremely lucky. Mihka had been huddled in those woods with hardly anything to protect him for a few days. Just a stone's throw from where they sat now, an old Akerfjorden woman had lost both her feet after a single night in a fierce blizzard.

The cost of flesh and bone was horrendous; Mihka would likely never be able to throw a lasso or cut an earmark again, would walk with a limp for the rest of his life. But at least he was alive.

He pulled the mitten back on and took another bite of reindeer. Tuomas did the same. To hear Mihka talking to him at all was progress, but he was still unsure.

"I'm sorry," he said. "I know how much it hurts."

"Well, I'm sorry for nearly breaking your nose," said Mihka, with the tiniest edge of a smirk.

Hope flickered in Tuomas's heart. The old Mihka was gone, but that sounded more like the idiot he remembered.

"Can we call a truce, then?" he asked.

Mihka looked at him. "I heard you freed the souls? My father?"

"*I* didn't," Tuomas admitted, "but I had enough of a hand in it, to see it done."

A shadow lifted from Mihka's face.

"Then that's good enough for me. Thank you. And thanks for coming and finding me in the woods."

"So... we're friends?"

Mihka shrugged. "I can't be bothered hating you anymore."

Tuomas regarded his white hair, remembering the black colour it had been until the beginning of the Long Dark. Never mind what was coming; something told him that things would never be the same between them, but he could part with Mihka on such terms. Any reconciliation, however strained, was better than none.

"Just so you know," he said, "I don't regret for a moment setting out to get your soul back."

Mihka held his eyes for a long moment, then nodded and returned to his meal.

After all the food was eaten, everyone headed to the shelters to sleep for as long as they could. Elin tried to pull Tuomas towards the hut, but he hesitated and twisted his hand free.

"You go," he said. "I'll be there soon."

"What's wrong?" she asked.

Tuomas bit the inside of his cheek so tears wouldn't form. If only she knew…

"I just need a little bit of time to myself before I go inside there again," he said.

Elin's eyes softened, then she stepped forward and put her arms around him. Tuomas held her as tightly as he could without hurting her.

"I'll make sure your sleeping sack goes in the old spot," she promised.

It was a simple gesture, but it made his heart wrench. He hurried away before she could see his pain.

Already, the village was deserted. The snow between the huts had been trampled thin by shoes, and in places he could even see dark patches of earth and grass poking through.

Everywhere shone a faint ethereal blue, reflecting what little light was cast by the stars and shimmering rip overhead.

As he walked towards the furthest hut, a circle of yellow surrounded him, as though he was holding a torch. But there was no flame save for those in his eyes, under his skin, flickering in sparks from his tail. Every movement he made brought it forth, without even needing to think about it.

He knocked on the door; Lilja opened it a crack and peered at him.

"I wanted to see you," Tuomas said. "Is Aki asleep?"

"Yes," she replied. "But come in anyway."

She pushed the door wide so he could duck through. The interior had been well-maintained by the Akerfjorden caretakers: the overlapping twigs on the floor were fresh and the hides only smelled a little damp. Lilja had brought all her belongings inside, but she hadn't unpacked; everything remained in leather bags, stuffed in the far corner. The only things Tuomas saw lying about were the sleeping sacks, a couple of cooking utensils, and her drum.

He swallowed when he saw it, suddenly very aware of the emptiness of his own belt.

"Where's yours?" Lilja asked, as though she had read his thoughts.

"I gave it as an offering to the Spirit of Death."

"You gave up your drum?"

"I had to."

Lilja surveyed him coolly, then sat beside a slumbering Aki and stroked his hair. He let out a contented murmur and buried deeper into the furs.

"The Spirit of Death," she repeated. "The elders told me you'd gone to the Northern Edge of the World. But you did more than close the gateway, didn't you, boy?"

"Yes."

"You took Aki across the Night River?"

"It was what the Great Bear Spirit instructed," replied Tuomas carefully. "Lilja, believe me, I didn't want to involve him. I was willing to go alone, but the Bear said it had to be Aki. It had a plan all along, to have him free the souls which the draugars took. I couldn't try to defy it again."

Lilja pursed her lips. "And I take it that not informing me was a part of that plan?"

"If I had, you never would have left him, to get the caretakers," said Tuomas.

"I never would have ended up with a broken arm, either," Lilja muttered.

Tuomas glanced at her sling. "How is it, by the way?"

"Healing fine," she said. "You did a good job."

Her voice was flat and quiet, but Tuomas still smiled. That was high praise, coming from her.

"How in the name of all the Spirits did you cross the Night River?" she asked. "Nobody's ever done that, not even the Great Mage. Let alone get back."

"It wasn't easy," Tuomas admitted. "But I think Aki might actually be the best one to talk to about it. *He* was the hero, Lilja. He freed the souls – Paavo, Sisu, Eevi, all of them. I just held his hand."

A soft warmth came into Lilja's eyes as she surveyed her son. She gently ran a thumb over one of his scarred cheeks.

"I'm glad you were there to hold it," she murmured.

She dug around for some herbs and tossed them into a pot to make tea. As she stirred it with a carved shinbone ladle, Tuomas turned his eyes to the pile of belongings. A small pouch was balanced on the top, and even in the shadows, he could see the long thin shapes of bone needles pressing against the skin.

"Are you still thinking of leaving?" he asked.

Lilja sighed. "I want to. Village life isn't for me, let alone being resident mage. I heard the elders talking about maybe keeping everyone combined for a while, staying here instead of going back to Poro and Einfjall. If that's the case, do they really need three mages? Can't one be enough?"

"Niina?"

"Or you. They can't get a better mage than you, can they?"

Tuomas swallowed and changed the subject.

"Why didn't you eat with us?"

"You've seen the way everyone looks at me, at Aki," Lilja replied sadly. "It's the way things are for people like us. As hated and mistrusted as we are respected. I'm sure you can sympathise."

"You're not hated," Tuomas said.

"I'm surprised they let *you* sit with them," she remarked. "You're not exactly difficult to miss now, are you?"

Tuomas smirked. He wasn't even sure how much of the glow on the walls was coming from the fire and how much was from himself.

"It happened when I was in the Deathlands," he said. "It's... a strange place. No colour. Nothing solid. It's like the World Above if all the stars disappeared."

Lilja cocked an eyebrow. "Well, without putting too fine a point on things, that seems to have already happened enough. When's your sister going to close the rip?"

Hidden from view, Tuomas gripped the hem of his coat.

"In one day."

Lilja blinked. "What's with that tone? Something on your mind?"

He didn't move. His thoughts beat against each other like hailstones. What was he supposed to say?

But then his eyes strayed to Aki again, and he knew exactly what he needed to do.

"I want to tell you something. He was the one who freed the souls, not me. But while I was down there, I asked the Spirit of Death to release Kari's soul."

Lilja dropped the ladle with a clatter. At the sound, Aki grumbled and rolled over, away from the hearth.

Lilja held a hand to the scar on her throat.

"You released…" she stammered.

Her eyes grew wide, then filled with tears. She didn't even try to hold them back; she crawled around the fire and hugged him. It was awkward with one arm, but was still the tightest embrace he had ever known from her.

Footsteps crunched in the snow outside. Tuomas's ears swivelled to listen.

"Lilja?"

She froze. It was Sigurd.

Without even waiting to be invited, he opened the door. He glanced at her, then Tuomas, and finally at Aki. A flicker of uncertainty passed over his face, but quickly melted into something softer.

Lilja glowered like a defensive wolf.

"What do you want?" she hissed.

"To talk," he replied. "Please. I don't want a fight."

"I'll go," Tuomas whispered.

"No," said Sigurd. "Stay. Please. You need to hear this, too. All three of us know the truth."

He perched in the space in front of the door. Lilja returned to her spot and sat between him and Aki. She laid a hand on her son's head and caressed it, to keep him asleep.

"Well, go on," she said. "Talk."

Sigurd licked his lips and rubbed the back of his neck nervously.

"Lilja, I'm sorry. I put you through so much and I never even stopped to think. It wasn't fair. I just want to apologise to you, and tell you I'm thankful for everything you did for my family. I don't deserve it. I respect you so much; I can't imagine what it must have been like for you."

Lilja didn't move. She didn't even blink.

"He's the best thing that's ever happened to me," she said in the end. "I have to thank you for that much."

Sigurd sighed, looked at Aki again.

"I can never acknowledge him, can I? Never share him?"

"Not unless you want everything destroyed," replied Lilja. She spoke bluntly, but the sharpness disappeared from her tone, and Tuomas recognised the faint notes of pity behind her words. "*I* can deal with it, Sigurd. I've done it for half my life. But can you? Can Alda, and Elin? Would you have him do it, too?"

She tossed her head at Aki.

"What happened, happened a long time ago," she said. "It cannot be known, and it cannot be fed."

"I know," nodded Sigurd miserably. "This is my fault. I'm so sorry, Lilja."

Tuomas glanced between them. Their eyes met, guarded yet mellow, a thousand words hanging in the silence.

Then Lilja fetched three wooden cups, filled them with tea, and passed them around.

"Bygones," she said, and all of them sipped at the same time.

283

Chapter Thirty-One

Despite tiredness tugging at his eyes, Tuomas refused to sleep. He tossed and turned in his sack, but eventually lay on his back and gazed through the smoke hole. It felt too strange to be in this shelter and not hear Paavo's snoring, or smell the lingering aromas of whatever he had last cooked.

In the end, he pulled on his shoes and coat, and slipped past Elin, out of the door. He stood alone for a moment and looked at the rip, felt the *taika* spilling over its edges. He spotted the constellation of the Great Bear Spirit, but there was no sign of the Silver One. She had turned her face away from the Northlands.

He glanced toward the storage hut, where Lumi was still hiding. She wouldn't come out now; it was too close to dawn. But he could imagine her, sitting there in the dark, and shook his head in bewilderment. He couldn't believe she had found it in her to apologise to her mother. He had, as a Spirit, spent generations with her in the World Above, but had a single winter together down here truly changed her so much?

He pushed the thought from his mind. He would have time enough to ponder it and speak with her soon. He couldn't say the same for the time he had now.

He wandered between the shelters, tracing paths he had followed for as long as he could remember. The torches and fires had burned out, but he saw perfectly; a faint ring of light followed him wherever he trod. He kicked at the snow, exposed the earth underneath. This beautiful white powder had lain on the ground since the end of autumn, and in another few weeks, it would be gone.

He approached the circle which Niina had laid around the village. For a moment, he worried how he might get through without a drum, but then shrugged and simply extended his hands. They glowed with fire and he felt the shell thin enough for him to pass. He ensured it was closed, and walked into the forest which surrounded Akerfjorden.

Several reindeer raised their heads to watch him, but didn't run. He regarded them as he passed, smiled when he saw the females with their calves. Several had died on the journey, but most had survived, albeit thinner than they should be. They would fatten up quickly enough on the rich milk of their mothers.

He didn't need to worry. Nature always found a way.

He broke free of the trees and climbed the rocky side of the Mustafjord. Heading to the top was too much – it was hundreds of feet high and would have taken him hours. Instead, he perched on a ledge close to a waterfall, let its spray settle on his face in a fine icy mist. The frozen water stood below like a long white ribbon, stretching out of sight on its route to the sea.

He stayed there as the stars faded and the sky lightened through shades of blue and purple. Eventually, the Sun Spirit rose in front of him and peeked her golden face over the eastern ridge of the fjord. Even though her light shone straight into his eyes, Tuomas felt no need to turn away. It didn't hurt, didn't blind him at all. The warmth of her touch washed over him, and he reached out his hands, so he could feel it on his skin one last time.

He let his *taika* swell, souls loosening, until they hovered just above him in trance. At once, he sensed his mother:

a waft of summer pollen, dry earth, open tundra bountiful with life.

Soon, my dear, she whispered.

I know, he replied. *But I will not choose you over your sister. You are both equal. Do not try to keep me from her.*

It is your choice. You should have it, for once.

Will you co-operate? Rid the Northlands of the trolls. I beg you.

You need not beg for anything, my sweet son, the Sun Spirit insisted. *It shall be done. But be prepared.*

With that, she pulled away from him, and Tuomas opened his eyes.

He stayed there for as long as he could. The cleft shimmered overhead, like a second fjord had carved its way through the sky, but Tuomas didn't allow himself to dwell on it and instead turned his attention to the village.

People emerged from the huts and set about their work: everything which they had been too exhausted to do the day before. Niina broke the circle before going to check on Mihka. Meat was laid across drying racks, old skins were shaken out, axes taken to trees so the firewood stocks could be replenished. A couple of people headed into the forest to check the reindeer, while others went to hunt.

Tuomas slowly made his way back down. He took his time, so he wouldn't slip on the icy rocks, and followed his own footprints until he returned to ground level. A few people threw him respectful smiles, or bowed their heads as they passed. He didn't have the heart to ask them to stop.

He ducked into his shelter. It was empty; he assumed Sigurd, Alda and Elin were making themselves useful. All their bows were gone, and their sleeping sacks neatly rolled against the wall.

Tuomas crawled outside again and kicked the door shut. Then he noticed a lone figure lying on a reindeer skin in the middle of the Mustafjord. He recognised it straightaway. Elin.

He started walking out to join her, moving in a zigzag to avoid the dangerous patches of grey ice. She had hacked a hole in front of her and was dangling a line on an antler tine, flicking it every now and then to check if anything had bitten. Beside her, a torch burned, to lure the fish closer.

She looked up as he approached, and kicked her bow aside so there was room for him on the hide.

"Mother asked me to try and catch something for tonight," she said.

"Can I help?" Tuomas asked.

In reply, she tossed him a spare antler and bone hook. He settled beside her, threaded the hook with sinew thread, then slid some bait onto the end and dropped it into the water.

"You were out early this morning," Elin remarked.

"I couldn't sleep," said Tuomas. "I've got a lot on my mind."

"You mean about the rip?"

"And other things."

Elin rested her chin on her hand and turned her eyes to him.

"So, when are we going up there?" she asked.

"Later. But it will just be me and Lumi."

"I'm coming too."

"No, you're not," Tuomas said firmly. "Not this time, Elin."

"You don't get to decide that for me."

"Yes, I do."

She gritted her teeth. For a moment, Tuomas thought she was going to smack him.

"You don't have to prove anything to me," he said. "I know you want to make up for things, but that's done now. You don't have to follow me. You *can't* follow me."

"If I can come across the Night River, I can go into the World Above," she insisted.

"This is different," Tuomas murmured. "It's too dangerous. Even Lilja never went there physically, and she's one of the most powerful mages. I don't want you to get hurt. Please just do as I ask."

Elin looked as though she wanted to argue further, but she held herself back. She gave her antler a half-hearted flick.

"I don't want you to get hurt, either," she said.

She spoke so quietly, with such vulnerability, that it broke something inside Tuomas as though an avalanche had slammed into him.

In a single fluid motion, he lifted the fox carving from around his neck and slipped it over her head.

Elin frowned. "Why are you giving this to me?"

"I already gave it to you, on Anaar," he replied, barely above a whisper. "Listen... I don't want you to go with me, because I'm not coming back."

She blinked in surprise, a tumult of emotions chasing each other across her face.

"*What?*"

"It's the truth."

"But you *will* come back!" she snapped. "You did last time!"

"That was before," said Tuomas sadly. "The Great Bear Spirit has decided I need to go there for good, as a Spirit. That means my life-soul will be gone, and I can't survive without one of those, you know that. So when Lumi closes the rip, it closes behind me, too."

"No!" Elin shrieked. She reared up and snatched his wrists. "You're coming back! You promised me you would last time, and you're going to do it now! Promise me you'll come back!"

Tuomas shook his head.

"Promise me!"

"I can't. I won't make a promise I can't keep."

As he spoke, tears dropped down his face. Elin was crying, too: desperate, hollow sobs which made her face blaze.

"Tuomas, I have never begged for anything," she said. "But I will beg you now. Don't do this!"

"I don't have any choice," he replied gently. "Please try to understand. I won't be coming back. But I'll always be watching you. That I do promise."

Elin broke. She put her arms around him and wept into his coat.

In a flash, he remembered walking into her shelter at Einfjall for the first time, when Sigurd had offered shelter from a storm. He thought of her solid assurance as she drew an arrow to her cheek, shot Kari's demon straight in the eye; all the times she had laughed and held his hand.

He pushed her back just enough to see her face. He studied her turned-up nose, her unkempt black fringe, the golden flecks dancing in her chestnut irises. She was the best friend he'd ever had; stronger than any other he'd ever known.

He held a hand to her cheek.

"I'm sorry," he said, then took a deep breath. "I've got to do this, at least once."

He leaned closer. Elin didn't even hesitate; she moved in and kissed him.

Tuomas closed his eyes. At any other time, he might have worried about making a fool of himself, but not now. Her lips were chapped and dry from the incessant cold, but fitted around his perfectly, as though he were touching the softest flower petal. He tasted her tears, and his own, made no move to wipe them away.

A shadow suddenly fell across the two of them.

Tuomas sprang back, looked around. The Sunlight was dimming by the second.

Elin gasped in horror.

"Look!" she cried, and pointed upwards.

Tuomas followed her finger. The Sun Spirit was still directly overhead, but the Moon was there too: a black circle, forcing her face in front of her sister's. The Golden One became a crescent, then she was hidden completely, and everything became dark.

Exclamations of shock echoed from the village as people streamed out of the huts. Even Lilja came running, followed closely by Lumi. She bolted onto the fjord, streaming the aurora in her wake.

A low groan drifted on the wind.

Then, with a great roar, the two trolls emerged from the cliffs, pulling themselves out of the rocks as though casting off a garment. The closest was still half-petrified, with an arrow sticking out of its eye.

It took one look at Tuomas, and bounded towards him.

Chapter Thirty-Two

Lumi leapt between Tuomas and the troll. She raised her hands and threw Lights into its face, knocking it backwards. But before she could shoot another, the second troll hurled its blade at her. It sliced straight through her snowy body, and she shattered, spilling across the fjord in a great green blanket.

Tuomas went to go to her, but Elin grabbed his hand.

"Come on!" she cried.

She snatched her bow and dragged him towards the bank. The air filled with the bellows of terrified reindeer and the thunder of hooves as the herd stampeded deeper into the forest. Sigurd, Alda, Stellan and the elders leapt onto the ice and readied their weapons.

"Hurry!" Sigurd bellowed. "Elin, Tuomas, run!"

The darkness became denser as the Moon Spirit blocked out the Sun. With every moment, the trolls seemed to grow in strength. Leering grins spreading across their grey faces; even the half-petrified one held a strange sense of triumph. All the mages were together, trapped by the sheer rocky walls and the slope at the back of Akerfjorden. There was no escape.

The ice cracked and groaned beneath their huge feet as they advanced on the villagers. Arrows started flying over Tuomas and Elin's heads, but as before, they had no effect, and bounced off the trolls' thick skin like splinters.

Flames flew from Tuomas's tail as it swept the ground. He glanced over his shoulder at the black disc in the sky. The gash heaved; he felt a huge tremor from the World Above and his head spun with pressure. His souls were clashing together like stones, twisting, trying to pull apart...

Then he remembered Lumi's words; the assurance that the Sun Spirit had given him that very morning. The celestial sisters had said they would co-operate to stop the trolls. How better than to create a false sense of night? A perfect trap to petrify them again?

But it would all be for nothing if the monsters reached the bank.

"Niina! Lilja!" Tuomas shouted. "Put up a shield –"

His shoes slipped and he crashed through a patch of grey ice.

Freezing water shot over his head. He panicked – this was exactly how he had died last time... It couldn't happen now, not yet...

He clawed his way back to the surface. As soon as he emerged, Elin snatched his wrists and hauled him to safety.

An idea leapt into Tuomas's mind. The ice was thin, scarcely able to hold a human. But a heavy troll, of rock and flint, twice his height and weight?

He twisted free of Elin and pushed her.

"Get over there!" he snapped.

Elin stared at him. "Are you crazy?"

"Just go!" Tuomas shouted.

Elin hesitated, but did as he said and sprinted towards the line of archers. She drew an arrow onto her bow and joined the fray.

"Move, you stupid boy!" Lilja screamed from the bank.

Tuomas ignored her and turned to face the trolls. They lumbered closer, blades flashing, limbs grinding against each other with a sound that set his teeth on edge.

Lumi swarmed to his side, twisted her Lights down to the ground, pushed them into arms and legs and a pure white tail.

"The Sun and Moon Spirits have done this on purpose, haven't they?" Tuomas asked.

Lumi nodded. "We do not have much time. We must keep the trolls in the open, prevent them from taking cover."

"I've got a better plan," said Tuomas. "Will you help me?"

Lumi locked eyes with him, and he knew she had realised what he was thinking.

Without another word, they both raised their hands. Lingonberries exploded across Tuomas's tongue as he grasped his *taika*, spun it around himself, hotter than anything else in the World Between. He let a fire form between his palms as Lumi conjured an aurora, and then they flung them at the trolls.

The half-petrified one moaned and went down on one knee. A loud crack sounded underneath it, but it didn't crash through. The other giant pointed its blade at Lumi threateningly.

In response, she ran forwards, coming apart in mid-step until she was pure Lights once again, and struck the giant where it stood. It was a terrible sight; the last time Tuomas had seen such viciousness was when she had attacked Mihka. The entire fjord glowed green and red with her fury.

A shockwave suddenly blew past Tuomas and almost sent him flying. He glanced behind, saw Niina and Lilja standing side by side. Niina was chanting as loud as she could – Tuomas felt her *taika* washing over him: crisp winter mornings, the sweetness of summer honey, the soothing sound of Aino's voice. And she held a drum; Lilja clutched an antler hammer in her unharmed left hand and brought it down.

Another wave flew out and the second troll roared angrily as its legs locked together.

A hail of arrows embedded into the ice. Tuomas peered at the sky. It was still as dark as night, the Sun Spirit only just managing to shine out from behind her sister in a brilliant white ring.

His eyes shifted to his hands. They were glowing brighter than ever before; his *taika* ran just below the surface like a raging fire.

Lilja wouldn't be able to keep beating the drum forever, weak as she was. There was no time; only one thing which would definitely stop the trolls now. He just hoped he could control it.

"Lumi!" he shouted. "Get out of the way!"

She drew back from the second giant, took her human form again and sprinted behind a boulder at the side of the fjord. The troll swayed on the spot, dazed. Another crack tore through the ice, but it still didn't break.

Tuomas grasped at his *taika*, drew it higher and brighter than ever before. This was more than splitting the avalanche, more than opening the gateway to the World Below... it sang to the part of him which had no name and no form. His body protested, but he forced himself on. He wasn't a human anymore, not now, not in this moment...

He became aware of everything around him: the crispness of the air, every hollow fibre of reindeer fur on his trousers, all the breaths taken by all the people standing behind him. He felt the tree which held the Worlds together, branches above and roots below...

He glared at the trolls, and at last, broke through the limit. A dazzling ball of light swelled between his palms. He opened his mouth, let out a staccato chant of the Sun: a perfect capture of everything warm and bright. The heat consumed him; it was going to tear him apart…

Then he raised his arms and let go.

The entire fjord filled with Sunlight. He staggered with the force of it, screamed as it tore him in a hundred directions. It was too much…

He fell to his knees. The glow subsided, and he eased his eyes open.

Relief filled his heart. The trolls were completely petrified: boulders carved into an alarming mimic of life. Their mouths were stretched wide in pain, tendons stood out beneath grey flesh like tight ropes.

Then, unable to bear the weight any longer, the ice gave finally way. The monsters plummeted into the Mustafjord, and the water swallowed them, as though they had never been there at all.

Cheers erupted from the bank, but Tuomas barely heard them. His heart was pounding, his lungs seared with every breath. The fjord rolled onto its side as he collapsed.

Hands appeared on his arms and pulled him onto his back. He stared up at Elin and Lilja, and they gasped in shock. Tuomas peered at his hands, and realised why. In places, they had turned transparent, and the skin split open under the pressure of the power he had summoned. A flickering flame-like glow seeped around trails of blood.

It had been too much. His human body was coming apart at last. It had never been meant to contain such heat, such fire…

Stardust showered upon him from the cleft. It was still dark, but the Moon Spirit was moving away now; daylight was returning to the World Between. A few moments, and it would be bright again.

"Lumi!" Tuomas gasped. "Where is she? Get her under cover!"

She appeared beside him, threw herself down. She landed heavier than he was expecting; when he looked at her, he noticed she was ringing wet, wincing in pain.

"Did I hurt you?" he wheezed.

"Never mind that," she replied anxiously. "We must go now. You have not long left."

"What?" Lilja blurted.

Elin snatched hold of Tuomas's face. He grasped her wrist with a shaking hand, clutched his chest with the other. He struggled to breathe; his heart was going to implode...

The Sunlight crept closer.

Lumi slid her arms around him. Tuomas pushed Elin away as gently as he could.

Realising what was happening, Lilja's mouth fell open.

"You're going back."

Tuomas looked at her, then at Elin. Even through the pain, a strange contentment came over him. There was no fear. He had seen death, and it was not the end.

"Thank you," he whispered.

Lumi lifted him. They rose into the air, surrounded by the greens and blues of the aurora. *Taika* flowed around Tuomas as they passed through the rip. The World Between became tiny; the huts and people shrank to pinpricks on the snow.

Lumi grasped the edges and pulled them together. The Lights blazed across the sky; he felt her power drawing the hole tighter and smaller, as he had done in the World Below. And then, with one final tug, it sealed shut completely: a door closed for all time.

Tuomas let out his last breath, and his sister carried him away.

Chapter Thirty-Three

Formless. Endless. Infinite.

Tuomas hung suspended. Around him, a maze of stars pulsed and sparkled. It stretched on forever, warm yet cold, surrounding him like a comforting blanket. He was still in his physical body, but it didn't matter. That body was dying.

The thought came to him distantly, as though in a dream. Yes, dying... the power of a Spirit had finally proven too much. His souls were pulsing, the Red Fox One within desperate to be free. The time was so close...

He raised a hand and touched his hair, imagined the blonde strands, felt his own blood run down to his scalp. He regarded the scars from when the draugars had bitten him, the frostbite from when Kari had almost murdered him.

All so far away now. All so unimportant. And yet he would miss it so much... those same hands had beaten Henrik's drum, played with Mihka, eaten Paavo's food, held onto Lilja and Aki and Elin...

He didn't breathe. He didn't need to. His lungs folded upon themselves like empty bellows. All that was keeping him alive now was his heart, and soon enough, that would stop, too.

Lumi guided him deep into the World Above, far from the reach of day or night; further than any mage had ever travelled. She spread her Lights as wide as she could. Already, she looked stronger, back in her own realm, away from everything hard and solid. Rivers of green and purple washed in every direction, and she spun through them: first as a girl, then as an orb, then as the celestial white fox.

A swarm of souls sprang out of the darkness. At once, she swept them close, held them against her and caressed them tenderly. Tuomas sensed their relief to be reunited with her; it rang through him in a silent song of joy. Without her up here with them, they would have had nothing to keep them together, no way to dance and know the contentment which came in that time between lives.

Tuomas allowed himself to feel it, too. It was like falling into the arms of family.

The stars and clouds twisted below; the entire sky pulled itself into the glittering face of the Great Bear Spirit. It gazed upon Tuomas and Lumi with its huge dark eyes, as endless as the void which encircled it.

You have both done as I asked, it said, in a voice which lingered between male and female, young and old.

Tuomas bowed low. *I'm sorry it took so long.*

It does not matter now. All is finished and done, and I thank you for it. Both gateways are closed, and I shall restore the taika as it was before.

The Sun and Moon Spirits rose on either side of the Bear. In his mind, Tuomas sensed them: two women, one clothed in flickering fire, the other in pale shadows. Gold and black hair knotted together as they hung back to back: light against darkness.

You saved us, said Tuomas. *You saved everyone, all the mages.*

Yes, beamed the Sun Spirit. *We knew it would lure the trolls out of hiding, give you a chance to finish them, my sweet boy.*

And even if you had been unable, trolls are simple creatures, added the Silver One. *They never would have escaped my sister's touch in time.*

Tuomas was stunned when he heard her voice in his head. The icy seduction was still there, but with none of the forcefulness he knew.

She reached towards him, stroked her thin fingers over his face, softer than a feather.

My son, she whispered.

Our son, corrected the Sun Spirit. *Our son, and our daughter. At last, you are home.*

Home... Tuomas repeated, as the Golden One's rays appeared on his other cheek.

Lumi swept her tail. The souls danced: a stream of white against the river of green. The World Between was too distant now – nobody down there would see the display – but it didn't matter. The distance was an eternity away... yet he still felt the phantom memory of ice under his back, water on his skin from when he had fallen into the Mustafjord.

How fitting... That was where he had died last time, too...

His heart jolted. He winced, clutched at his chest.

It hurts... he whispered.

The Red Fox One seeks to be free, said the Great Bear Spirit. *Are you ready?*

He nodded. *Let it be done.*

Lumi held onto Tuomas's hands. He watched as the Spirit of Passage drew close, in the form of a billowing blue cloud. He swept around Tuomas and touched the scar over his breastbone. Behind his ribs, inches away, the Spirit of the Flames pulsed and shone.

Red Fox One, said the Spirit of Passage.

Tuomas. Let me have that name one more time, Carrying One.

He closed his eyes.

Wait!

The Spirits all turned; Lumi's grip tightened on his hands. A soul was swimming forward, out of her Lights. She waved it closer, until it was hovering before Tuomas's face.

He stared at it in shock. Behind the bright starry glow, he saw a trace of the being it had been in its previous life, like the outline of a face pressed into virgin snow. He sensed the aroma of delicious food, hair the same blonde as his own, the kindly eyes which had greeted him every morning...

It was Paavo's.

This must be done, said the Sun Spirit. *Do not interfere. Let it be over quickly, and save him his pain.*

I understand, the soul replied, *but I make an offer to you, Great Bear One.*

If he was still able, Tuomas would have shed tears. Even though the voice was only in his mind, it sounded so much like his big brother.

The Spirit of Passage hesitated. The Bear blinked its fathomless black eyes.

Speak, it said.

The soul turned and danced on the spot. Lumi sent out another wave of green to keep it close.

When this life-soul is taken, replace it with me. This boy was once my family. Let my next life be a continuation of the one he already lives.

Tuomas stared. Did that mean what he thought it did?

You would go into his body, so it may survive? asked the Moon Spirit. *So it may return to the World Between?*

I would, replied the soul. *Let the Red Fox One remain here, and let the boy's life go on.*

Lumi glanced at the Great Bear. *It has never been done.*

The Bear inclined its starry head. *It can be.*

You knew this was possible? Was this part of the plan, too?

I knew it was a possibility. Rare, they may be, but there are occasions when balance need not require my intervention, White Fox One.

What is this? Tuomas asked incredulously. *I can go back?*

It will not be completely as the individual you have been, the Bear warned. *Memories belong to the life-soul, and if you agree to the replacement, you will be like a newborn, with no recollection of your former self.*

I am willing to grant him the memories we have shared, Paavo's soul insisted. *He will know those who we both knew in life. Will you accept this, Great Bear One?*

The Bear let out the smallest hint of a smile.

I shall. I honour your offer.

I agree, Lumi added. *He should have a chance to continue his life.*

Wait, said the Silver One. *This is your choice to make, Tuomas Sun-Soul.*

Tuomas spun between all of them. It would be so simple to refuse, to stay here, and be still, and know the dances of the World Above. Could he even manage to survive if he returned in this body? It was falling apart, crossed with scars, torn by more *taika* than should ever have been contained in a single form…

The Spirit inside me was the mage, he whispered. *I'll never be able to enter a trance again, or speak to you, will I?*

You may be able to re-learn the skills and take your test again, replied the Golden One, but there was an uncertainty to her tone which wasn't lost on him. It was a chance which could fall in either direction. And when he did die, it would be as two souls, just like every other creature in the World Between.

He turned to Lumi. She transformed, so he could look into her human face, and a tear fell down her cheek.

I choose to return, he said.

Pain flashed through her eyes, but she nodded.

Carrying One, you are not needed to take this life, said the Great Bear Spirit. *The White Fox One is able to pull out a single soul. She can replace it, also.*

Very well, replied the Spirit of Passage. *In that case, I must leave. There is a hare which calls to me.*

With that, the shifting cloud disappeared and dived towards the World Between. Tuomas watched him go, then looked between his two mothers. The Spirit in his heart shifted impatiently and he bit his lip so he wouldn't cry out.

I thought you would choose this, Lumi muttered. *I cannot blame you. As you said, you should have your life. More than fifteen years of it.*

Tuomas held onto her arms. *But you still have me, all of you. The Red Fox One, I mean. And you'll always be Lumi to me, no matter what.*

Yes, she smiled, wider than he had ever seen. *And I will be with you, Tuomas. Even if you cannot see me, I will look down on you, and I will run beside you under the frozen skies.*

She placed her hand on his chest.

Goodbye, my brother, she whispered, then pushed.

Tuomas gasped as her fingers forced their way into him, latched around the Spirit. She pulled back, and through tear-blurred eyes, he saw it in her hands: a glowing orb, as bright as the Sun, sparkling with power…

The weightlessness ended. He tumbled through the sky, and she chased after him. She caught him in mid-air and drove Paavo's life-soul into his body.

Wind... air... falling...

He landed, and opened his eyes.

Overhead was a bright afternoon sky, tinged with the faintest wash of green. A crowd of people surrounded him.

He frowned. Did he know them? Some of them looked familiar...

He suddenly remembered he had lungs. He sucked in a breath, let it out, and the onlookers drew back with a gasp. At first, he didn't understand why, but then he saw it misting in the frigid air, and watched in awe.

Within the cloud was the distinct shape of the Great Bear's head. It was there for a moment – a heartbeat – and then it was gone.

Chapter Thirty-Four

It was though he had spun in a hundred circles. The smallest movement made him feel sick. The Sun Spirit shone overhead, with the faint disc of the Moon hovering at her side.

The sky looked different to how he remembered. Hadn't there been something wrong with it? The stars had been falling...

He squinted at the faces, trying to place them. He knew these people. Somehow, from somewhere, he knew them.

He focused on the one closest to him. It was a girl with black hair. Lines from tears had dried on her cheeks.

"You're not dead!" she was crying in disbelief. "You came back!"

The others started muttering amongst themselves. The words tumbled over each other in his ears.

"He fell out of the sky again..."

"He isn't glowing..."

"His eyes are blue again. What happened?"

"Where are the ears?"

He frowned. What was wrong with his ears?

He brought his hands up, felt them. They were cool, but normal: fleshy and rounded. Then he explored the surface he was lying on. It was hard and cold, a little wet to the touch. Ice.

Then he inspected himself. He was wearing a coat of white reindeer fur, soaked through with freezing water. He had two arms, two legs. His chest burned as though he had been punched. His skin was covered in scars, and his palms were bleeding and burned. A couple of fingertips were missing;

frostbite had done that. He couldn't remember it, but he knew that was what it looked like when winter killed living tissue. He'd seen it before: an old woman who'd lost her feet…

Why was he so injured? Where had all the scars come from? They looked like bite marks, and not too old, either…

He opened his mouth, but nothing came out. His tongue felt heavy. He swallowed, trying to get it to work, and managed a tumble of sounds. The black-haired girl sprang forward and looked deep into his eyes.

"Are you alright?" she asked tearfully.

He tried to speak again. This time, it worked.

"Elin."

She grinned from ear to ear. He was correct, then. That was her name.

"Back off, everyone. Give him some air," snapped another woman, behind Elin. She was older – in her late twenties – with two long sandy blonde braids hanging over her shoulders. One of her arms was in a sling, and the other was wrapped around a little boy.

"Lilja?"

The sling-woman nodded.

"And… is my name Tuomas?"

Elin frowned. "Of course your name's Tuomas."

"Where am I?" he mumbled. "I am called Tuomas… yes…"

"What's wrong with him?" a third woman asked; a redheaded teenager – he vaguely remembered her name was Niina.

"Nothing's wrong," Lilja said. She disentangled the boy from her hip, then came forward. "Tuomas, are you the Son of the Sun?"

He trembled. Those words meant something… or had meant something…

"Who were you in your last life?" Lilja pressed. "Do you remember?"

Slowly, the answer drifted into his mind.

"I was called Paavo," he replied. "But now I am Tuomas."

Understanding dawned on Lilja's face.

"He's swapped his life-soul."

"What?" Elin blurted.

"Is that even possible?" Niina asked. "Tuomas, what happened? Where are your ears and tail?"

Ears and tail? What was she talking about?

"Easy does it," said Lilja, not taking her eyes off him. "Can you sit up? Elin, help him."

"I don't understand," Niina hissed. "Why doesn't he know who he is?"

"The Lights took the Spirit out of me," Tuomas said. "And I came back."

Lilja nodded slowly. "Lumi's replaced the soul with Paavo's. He only remembers what Paavo did, and up until the moment he moved on."

Elin gaped at her. "So, nothing since then? When we first got to Anaar?"

"It doesn't seem so," said Lilja.

Elin choked on a sob. Why was she so upset?

The little boy stepped closer. Tuomas peered at him, but couldn't place him in his memory. Those puckered scars on his cheeks looked familiar. Hadn't he been covered in water? And weren't his eyes supposed to be white, not blue?

"Who is that?" Tuomas whispered to Elin.

The boy looked stung.

"It's me!" he cried. "Aki! Don't you remember me?"

Aki? He'd never heard that name before. Where was this kid even from?

Lilja quickly bent so she was at the boy's height. Was he her son? Yes, he looked like her. Had Lilja ever mentioned anything about a child?

"It's alright, baby," she said gently, kissing him on the forehead. "Tuomas has a new life-soul. He knows me, because both him and Paavo met me. That's how he knows Elin, too. But Paavo never met you."

"Yes, he did," Aki protested. "Paavo was one of my friends!"

At that, Elin and Niina shuddered. Lilja shot a warning glance at them.

Guilt gnawed Tuomas's heart. Had he truly known this little boy? How could he have forgotten him? Were there other people he didn't know? How many?

He looked around, at the rocky cliffs on either side, lined by waterfalls and hardy trees clinging precariously to ledges. The ice was broken nearby, as though something huge had sunk through it. And on the far bank, in front a snowy forest, was a little village.

Akerfjorden: the southernmost settlement in the Northlands, at the end of the Mustafjord. Home.

He started shivering. Why was he so wet? Nobody should be out in winter in wet clothes, it was a death wish…

Niina immediately pulled an arm across her shoulders. Elin took his other one and together they helped him to stand.

"Come on, we need to get you inside," said Niina.

They started walking him towards the huts, each foot placed carefully to avoid the thin patches of ice. Lilja followed, holding Aki's hand while the little boy wept into her sleeve.

Tuomas wanted to talk to him, learn how he knew him, but he didn't have the energy. Every muscle in his body ached. No, not ached – that would mean they had been used. It felt as though he had *never* used them before, at all.

Eventually, they reached solid ground. Elin and Niina wedged open the door to the nearest hut and laid him on a sleeping sack. A teenager was sprawled over some furs in the corner. He looked up in alarm, and Tuomas saw a shock of white hair. Mihka.

"What happened?" he demanded. "What was all that noise? Why did it go dark? Tuomas?"

"I'll explain in a moment, hold on," snapped Niina as she threw more logs onto the fire.

The shelter was already deliciously warm, but Tuomas winced as heat began to work its way back into his frozen muscles. Niina stripped him out of the white coat, then the rest of his clothes, and wrapped him in the sleeping sack.

He vaguely recognised this place, more from smell than sight. The aroma of herbs and strong tea had worked its way into the walls. His younger brother had spent hours in here, chanting and talking with the old mage, Henrik.

No. There was no younger brother. *He* was the younger brother.

He held a hand to his head. Why was it all so confusing?

A crowd gathered at the door, but Lilja shooed them away.

"Leave him," she said firmly. "He needs to recover. He's not immune to the elements like he was."

"Do you mean he's not the Son of the Sun anymore?" someone asked – a woman. Maiken.

"No," said Lilja. "Listen, I think he'll be fine, but it won't happen any quicker if you swarm him. Just get people to find jobs to do; corral the reindeer, or something."

Niina bent over Tuomas and checked his temperature.

"You seem alright," she muttered. "By the Spirits, I didn't think I'd be doing this again so soon..."

Her voice trailed off. His head was spinning; he closed his eyes to try and get away from it. The sounds faded, then blackness engulfed him. It was all too much.

He didn't know how long he slept for, but when he awoke, the sky through the smoke hole was dark and dotted with stars. He wiggled his fingers, found them covered in bandages, and remembered the wounds on his hands. He no longer felt cold; someone had dressed him in dry clothes, with the fur on the inside. But he was still aching, as though he had run for a hundred miles. Even his heart hurt.

What had happened to him, to make him so tender?

He glanced around. Elin was nestled beside him in another sack, clutching a bow as a child might hold a toy. On the other side of the hearth lay Niina and Mihka. All three were sound asleep.

More logs had been added to the fire: thick ones, to burn slow. Many had collapsed into glowing red embers, so hot that the air trembled around them. It prickled Tuomas's skin and he shuffled away. It was too warm; he needed to get out.

Moving carefully so he wouldn't wake anyone, he found his shoes. His fingers shook as he tied the ankles shut. His brain felt almost separate from his body; there was a delay in every movement. He shook his head hard, grasped his coat, and crawled out of the hut.

Fresh, cold air stabbed at his lungs, rushed into his blood. The temperature immediately chased away the final dregs of tiredness. He hunched his shoulders against it, hobbled stiffly along the paths like an old man. Smoke drifted into the sky from numerous fires, but the entire place was quiet; the only sounds he heard were faint snoring and the soft jingle of reindeer bells in the forest.

He walked to the shore of the Mustafjord and looked across the ice. The giant hole was still there, gaping black in the distance. The Moon Spirit had turned her face away, so the only light came from the stars and a couple of torches at the edge of the village.

He tried to think. If the waterfalls had thawed on the sides of the fjord, then that meant it was spring. But why were people in Akerfjorden in spring? Hadn't they driven the herd to the coast? He remembered doing that…

A faint green glow flickered in the sky. As he watched, it spread, grew brighter, waved tendrils of pale fire through the night.

He lowered his head in reverence. It was important to show respect to the Spirit of the Lights, lest she come down and strike. That was what had happened to Mihka.

A name suddenly swam into his head.

Lumi.

In an instant, he saw a girl with skin like snow, fox tail sweeping the aurora behind her. She had been his sister, in that other life, when his soul was that of a Spirit. He had been the Son of the Sun; a mage; someone who had done something very wrong – then set it right.

"Tuomas?"

He turned around. Elin was standing a few feet behind him.

310

"What are you doing out here?" she asked.

"I just needed some air," he replied.

Elin walked closer. The aurora reflected in her eyes.

"Beautiful," she said, with a bow. "Do you... know who she is?"

"Yes."

"I thought I'd never see you again. You said you weren't coming back."

Tuomas frowned. Had he said that?

"I don't remember," he admitted. "I'm sorry."

Elin went still. "You remember *me*, though. Don't you?"

He tried to think. She had stayed in Akerfjorden and come on the migration to the islands. She was a good shot with a bow and arrow. She had mittens made from white hare fur. She'd been sick with something which had ravaged her souls.

No, there was more than that. What had his other soul felt, before the Spirit of the Lights took it away? Who was she?

He looked at her. She was his age, a couple of inches shorter, but toned. A fox head, carved from bone, hung around her neck. He knew her face...

"A lot of it's fuzzy," he said slowly. "I don't know what to think."

Elin bit her lip so she wouldn't cry. "So you don't remember."

Her voice was so sad, it almost broke his heart.

She went to draw away, but Tuomas reached out and grasped her hand.

"Wait," he said, glancing at her lip again. "Is it true that I kissed you?"

Elin's eyes lit up. "Yes."

"Out there. On the ice."

"Yes, you did."

311

A smile broke across her face. Then her composure snapped and she threw her arms around him. The Lights blazed overhead, as though dancing with joy.

"Don't worry," Elin whispered. "I'll tell you everything you need to know. We all will. It's going to be alright now."

Chapter Thirty-Five

The Moon Spirit circled through the skies above the Northlands, waxing to full, then waning to new. The last of the snow melted; the rivers and streams broke free of their icy purgatory. Heathers, saxifrage and cowslip transformed the once-barren tundra into a rich carpet of colour.

Nights became equal with days, and then gradually shorter, until the Sun Spirit lifted her golden glow high and never set. The Long Day arrived: two whole months without a single moment of darkness. And in the very middle of it came midsummer.

In the corral at the rear of Akerfjorden, Tuomas stood in the centre of the herd, along with Aslak and several men from Einfjall and Poro. Reindeer stampeded around him in a frantic circle. The calves had matured and the females began growing their antlers back again – the air was filled with the sounds of them smacking together. Above, a cloud of mosquitos buzzed relentlessly; Tuomas smacked them away as they landed on his arms.

He held a lasso, searched for any calves with his mark cut into its ear. He spotted one and flung the rope. It landed around the animal's neck, and he pulled it close, flipped it onto its side so he could check its teeth. Everything looked good, so he let it go.

He wiped the sweat off his forehead. Aslak had said they wouldn't usually corral the reindeer at this time of the year, but after coming back to the winter grounds early, it was best to make sure they were all still healthy. It had been difficult work, but now they had managed to check every calf from the three villages.

Though he had no personal memory of what had happened after the arrival at Anaar, Elin and the others had been true to their word and told him all the details. Now, there was little he didn't know, and he'd kept an open mind, to re-learn the skills which he had lost.

He hung the lasso on one of the fenceposts at the edge of the corral. Aslak approached and clapped a hand on his shoulder.

"You're getting the hang of things again," he noted. "But, to be honest, Paavo never did have the best aim."

Tuomas smirked as he fetched his coat and belt from a nearby branch.

"I'd have thought I might have turned into a better cook, though."

"Don't push your luck. It's still early days."

"It's been three months. Hardly early days."

"Three months is nothing compared to three years," Aslak replied, throwing a glance at the Sun's position in the sky. "Speaking of which, we'd better head back. It's almost noon."

The herders opened the gate and let the reindeer run out into the forest. Then they walked down to the village. The Mustafjord sparkled a stunning cerulean blue, the light reflecting off the surface like a thousand diamonds.

People were moving onto the bank, ready to celebrate midsummer. A huge fire was already roaring in the central pit, ready for the dancing and feasting which would follow. Everyone settled on the shore, as they had done for generations; talking amongst themselves, passing around pieces of fish and blood pancake.

Only Tuomas hung back, waiting at the edge of the gathering for Lilja and Niina.

Eventually, they appeared. Lilja's injuries had healed now, but she still held her arm stiffly, wary of jolting it. Aki walked at her side, clutching Enska's ceremonial antler headdress. When he saw Tuomas, he ran over and hugged him around the waist.

"Hello, Aki," Tuomas grinned.

Aki beamed, showing a gap where his two front milk teeth had fallen out.

"Happy birthday!" he said. "How old are you now?"

"Sixteen," replied Tuomas. "I don't feel it, though."

"Well, you're not, in many respects," said Niina with a smile.

She pulled her drum off her belt, caressed it with one hand. She was a full mage now: she had admitted that the journey back to Akerfjorden had made something click inside her, and Lilja wasted no time in confirming that her test was passed. Aki had undergone his test as well, with the crossing of the Night River: the feat unmanaged by any before him. Now, he was the youngest mage in living memory, but Lilja insisted that he remain her apprentice for a while. The full burden of working magic was too much for a six-year-old to bear.

"Can you hand me those, please, baby?" asked Lilja.

Aki held up the headdress. Lilja took it from him by the antlers, kissed him on the cheek, then positioned it atop her head.

"Well, here we go," she said, with a strange resignation in her tone. "Are you all ready?"

In response, Tuomas reached under his white coat and withdrew his new drum. Over the spring, he had sat for hours with Lilja, painstakingly making it: wetting the wood and then letting it dry into the shape of the frame; stretching the skin across it; painting symbols with alder bark juice. He could hardly do anything yet – shockwaves and trances were a distant hope – but it was a start.

He couldn't believe that, not long ago, he'd been able to walk through flame, split avalanches, speak the silent language of Spirits. If so many people hadn't insisted it was real, he might have thought it a story, told around the hearths on a cold winter's night.

"Come on," said Lilja.

The four of them stopped at the fire pit, mixed some ash with water, and daubed it across their faces. Then they walked in a line towards the Mustafjord. The crowd fell silent as they passed, and lowered their heads in respect.

Tuomas sighed as he stood by the lapping shore. This time last year, Henrik had been in this exact spot, and Tuomas himself had watched from the crest where Mihka now sat, imagining the day when he might do the same.

Just one year, and so much had changed.

He raised his hand and touched his ear. What must it have been like to have the pointed red ones everyone had spoken of? Or the tail, which swept fire and sparks whenever he moved it?

It didn't matter. It was a dream, from another life. The Spirit of the Flames was back in the World Above now, where he belonged, dancing with his sister and basking in the glows of his mothers.

Tuomas surveyed the faces before him. He found Elin with her parents; the elders of all three villages clustered together. It had been confirmed, at the spring equinox, that Einfjall and Poro would remain a part of Akerfjorden for the foreseeable future. Tuomas knew they would have to part again at some point – there was no way the forest and lichen could support such a huge herd for an extended period – but for now, there was harmony. New huts had been built, the village expanded, and the community was stronger than ever.

And when Tuomas looked out at his neighbours, he noticed how *they* were looking back at *him*. There was no fear, no worry about offending – at least, no more than would be shown to any mage. He might still be re-learning the skills of the craft, but he, Aki, Lilja and Niina were all equal now.

Lilja raised her hammer. Tuomas and Niina readied themselves to begin drumming with her, but to their surprise, she didn't move. Then Tuomas realised, she had only lifted it to make sure everybody was paying attention.

"Today we celebrate the highest reach of the Golden One," Lilja said. "We will enter the trance, sing the chants, and thank the Spirits, as we have done for a thousand generations. Let us accept ourselves as a part of nature, not greater or lesser than any other living thing in this World. We give thanks for the bountiful summer, and the lessons winter has taught us, and we remember those who fell."

She hit her drum, hard enough to have sent out a shockwave. But that didn't happen. Instead, the villagers all cheered and lowered their heads in respect.

"There's one more thing I wish to announce," said Lilja.

Tuomas eyed her. There was a sudden shadow to her words, as though a cloud had passed overhead.

"We are all as one people now, for the first time since the Great Mage walked among us," she said. "As such, there is hardly need for three mages any longer. And so, I shall be stepping down as the Poro mage."

A startled gasp flew from the crowd. The only ones who didn't react were the elders – Tuomas realised she must have already discussed this with Birkir and the others.

"Lilja, are you sure?" Niina hissed.

"Positive," she replied. "Now, come on, let's get things going. The sooner we're done here, the sooner people can be merry."

Without another word, she struck up a beat. Niina and Tuomas exchanged a glance, but nevertheless joined in and hit their drums in unison with her. Lilja began chanting: a light, airy song, which seemed to hold the very essence of summer. Niina sang too, and then finally, Tuomas himself.

He let the *taika* flow through him as Henrik had once taught him. It was much lesser than it had been, like strong tea diluted to nothing, but he didn't care. It danced and wove with that of his fellow mages, as well as it could without the soul of a Spirit: entwined but never joined.

After the ceremony, everyone gathered at the fire, joined hands, and spun in circles. Chants and laughter filled the air long into the night, even though the Sun Spirit didn't set. Tuomas linked arms with Maiken, then Alda, then Ritva… too many faces to count. Soon, his legs were burning and he stopped to catch his breath. Many others had had the same idea and began flocking around the secondary fire, where a large helping of stew had been prepared.

Elin appeared, two cups of tea in hand, and passed one to Tuomas. He took it with a grateful smile and they drank at the same time.

"Getting tired?" he asked.

"A little," she admitted. "I don't know, I always find it a little harder in the summer, with the constant daylight. The Long Dark seems easier, somehow."

"Speak for yourself," smirked Tuomas.

Elin jostled him with her elbow. The bone necklace bounced against her tunic as she moved, and its white colour shone as the Sun struck it. Tuomas took the opportunity to quickly lean in and kiss her on the lips.

"By the way," he said, "have you seen Lilja and Aki anywhere?"

Elin shook her head. "They've probably just gone to eat alone again. Or to bed."

At any other time, he would have agreed with her, but after Lilja's words, he wasn't so sure.

"I'm going to check on them," he said.

"I'll come, too," said Elin.

"You don't have to follow me everywhere."

"I know. But I suppose I've gotten used to it."

She flashed him a toothy grin. Tuomas rolled his eyes, but didn't protest.

They set the cups aside and walked towards the hut at the edge of the village. Even though new shelters had been built, Lilja's was still firmly on its own.

He knocked on the door, but there was no answer. He pushed it open.

Lilja and Aki's sleeping sacks were gone, as were her healing supplies and the rest of her belongings. The hut was completely empty, save for the hearthstones and the reindeer skins on the birch floor. And, hanging from a notch in one of the roof beams, was Enska's headdress.

"I was just coming to find you."

Tuomas spun around. Lilja was standing by a nearby tree, a reserved expression on her face. He read its meaning at once.

"You're leaving."

Lilja nodded. "I said my piece, cast off that mantle at last. I'm going to slip away now, before anyone notices – I've had our things packed and ready since last night. You two are the only ones who I wanted to tell."

Tuomas frowned. "Are you going back to Poro? Why not just leave when everyone else does? And why aren't you taking your headdress?"

"I don't want it anymore. It can be yours now," replied Lilja softly. "And I'm not going to Poro. I'm the wandering mage, remember? It's about time I wandered again."

"Where to? You've been everywhere."

"Not quite. I thought I'd maybe see what lies south, outside the Northlands – the snow and tundra can't go on forever, can it? Maybe there's another forest. Maybe I'll find other mages, and Aki can learn new types of magic. He is the next generation, after all."

Tuomas's tongue stuck to the roof of his mouth. A part of him had suspected this day might come – when telling him his memories, Lilja had made no secret of her wishes. He had hoped she might reconsider, or that it would happen far in the future. But she had spent half her life rootless, always on the move. If he wanted her to stay, he'd have to cut off her feet.

Lilja tossed her head.

"Come. Walk with me."

She led them out of the village, through the forest, and up the slope which curved round to the tops of the cliffs. The sound of the celebrations faded with every step. It took a while to scale the rocky walls, and by the time the ground levelled out, all three of them were gasping for breath.

Tuomas looked upon Akerfjorden and the sparkling waters of the fjord. Everything seemed bathed in a soft blue colour, from the sky down to the sea.

Then he heard a child's giggle. Aki was clutching the ropes of Lilja's two reindeer in his little hands. Each was lashed to a small sled, carrying all she owned. Tuomas spotted the sleeping sacks, bags of lichen, utensils, equipment to erect a tent, even a pouch of bone needles. He wondered if they were the same ones which Alda had given her, all those years ago.

"Tuomas!" Aki grinned excitedly. "Are you coming with us?"

Lilja stroked his hair. "No, baby, they're not. They're needed here."

"Aw!" Aki protested. "Please come with us, Uncle Tuomas! It's going to be an adventure!"

Tuomas's heart jolted. Aki had never called him that before.

He knelt so they were the same height. Aki ran to him and hugged him.

"An adventure better suited to you two, I think."

"You've had enough adventures to last you a lifetime," Lilja muttered. "Well, if you think about it, they *did* last a lifetime."

Tuomas smirked. "You can say that again."

He eased Aki away and playfully flicked his nose.

"Be a good kid," he said. "Do as you're told."

"You never did what you were told," Aki pouted.

"Yes, and look at what happened," Tuomas replied. "You'll be fine. Look after your Mama, alright? And I know her arm's better now, but don't swing off it. Promise me?"

Aki snivelled, but nodded.

"I promise."

Tuomas pulled him in for one last embrace. Then, to his surprise, Elin bent down and joined in.

Tuomas looked over Aki's shoulder at Lilja. Her eyes shone with tears. When the three of them drew apart, she walked closer and cupped Elin's cheek in her hand.

"Thank you," Elin smiled.

Lilja blinked hard so she wouldn't cry.

"You just take care of your family," she said.

"Will we ever see you again?" asked Tuomas.

"Maybe. Maybe not. We'll see how interesting life decides to be," replied Lilja. "You know something? I think I figured out why the Great Bear Spirit saved my life, back when I was a kid."

"Why?"

"Because it knew I'd be needed in the future. Needed to help with your birth, to help tutor you. And I'd need your help, too." She twisted one of her braids in her fingers. "I'm honoured to have shared in your story, boy."

Tuomas shook his head. "I barely remember my own story, Lilja."

"Yet," she replied shrewdly. "But others do. And they will never forget it."

She opened her arms.

"Now, I'm going to ask you for something. Will you come here and give me a hug?"

A laugh and a sob tangled together in Tuomas's throat. Without hesitation, he stepped forward. Lilja held him tightly, caressed his face, and pressed her lips to his forehead.

He could have stayed there all night, but she let go of him. She took the lead reindeer's rope in one hand, Aki in the other, and looked back over her shoulder.

Tuomas raised a hand in farewell.

"Go in peace," he said.

Lilja smiled. "Stay in peace."

Before there could be any more tears, she walked away.

Elin came to Tuomas's side and slipped her fingers into his. The two of them watched as the little caravan turned off the clifftop, then headed due south, into the dense line of trees which stood between the Northlands and whatever lay beyond.

Author's Note

I knew I wanted to write a story set in a frozen world ever since I was a little girl, tucked into bed and listening to my Mum read Hans Christian Andersen's *The Snow Queen*. Then, when I was ten, I discovered Philip Pullman's *Northern Lights*, and, to borrow a line from that book, my fascination with "the idea of north" grew. Finally, in 2015, I came to Lapland for the first time, and my love for the Arctic, for winter, for dark and cold, snow and auroras, was frozen onto my heart.

That winter, I also heard another story. It wasn't one of ice palaces or armoured polar bears; it was of a magical fox that swept up the snow with its tail to create the northern lights. This is the legend of *revontulet*: the fire fox, which even today is the modern Finnish word for the aurora borealis. It is a legend that has so fascinated me, The Foxfires Trilogy isn't even the first time I've explored it – another of my retellings, the short story *Talvi and the Stars*, won the Fairytalez.com Best New Winter Fairy Tale Award in 2019.

My first Arctic winter was in every way the dream I envisioned. By the time I returned to England in early 2016, my own tale was fully formed in my mind, and I set to work. Every story I write is special to me; each one like a child which I've birthed, raised, and finally let go. And like children, each one has its own personality. This one in particular grew like a snowflake and was a joy from beginning to end. The three books also hold a very special place in my heart – not only because of the place and tales which inspired them, but because they were written to coincide with what would have been my late younger brother's eighteenth birthday. And now, in 2020, their publication coincides with his twenty-first birthday. His name was Thomas Hibbs.

I called upon many sources to create the Northlands and their neighbouring Spirit realms, mainly my own experiences of the Arctic and shamanism. At the time of writing, I've been fortunate enough to spend five winters in Lapland: a place which has become my second home. I have eaten reindeer meat, had tears freeze on my eyelashes, been attacked by a very vocal ptarmigan, suffered (mild) frostbite, and sat around fires under skies filled with stars and northern lights. I was also greatly inspired by the mythologies and peoples of the north, including the Inuit, Nenets, Eveny, and Sámi. This latter group were a particularly heavy influence, since I've had the pleasure of experiencing their beautiful culture first-hand and have several Sámi friends who graciously shared their way of life with me. However, I wish to stress that the people of my story are not Sámi, nor any other named indigenous group, and are not intended to represent any of them. The entire Trilogy is a work of fiction, and while it weaves threads of our own Arctic, it's ultimately up to you to decide whether the Northlands are in our own world, in the distant past or future, or in another world altogether.

And so, this Trilogy is many things: a celebration of life and nature, a respectful tribute to indigenous peoples and shamanistic beliefs, a personal love letter to winter and the frozen north, a birthday present and memorial to a brother from his sister. It may be told through a lens of fantasy, but I would also like to think that lens is as clear as a sheet of ice. These are my reasons for bringing it into the world, but it's your story, too. My child is free and making its own way now. If you, dear reader, can take the same beauty and hope and warmth from its snowy pages, then I've done my job right.

May *taika* fill your heart forever.

E. C. Hibbs
Sodankylä, Lapland, Finland
December 2019

Acknowledgements

I may have written this series on the page, but it wouldn't have come into existence without the hard work and support of many other people to whom I owe immeasurable gratitude.

First of all, my amazing parents for their never-ending love and support in all I do, no matter how crazy the adventure might turn out to be. Extra special thanks to my Mum, who not only serves as my editor and confidante, but also my companion in beautiful Lapland.

Thank you to my second family: my friends and colleagues out in Lapland. You are all so special and I'm honoured to have shared that time with you. Thank you to my taller twin, Tara, who brought me out in the first place and with whom I passed five wonderful winters. So much of this story rests on your shoulders.

Thank you to the incredible reindeer herders of Poropuisto Kopara in the Pyhä-Luosto National Park; especially Anssi Kiiskenen, who shared a treasure chest of knowledge of reindeer behaviour, and the fascinating history and traditions of the ancient herding way of life. I learned more in just a few conversations with you than I would have in a hundred books. Kiitos paljon!

Thank you to the fantastic beta readers who volunteered their time to read the story and help me unleash its potential with their honesty: Ryan Carley, Carl Smart-Smith, Alan and Becky Kilfoyle, Jaime Radalyac, Penny-Jane Poulton, Pat Nelson, Matthew Ashman and Elizabeth Vaughan. Thank you also to the editors at Cornerstones Literary Consultancy for your invaluable advice, and to all the bloggers, bookstagrammers and reviewers who helped to push this story into the light. Special thanks to my fellow authors and dear friends Anthony Galvin-Healy and David Fingerman, for a depth of support which I still can't wrap my head around.

Thank you to all my friends from around the world who have supported me and stood by me. If I mentioned you all then this section would be another book in itself, but you know who you are, and I love you. Rhian, my Number One Batty, and the entire Jones family; Nasha and Roger; Sally and Josh; Courtney, Carter, Emma, Holly, Fletch and Iona; the Tenerife family: Karolina, Charley, Eve and Jensen; Donna; Emily and Matt; Christine; Hannah, Zoë, Dani, Lizzy, Jo and everyone from work. Special thanks to my Sámi, Finnish and Norwegian friends: Maiken, hot chocolate connoisseur and Nordic history buff; Niina, my fellow fairy lady and folklorist; Pirjo and Heli for your delicious Lappish cuisine and warm company; Meeri, my treasured WhatsApp pal; as well as Mikaela, Ari and the two Jonis at Kopara for many hours of chatter; and Saara at the Arctic Husky Farm for teaching my clumsy butt how to drive a dogsled.

Thank you to the following people who shared insight and inspiration: Ronald Kvernmo, Elin Kåven, Freyia Norling, Jungle Svonni, and National Geographic photographer Erika Larsson, who kindly gave up her time to speak to me about her experiences living in Sápmi. Thank you also to the many resources I drew on for research and inspiration, namely works by Hugh Beach, Barbara Sjoholm, Emilie Demant Hatt, Evelyn C. Rysdyk and Mike Williams; and the older epics: the *Poetic Edda, Prose Edda*, and *Kalevala*.

In a story where the soundscape is just as important as the landscape, I want to thank the music artists who influenced the drums and voices of the Northlands: Mari Boine, Elin Kåven, Jon Henrik Fjällgren, Jonna Jinton, Sofia Jannok, Keiino, Cantus, Frode Fjellheim, Angelit, Heilung, Wardruna, Skáld, Eivør and AURORA.

To the real Tuomas from the real Lumi: I thank and salute my little brother Thomas Hibbs. I might not have gotten the chance to know you, but if I had, I can imagine the two of us running and dancing side by side under northern skies. You live in these pages, and you will never be forgotten.

Thank you also to my friends and family who are no longer with me but drove me towards great things: Grandpop; Nan; Grandma; and Katie, my sister in all but blood.

And finally, thanks to you, for standing by me through this long journey, whether that's by reading my stories, watching my videos, commissioning my artwork, or sending me comments and reviews telling me how you appreciate what I create. Special thanks to those who support me on Patreon, including my Phenomenal Batty Mariletty Blackrose.

To all of my Batties: none of this would be possible without you and there are not enough words to say how much your support means to me. Never stop being awesome.

Printed in Great Britain
by Amazon